PRAISE F

Moving Day

"Crisp, elegant prose distinguishes this exceptional crime thriller from Stone."

—*Publishers Weekly*, starred review

"From the author of the Julian Palmer series (*The Cold Truth*, *Parting Shot*), this is a compelling mystery with a moral foundation."

—*Library Journal*, starred review

"Well-developed characters, vivid settings, and tautly written suspense make this a true page-turner, sure to appeal to Harlan Coben and Laura Lippman fans."

—*Booklist*

The Teller

"Stone's plotting is tight as a drum, and his writing lean, with short, staccato sentences that create an immediate and immersive experience. Fans of Stone's other suspense titles will be thrilled, and newcomers will scramble for more."

—*Library Journal*

"This fast-paced shell game of misdirection, in which it's hard to tell the good guys from the bad, is reminiscent of *Found Money* by James Grippando, and *Good People* by Marcus Sakey."

—*Booklist*

Two for the Show

"The surprise-filled plot shifts rapidly between illusion and reality, keeping the reader constantly—and entertainingly—off-balance."

—*Publishers Weekly*

DAYS OF NIGHT

Other Titles by Jonathan Stone

DAYS OF NIGHT

A THRILLER

JONATHAN STONE

THOMAS & MERCER

Text copyright © 2017 by Jonathan Stone
All rights reserved.

Published by Thomas & Mercer, Seattle

www.apub.com

Amazon, the Amazon logo, and Thomas & Mercer are trademarks of Amazon.com, Inc., or its affiliates.

ISBN-13: 9781542045841
ISBN-10: 1542045843

Cover design by Brian Zimmerman

Printed in the United States of America

On 11 May 2000, astrophysicist Dr. Rodney Marks became unwell while walking between the remote observatory and the base. He became increasingly sick over a 36 hours period, three times returning increasingly distressed to the station's doctor. Advice was sought by satellite, but Marks died on 12 May 2000, age 32, with his condition undiagnosed . . .

The cause of Marks' death could not be determined until his body was removed from Amundsen–Scott Station and flown off the continent for autopsy. . . A post mortem established that Marks had died from methanol poisoning . . . The case received media attention as the "first South Pole murder."

—*Wikipedia*

The only thing that's the end of the world is the end of the world.

—*Barack Obama*

PROLOGUE

He's a scientist. A biologist. *So he's cursed with knowing.*

The sudden profuse sweat, out here in fifty below. The sheen of it across his face, his hands; his arms and legs suddenly soaked in it beneath his heavy clothing.

He tears a glove off to see the telltale sign he suspects. His fingers suddenly gray. Blood circulation to his hands stopped. Far more sudden and severe than the white of frostbite.

He knows too that the angry, shocking look and color of his skin—his hands, his abdomen, his neck—will retreat to normal, to undetectable, in the fifty-below temperature. It's visible to him momentarily. It will never be visible to anyone else.

He can picture it. He's cursed with knowing.

The steady, relentless spread from his veins to his organs—lower intestine, bladder, pancreas, upper intestine.

He can visualize the different cells of each organ, their different mechanisms, taking it in, trying to defend themselves, being overwhelmed, passing the compound on, helpless, defenseless, ambushed.

He knows by the sudden painful bloat of his stomach that all his organs have gone into free fall together.

He can feel the paralysis set in. Extremities first—toes, fingers, like frostbite but hot, sizzling, followed by nothing, no feeling.

He's cursed with knowing—by the pace of it, climbing his biceps, climbing his thighs, like a liquid knife cutting through the nerves, like a mad explorer slashing forward—that he has maybe a minute left. He knows he has been poisoned.

He knows he will soon feel a shortness of breath as the poison—whatever it is—finishes its journey through his bloodstream to his heart.

There it is. The shortness of breath.

He can picture his bronchial cells, their own version of violent protest, their own shutdown.

He feels dizziness but no need to vomit. He knows, from this, that he will not be expelling any of the poison that way. It acted too fast to let his stomach and intestines defend themselves. Which eliminates certain classes of poisons but leaves plenty of other possibilities.

He can think of a dozen poisons that could have this effect. He doesn't know how this one got into his system. Or how it lay in wait, to unleash at this perfect time and temperature, when he is by himself, out in fifty below.

He knows he will lose muscle control in a half minute or so and will find himself facedown on the frozen tundra.

He is facedown on the frozen tundra.

He never liked it here. Some people thrive here. For him it was too alien, uncomfortable, challenging.

He knows he's about to black out. No blood flow to the brain.

He's a scientist. A biologist.

He knows this is where the knowing ends.

He knows it's the last thing he'll be cursed with knowing.

BOOK ONE: DAY

1.

Heller comes in on a supply plane toward the end of the season, during the long summer days of late February, when the weather is predictably clear, windless, and warm.

Relatively warm.

Endless blue sky. Searingly bright sunshine. (Do not take your sunglasses off when you're outside, he was told. Seriously. You need them there. No fashion statement. You'll damage your corneas. Repeat: do not take them off.)

Supply plane, yes—but not what that phrase once conjured. Not some bushwhacking, barnstorming, belly-churning contraption setting down anywhere on the ice, sliding and spinning to a stop in a haze of cold, dusty whiteness. Not like the wing-and-a-prayer old days, of which he had already heard so many stories.

Nowadays, a converted US Army 747, gray, massive, in full-cargo configuration. Specially outfitted for this service. A supply ship of the twenty-first century. He is one of about twenty passengers, in familiar, standard airplane seats of five-across rows that would seem like any other 747, except the rows are bolted to the aircraft's bare metal floor, like an afterthought, amid an inconceivably large airborne warehouse of food, clothing, medical equipment, and scientific supplies surrounding them, most of it secured behind cargo netting. Cartons, crates, Bubble-Wrapped equipment. Snowmobiles, motorized sleds. All for the benefit of humans, but the humans on board have no choice but to feel secondary, small.

Arriving on the supply plane. Entirely appropriate, Heller thinks. Because he is a kind of supply, after all. A commodity they haven't needed until now.

He has been looking out the window for the last half hour, silent, riveted, as the previous and known world disappears behind him, and this new world spreads out majestically in front of him, and he continues watching intently for the entire landing. The landing strip is simple, unadorned, but clearly demarcated by blinking light poles.

Everything he has seen on approach—the blue horizon, distant white summits (crisp, not hazy), the intense white sheet stretched taut and featureless to the horizon—is expected, just as imagined. Yet at the same time, everything is new, and remarkable.

He suddenly realizes why that is: He had imagined the sight of it. But he had not adequately imagined the feeling.

On board he has learned—unsurprisingly, in retrospect—that this is the same aircraft that carried the body out. The body that had been flown twenty thousand miles for an autopsy. A record, probably. The dead body that is bringing his live body here. Cause and effect. Tit for tat. A weird trade. As if he is a sort of replacement.

On touchdown, a skirt of white erupts instantly around the wheels and lower fuselage. The white skirt falls away by the time the plane spins slowly, balletically, almost ceremonially on its own axis at the end of the runway. It taxis, then stops, and the pilots cut the engines. Heller sits listening to the sudden silence for a moment.

Following the cue of the others now moving around him, veterans of this flight, he zips into his orange parka, provided to him under the auspices of the US scientific community. They're all identical subzero orange parkas—with name tags so that (he understands instinctively) you can identify one another without seeing a face or hearing a name.

He grabs his duffel, heads back with the others to the cargo bay.

A crewman throws levers. The cargo bay hydraulics hum and strain. The cargo ramp descends magisterially.

There's something laughable, absurd about the blast of cold.

A cold that is mute, still, overwhelming, ungodly, a fact of life—for a moment the *only* fact of life as he descends the cargo ramp.

Bringing his breath up short. Freezing his brain for a moment, in a delirium of new sensation. He's anticipated it, of course. He's been told about it. He expects it. But it's so far outside his previous experience. *I'm gonna LIVE in this? I shouldn't be here. Nobody should be here.*

But more than all that, it's a reminder—on his skin, boring into his bones—that he is venturing into something extraordinary.

Like the views on arrival.

Like everything about it so far, he muses.

Totally expected.

Totally unexpected.

Heller notices how deeply it is both.

And is thereby prompted to remind himself—it's at the moment when you think you know something that you really, suddenly don't.

• • •

At the bottom of the ramp, he steps carefully for the first time, but with no sense of ceremony, onto the ice.

A bearded, compact man in a yellow parka approaches him. Swarthy, elfin—qualities apparent even behind the sunglasses and under the knit black cap. "Joe Heller?"

"I'm Heller."

A gloved hand is thrust out in greeting. "Manny Hobbes." Emmanuel Hobbes—the station manager he's been e-mailing with for months. Smiling, jovial. "Welcome to the end of the world."

At the time, of course, Hobbes means it only geographically.

Only genially.

7

Only as a good-natured, friendly greeting.

Nothing more than that.

• • •

The landing strip is just a few hundred yards from the center of McMurdo Station, and most of the orange parkas, he notices, begin to hike toward it, lugging their duffels, in the bright February summer sun. But Hobbes has an ATV to take Heller—minor VIP treatment, maybe his first, maybe his last?—and Hobbes sets Heller's duffel into the corrugated metal bed in back.

They can't really talk above the unmuffled engine, so Heller looks around him during the quick trip. Ahead of him is the closely packed community of McMurdo Station. He can already see a haphazard jumble of dozens of buildings, constructed over decades with no discernible street pattern, simply thrown up ad hoc, some buildings sixty years old, others sleek and new. Part ramshackle frontier town, part interplanetary settlement. A community he must penetrate somehow. That he assumes he will find unfriendly, unwelcoming of the task they've given him. *Solve it. Solve it quickly. Involving as few people as little as possible. Don't rattle what we've built here. Don't derail our ambitions, our dreams. Get this taken care of. Figure it out for us; then get the hell out of here and let us go back to our science, our work, our way of life.*

He turns and looks out onto the horizon. Empty field, warm enough at this time of year to grow some things—a hardy bit of flora, stubby, surprising hints of green punching up through the frozen earth. And beyond it the sea—blue, gray, dark green, a roiling reminder of their insignificance in the face of nature.

He sees someone in a parka—from this distance, not much more than a floating, puffy, bright-red dot—standing motionless at the edge of the sea. A moment of contemplation and meditative calm? Or of churning fear? Suicidal impulses? Absorbed in the ocean's vast beauty?

Or in his or her own tyranny of thoughts, the ocean only secondary, happenstance, a blue-and-gray canvas for the ceaseless splashing of internal turmoil.

The figure's posture gives nothing away of motive or inner life. Just that lone figure and that vast panoramic sea.

Man's smallness, nature's vastness, as if posed purposely for Heller.

The puff of parka now moves a little along the shore.

And Heller turns his attention back to the bump and rumble of the ATV beneath him and the growing presence and bustle of McMurdo Station before him.

● ● ●

Less than a minute later, the ATV pulls up to a thick, low, drab Quonset-style building, and Hobbes cuts the engine.

"Visitor's dorm. Here's your key, room 109. Go ahead and unpack, get cleaned up, use the john, relax a little after that brutally long flight. I'll pick you up right here in an hour to take you over for the briefing."

A nod. A smile. Hobbes starts the engine again and is off.

2.

People don't know the first thing about Antarctica, thinks Heller. They don't even remember what they learned in grade school. The other continents have centuries of civilization and culture, a couple of millennia of human presence, travel and trade, generations of explorers, then settlers, then tourists, tying all the continents together, bringing them alive in the common imagination, so that even grade-school kids have pretty vivid mental pictures of dozens of places in Europe, South America, Africa, and the Far East, the native garb of their inhabitants and the distinctive sound of their languages, yet in that same common imagination, Antarctica is merely a single image of frozen white.

People don't know there's hardly any actual land; it's ice, miles deep. Shifting ice. Shifting so much that the flag marking the South Pole has to be adjusted by ten meters every year, to keep it placed correctly. People assume global warming is affecting it, but much of Antarctica is actually getting colder, and some of its areas are seeing an increase in sea ice. People don't know its most basic geographic facts. That East Antarctica is elevated, hence colder, than West Antarctica. They don't know that it's technically a desert (because there's no rain), with only an occasional dusting of snow (because it's generally too cold for clouds and precipitation to form). That the only real weather, the only real storms, are windstorms. Like on Mars. That its weather has nothing to do with the rest of the globe's; it's a weather system unto itself, closed, locked. That it's the size of Europe or North America, but across 98 percent of its mass, it is geologically, climatologically, and biologically identical and unchanging. That the Antarctic Peninsula, at sea level, can warm up to nearly sixty degrees for a few precious days in the summer, but at the South Pole, fifteen hundred kilometers inland, it never gets above freezing, and more typically remains at sixty or seventy below—and at Amundsen-Scott Station, right next to the pole, it sometimes registers a hundred below or more.

None of which he knew before he boarded the plane. All facts he picked up browsing the Internet on his smartphone, drifting in and out of sleep on the long flight down. (His smartphone that will soon be useless. There's no cell phone service at the American bases in Antarctica. The Australian bases, the Argentine base, yes. The American bases, no.)

He laughs—trying to learn about an entire continent on a single plane trip, on the way there. An infamously dangerous continent. Spending a few minutes on some facts about survival—that doesn't feel very smart. That can't be a good thing.

But how could he say no? The call had come out of the clear blue, literally—from the US Marshal's office in Hawaii, which, to Heller's understandable surprise, has jurisdiction over serious crimes at the American bases in Antarctica, through a recent agreement with the National Science Foundation, which operates the bases. The Marshal's office informed him that they needed to subcontract an experienced homicide investigator to fly in, assess the situation, and begin to gather evidence, and he was their first choice, but there were other solid candidates too—so take it or leave it—and then they told him the pay, and with so little saved at this point and so many bills and looming alimony and Amy's tuition, saying no wasn't really an option.

Tuition. Alimony. And the unnerving headlines screaming from the newspaper in the seat next to his: renewed nuclear testing and territorial posturing from Russia, China, and North Korea in response to the chest thumping of a chaotic, unpredictable administration. It's a world of escalating tensions, both personal and global, that Joe Heller is happy to temporarily escape. Antarctica seems like a good place to avoid all the fallout.

He thinks about the bills again and laughs at the irony. A job in Antarctica as a matter of survival.

3.

The little briefing room is warm, tight, a little claustrophobic. No windows. Not many windows generally in McMurdo Station, he's noticed; windows just invite in weather and cold and trouble. Sealed off is a way of life. Is it also an attitude? Even among supposedly open-minded scientists? He'll soon see.

Heller joins three men and a woman already gathered around a conference table. "Sorry it's so stuffy in here," Hobbes apologizes. "This building is pretty airtight, and we always shut the heat in from previous meetings. Less fuel use. That's the ethic here." A twinkle in his eye, his elfin smile. "On any other continent all our trapped BO would stink, but Antarctica is so dry. It's not too bad, is it?" Hobbes tilts his head, sniffs the air. "I'm trusting you to tell us otherwise, Mr. Heller. We all lose our sense of smell over the Antarctic winters."

A few chuckles.

Heller smiles back gamely. "No smell."

Hobbes's intent is clear, of course: to relax everyone a little, informalize the grim business to come, open the proceedings with a joke, lighten things—if only briefly.

Heller notices a phone in the middle of the table. For conference calls with the mainland, he assumes. But no one is on the phone now.

Hobbes gestures around the room: "Joe Heller, homicide investigator, meet Ron Stanford, chief of science, Colonel Wick Simmons, base administrator, Antoinette Bramlett, supply-chain command, and me you've met. I'm the station manager." Head nods, and brief smiles of acknowledgment. Nothing as formal as a handshake.

Hobbes then introduces a fifth person at the meeting, by slapping a thick manila file onto the center of the table.

"Meet Sandor Lazo-Wasum. Sandy to his friends. Austrian. Thirty-eight. PhD in biology. Stanford, MIT. Five foot eleven. Two hundred ten pounds. A little overweight over the winter, like all of us."

Lazo-Wasum's photo ID is part of the file. Heller spins the photo toward himself, looks at it, mainly to be polite. Black bearded, wire-rimmed glasses, black eyes seeming to blink for the camera. Strong jaw. Generically good looking—like a stock photo of a scientist. But in that moment of the photo, he appears befuddled—a hint of personality that is not stock.

"Body preserved frozen until the cargo four-seven can get back in here, and is then sent for an autopsy," Hobbes recounts. "Inadequate forensic facilities here at McMurdo. We hoped it would be suicide. Harsh as that sounds. We *assumed* it was suicide. We have our share, not surprisingly. Or natural causes. Heart. Lungs. Aneurysm. The biometric extremes here tend to bring out any latent physical problems. We screen for health problems, of course, pretty intensively, but we nevertheless have a higher-than-normal incidence of undiagnosed issues, given the environmental stresses."

Hobbes slaps down a second manila folder next to the first. "Autopsy and toxicology report." He looks up. "As you've heard by now, Heller, a mess. Degradation of corpse in inadequate tempera-ture during months of storage, due to a refrigeration-unit compro-mise that went undiscovered for weeks because its sensors were not adjustable to the outside ambient temperatures of Antarctic win-ter—like nothing is, after all. And when it was finally discovered, we did not have the necessary parts for repair, so our facilities team jury-rigged something, but the damage was done, probably." He continues with a sigh. "Further degradation because of inadequate precautions during transit . . . temperature swings, cabin pressure shifts . . . key minutes lost in cross-border paperwork issues arising from his Austrian citizenship . . . more minutes lost in drop-off at the first forensic lab, which had the transfer time wrong and no one there for receiving. A second, independent forensics-lab exam was commissioned based on the shortcomings of the first, producing— need I even say it—contradictory findings." Hobbes now picks up the second folder, waves it in the air for them, shakes his head, rolls his eyes in generalized frustration, before continuing. "Toxicology and autopsy results: traces of phenobarbital, cannabis, and alcohol." He looks at Heller, explains. "Not surprising for a young guy wintering over here, just so you know." Looking back down at the report. "*And* bacterial traces of several chemical compounds and toxic residues that *may* indicate poisoning. Accent on the 'may.'" Hobbes slaps the folder closed. "Poisoning. A highly provisional finding. And that's the best we're going to get."

"Which could easily have been *accidental* poisoning," explains Simmons, the base administrator, interjecting eagerly. Tall, lean, jumpy, voluble. "Our scientists work with lots of toxic chemicals. Or maybe something in the air supply systems. Or the waste disposal systems. Who knows what could have happened."

"Or not accidental at all," says Ron Stanford, chief of science. Stocky and tanned, he wears his thick white mane long in the back, a scientist ready to host his show on public television. "We're almost a hundred scientists. Botanists, chemists, chemical engineers, lots of advanced degrees. It could have been any of us."

"You mean 'any of us' as victim or as perpetrator?" asks Bramlett, the supply-chain woman. Pale skinned, jet-black hair in a bun, oversize black-rimmed glasses. A prim career bureaucrat.

"Either," Stanford says with a shrug.

"That's the thing, Detective." Hobbes smiles. "We don't really know anything. All these smart people, and we don't know anything. Blank slate. Just like Antarctica."

"And the refrigeration issue and the transport issues and the clerical issues in receiving . . ." Simmons shakes his head. "One more case where the best of intentions—good scientific thinking and reasonable planning—get trumped by uncontrollable outside forces."

"That's Antarctica in a nutshell." Hobbes smiles again. "Welcome to it, Mr. Heller."

• • •

Over the next half hour, the conversation ranges broadly. A little impromptu, incidental, and practical education for Heller from hosts who want to be, or at least to appear, cooperative.

"There's only five thousand people on the whole damn continent," says Hobbes. "Most of us, nine hundred or so, here at McMurdo. And wintering over here last season, just one hundred fifty-seven, which is typical." He brings out yet another manila folder. "Here's the list. I knew you'd want it."

"Your names are included?" It's the first thing Heller has said in the briefing. He looks around the room. *This will be thorough. No favoritism. I'm a cop.*

"Of course. Our names are included. We were all here on the continent when Lazo-Wasum died. All four of us." Hobbes leans back. "One hundred fifty-seven people. It's finite. A twenty-first-century variation on the locked-room mystery, isn't it?"

"Locked-room mystery?" asks Stanford.

"You've never heard that term, Stanford?" Hobbes shakes his head, smiles. "Labs and cages and white mice all your life, Ronnie." Hobbes explains patiently. "That's when the murder takes place in a castle or at a dinner party or on an island, so the killer has to be someone in the room, and Inspector Holmes or Poirot or Maigret or whoever has to figure out the culprit. It's a whole literary genre."

"Doesn't Trebor read those things?" asks Bramlett.

"Yes, loves them—has a whole shelf of them."

A shrug from Stanford. "One of my researchers reads botany texts. Another reads the DSM." Heller knew the reference. The *Diagnostic and Statistical Manual of Mental Disorders* of the American Psychiatric Association. Interesting pleasure reading. Heller will ask Stanford who's reading that.

Hobbes explains to Heller, "You've got to tackle something over the winter. You've got to have some project. And as far as what it is, *de gustibus non est disputandum.* To each his own."

Hobbes shifts in his chair, frowns for a moment, and starts to summarize, in a way, everything that Heller has been hearing. But it's also clearly something that Hobbes has been waiting to say.

"It's different here, Mr. Heller. You think differently. It stresses you in unpredictable ways. Someone otherwise normal may have gone off the deep end, and only temporarily. Maybe doesn't even remember." Hobbes leans back in his chair. "And you've got no resources here for your investigation. In that way, it's primitive. But at the same time it's highly advanced here. Lots of educated people, with access to lots of technology. You could be dealing with a clever criminal, because it's one of us. A potentially tough case, Mr. Heller, right from the start."

And then Simmons, the base administrator, jumps in, energetic, excitable, with what, Heller realizes, he has also been waiting to say to Heller. "And then, depending on what you find, we've got no mechanism in place for prosecution. If you've got perpetrators and victims who aren't Americans, like Lazo-Wasum, the legal system breaks down. It's just a collegial partnership of countries, and no nation's legal system is binding."

Heller knows the problem—and the precedent. They all do. A possible homicide in 2000. An Australian astrophysicist named Rodney Marks, thirty-two. Felt sick walking from the telescope observatory back to his barracks, went straight to the doctor, complained of headaches, expired a few hours later. Body kept frozen for six months, until it could be flown to Christchurch for an autopsy. Methanol poisoning. Marks was newly engaged to a maintenance technician here, had no financial troubles, was well liked, popular. Suicide was ruled out. But America and New Zealand had squabbled over jurisdictions and procedures, his room had been cleaned out, and thus any latent evidence destroyed; the forty-nine others who had wintered over with him at the Amundsen-Scott South Pole Station were never interviewed, then dispersed across the globe. Marks had Tourette's, and doctors made a plausible case that his death was related to that. In the end, only a suspicious death. Inconclusive. Could the same killer have managed to keep a lid on it for fifteen years and then struck again? No—no one who wintered over at Amundsen-Scott or McMurdo had service of more than fifteen years. But the Antarctic authorities didn't want an outcome like that again. An outcome of no outcome. Then again, in the intervening years, not much had changed, and "inconclusive" loomed again in the little conference room.

Of course, it would make sense if it was a suicide—Marks's ingestion of methanol, and Lazo-Wasum's death too. All that alcohol and marijuana in Lazo-Wasum's system. It's a lonely, difficult place over winter. Suicides are not common, but not unheard of. But they need to know if it was *not* a suicide—because justice has to be served. Or does it? What kind, what version of justice? That will be up to them, thinks Heller. Over his pay grade.

"It's a legal minefield," admits Hobbes. "What do we do with the perpetrator or perpetrators when and if we catch them? Depends on the nationalities of the perpetrator and the victim. But why should it, when nationality doesn't mean anything here?"

"So why are we even looking into it, if we can't necessarily take any action?" Simmons asks the room with rhetorical frustration.

"Because we need to protect our little society, such as it is," says Stanford. "If it is a homicide, we can't have another one. We can't have some monster loose among us. We have to feel secure. Plus, this is a community of scientists. We search for and value the truth, just for itself. We want the facts, deserve the facts. Whatever happens or doesn't happen as far as prosecution or punishment."

Bramlett adds quietly—but with a little waver of emotion in her voice—"And . . . well . . . societies have to be just. Even ad hoc ones like this. We have a responsibility. To Sandor's survivors. To his family in Austria. To all of us. It's the mark of a civil society."

"Truth is, we're in two camps," Hobbes admits to Heller, "as you're beginning to gather. The utopians, who want to leave this alone as an isolated incident, let it go, keep our utopia intact. Maybe it was natural causes, maybe suicide, why not leave those as convenient possibilities. Versus the, I don't know, *justitopians*? . . . *authoritopians*?"—he looks vaguely around the room, seeking tacit approval of his made-up word—"who feel we have to provide and follow *some* set of rules, in order to protect our society. It's an ongoing internal debate." A wry smile.

Beyond his e-mail exchanges with Hobbes, Heller doesn't know any of the people in this room. But he does sense how well they know one another. Days together, weeks together, seasons together. He knows that there is likely to be, beneath the collegiality, some annoyance, some different points of view, some tensions, minor or substantial. The utopians versus the authoritopians. But there are probably more nuanced points of view than that.

Over the next weeks and months, Heller will come to understand these differing points of view, differing visions for Antarctica. But uniting them, he will see, is their common love of the continent they are on. For some of them, an allegiance far beyond any to their land of origin—an accident of birth, after all, because this is the land of their dreams, their ambitions, their souls, and their free choice.

Heller could understand the utopians. Hell, in just a few hours, he could sense it. For many of them, mankind's last continent. Mankind's last hope. Mankind's fresh start.

But mankind being mankind, it has finally happened.

Amid the scientists, the political philosophy, the camaraderie, the spirit of international cooperation, the pursuit of scientific knowledge that crosses national boundaries so fluently, the common bond of discovery, the common bond of survival, the dreams of a better world, it has happened.

In this borderless collaborative community, a nation of no nations, a place of shared purpose and aspiration, it has happened.

Inevitably. Ruefully. Its own loud, silent comment on mankind.

A homicide.

A murder.

The utopians may still doubt it, but Heller is pretty sure of it already.

Heller is no scientist. He's a cop. One who left the force several years ago, trying to put it behind him, creating a quieter life for himself, remaking his identity from cop into amateur astronomer. But someone in the US Marshal's office unearthed his name and career from the digital record, double-checked it, Heller assumes, with phone calls to his former department, proposed him to Hobbes and his administrative team, and here he is. The continent's first cop, presumably. The continent's only. Manny Hobbes, as McMurdo's station manager, is technically a Special Deputy US Marshal, approved for light law-enforcement duties—issuing tickets, disciplinary recommendations if an argument becomes physical—but it's a largely ceremonial role, and he has little training—an annual paper test administered from afar by the US Marshal's office in Hawaii—and no actual police experience.

Right now, Heller's thought is far more concrete than any of the philosophical discussion across the table from him.

The faster he solves it, the faster he can get home, the faster the justitopians can get it off their plate, and the faster the utopians can return to their dreams.

And an accompanying, inverse thought: as far as solving it fast, he already knows he's deluding himself.

• • •

After the briefing ends, and the parties disperse with professional smiles and, now, handshakes, Colonel Simmons and Ms. Bramlett linger a little to offer some further insights. As if the presence of someone new, outside their circle, is a chance for a moment of broader perspective.

"America has traditionally dominated here," Simmons tells Heller, "but that's changing. The Russians and Chinese are making a bigger commitment. Argentines and Chileans committing to it too, with their maturing economies and their proximity. The treaties all come up in 2048, and there are abundant natural resources everyone will be competing for. It all looks like collegial science right now. But we're talking about oil and gas and minerals, and the means of extraction have advanced enormously, so all these countries are salivating. Mark my words, our little utopia will become a war zone." A shrug. "A little context for you, Mr. Heller."

He thought he was escaping the world's escalating tensions. Only to land in a place where they could bubble over.

"But that's the future," says Ms. Bramlett, touching Simmons's sleeve as if to calm him down. "And the future is uncertain. Mr. Heller is here for a more practical problem."

A minute later, it's only Hobbes left in the briefing room with Heller.

"Hey, everything is tougher in Antarctica," Hobbes says. "Food. Waste. Power. Transportation. Communication. Daily life. Why should police work be any different?" He shrugs. "That's why there are no kids, no pets allowed here. It's a place for grown-ups. And if you're not one already, it grows you up quick."

Yes, a homicide investigation is going to be tougher in Antarctica.

Though Heller will look back on this as the easy time.

Before things got tough.

Really, *really* tough.

4.

They've given him his own room. A bed, a dresser. A small desk and chair. Shared lavatory and shower down the hall. It's like a boarding-school dorm room at the bottom of the world. Many of the permanent staff share a room, but his guest status earns him his own quarters.

Unpacking had taken just ten minutes. Stack of thermal underwear, bib overalls, snow pants, gloves, boots. Everything had been specified in e-mails from McMurdo administration; there were few choices.

He's impressed that there are electrical outlets. Amazing, really.

Now, he turns on the little desk light. Efficient, multidirectional.

He spreads out the names in front of him. One hundred fifty-seven names.

The list is broken into function, department. An attempt by Hobbes to make life a little easier for him. Or Hobbes the scientist, offering up taxonomy, the botanist's sorting of the fauna, dividing the species into genus and phylum.

Under medical personnel, there's Dr. James Calloway. And his nurse assistant, Anita Sorenson.

Under executive administrative staff, of course, there's Hobbes. Stanford. Simmons and Bramlett.

Under communications support staff, there's Daniel Pritchard and Patrick Dolan. He already knows from the reports they're the ones who discovered and brought Lazo-Wasum's body straight to Calloway and Sorenson in the infirmary.

One hundred fifty-seven names.

Just names still.

With no faces yet, no stories yet.

It's a finite list, after all. No one slipped in or out of McMurdo by kayak or tractor sled or aircraft. No one came over from one of the other international science stations—too tough to make it over in winter—and no one was able to travel in or out during the weeks surrounding the murder. It's a more finite list, a more finite starting group, than most in typical police work. You'd think that would make it easier. His instincts tell him that won't be the case.

He's like a teacher at the beginning of the semester, with a very large lecture class, just names, and he will fill them out slowly, with their grades, little red- and blue-coded marks, with their "aptitudes" and attitudes. Getting to know the class and the classroom.

Or like a tournament director—the starting draw is in front of him—and the competitors will be gradually, steadily, or quickly eliminated, the draw will continually narrow, until there are just a few left standing, and their skills will be closely scrutinized, their play will be closely observed, until there is a "winner."

A couple dozen people on this list, he already knows, are no longer here. Part of his job will be tracking them down, wherever they are now working and residing, interviewing them, checking them out, checking them off. The perpetrator could easily have been one of these itinerant, transient part-timers, committing the crime and then getting far away from it. But his instincts are already telling him otherwise—that if it is indeed a poisoning, it is more likely an insider or insiders, someone who has plenty of ongoing experience with McMurdo's routines, procedures, and materials, who knows how to pull it off undetected and how to stay hidden.

Somewhere among these names is the truth. Somewhere on this list a story, an explanation, a terrible truth or series of truths.

It's a strange feeling to know the answer is already there, somewhere on the spreadsheet in front of him.

In his thirty years of police work, he's never had the experience of the answer being handed to him—and he just has to find it.

It's a larger sense of responsibility. Because it's already in his hands—literally.

A spreadsheet. Science. He smiles. He feels like a provisional member of Antarctica's scientific community.

Though he senses already, with those thirty years of experience, that it won't all be science. Because science hasn't delivered the answers yet, there will be art—intuition, instinct—involved.

Despite DNA, toxicology, autopsy, it is rarely all science.

The word will spread quickly—probably has already—about who he is and why he's here. It's like a small town, he senses. A small town of specialists and scientists at the far end of the earth, but a small town nonetheless, with the typical small-town virtues, he's sure (friendliness, camaraderie, watching out for neighbors), and small-town vices (pettiness, grudges, secrets).

He sets aside the spreadsheet, the autopsy and toxicology reports, looks again around the dormitory room. Spare. Unadorned with anything personal, of course.

A bed. A dresser. A small desk and chair.

A motel room really, at the end of the world.

A room that requires, he can't help but notice, no adjustment at all for him.

Because he can't help but notice that it's no different, in look and feel, from where he's been living. Or how he's been living.

He reaches up in his bunk, turns out the light, lies in the dark—strange and familiar—and slips into sleep.

5.

Dr. Calloway is trim, extremely handsome, early forties, seemingly straightforward, immediately cooperative, and will prove largely useless.

Heller knows it right off, because he senses right away that Calloway is a short-timer. He is doing his two-year stint as the doc-for-hire and will be happily gone and replaced at the end of this season.

Calloway gives him an impromptu tour of the infirmary before they talk. The infirmary is small but extremely well equipped. The most up-to-date EKG and diagnostic devices, ER-level monitors for vital signs, the latest in medicated patches and chemical treatments for frostbite and other extreme-temperature issues. Drug supply ample and triple locked. "I follow all the protocols carefully."

He motions Heller to sit at the only place available, the rolling stool at Calloway's small corner desk. Calloway sits on the examining table. How appropriate, Heller thinks. Both of them smile at the minor awkwardness.

"I've been a doctor on several expeditions to Everest and up K2, so I was well qualified for service here. But medical work on those trips is exciting, pulse-pounding sometimes, while here, it's mostly babysitting. This is a glorified school nurse's office. I'm heading back to the mainland at the end of the season. This isn't for me."

"Can you take me through what happened last June?"

Calloway smiles. "You mean on the night in question." He's enjoying meeting a detective. A change in routine.

Heller nods. "Yes, on the night in question."

"Sure." He shakes his head in frustration. "The one exciting, out-of-the-ordinary thing that comes my way all winter, and it was immediately apparent to me that I wasn't equipped to handle it."

Heller nods, waits for him to explain.

"Sandy . . . uh, Mr. Lazo-Wasum . . . was rushed in here by Pat Dolan and Dan Pritchard, the comm team. Dan radioed ahead on a walkie and told me they were coming, told me they stumbled on him unresponsive on the ground when they went out for dawn comm and weather check."

"What's that?"

"At McMurdo, Pritchard and Dolan physically check the comm tower and weather tower elements, to be sure everything's working. We can't risk any compromise in our communications or weather-reporting systems."

"Okay."

"I called Sorenson, our nurse, who hustled over to the infirmary to help me. We took Lazo-Wasum right in here, right where I'm sitting. Checked vitals immediately. No breath. No pulse. Skin blue. Skin temperature extremely low. Not icy yet, but cold. I cut through his parka and clothes in about five to ten seconds. We've got a special tool for that." Calloway holds up a finger—*wait*—opens a drawer behind him, pulls out a kind of electric knife, turns it on, and the fierce high whine and blinding-bright blade make his point for him. "The clothes fell to the floor around him. I administered a dose of adrenaline into his chest, and Sorenson prepared paddles.

"No apparent signs of bruising or asphyxiation or distress. In fact, no outward evidence of injury at all. I was keenly aware, believe me, that his near-frozen body might be preserving some clues about his condition and demise—that's the good part of living in a world of ice, Mr. Heller—and I was aware that every second he was warming up in here, as we tried to treat him and save him, I might have been losing those clues." He shakes his head, reliving the frustration.

"And that's when I saw it. Well, happened to see it. Truth be told, it's Sorenson who happened to see it. Just lucky. A pinprick at the base of the neck. A little dot of red. Could have been easily mistaken for a pimple or mark on the skin, but the recency told me it wasn't. And let me tell you, it was a little pinprick to my brain, seeing that. Because right away, if it's from a drug, it's from a drug that Lazo-Wasum did not administer to himself. Drug addict or OD? In the arm, sure, or even between toes or under the testicles to hide his addiction, I've seen that, but back of your own neck? Pretty much impossible. And if it's from a drug, and whoever administered it came up from behind him, then he might not have even known it happened. Maybe at night. Maybe never even felt it. This is all the stuff that was going through my mind right away, seeing that red needle mark. Now, I'm not a forensic technician, I'm a mountaineering medic, for Chrissake. I was way out of my depth on this, and I was sure right away that if I administered a standard toxicology protocol, it was not only going to risk missing this, it could even fuck up the evidence, taint it."

Going through Heller's mind are different questions: How did Nurse Sorenson happen to see it, when the doctor didn't? When the doctor implied it was unlikely or surprising that anyone would? Did she know it was there? And did she purposely have to point it out to the doctor, when she saw that he'd missed it, didn't see it for himself?

He'll be talking to her soon. Or holding off talking to her till he knows more. His first interview, and things are permutating already. The tentacles are already stretching out . . .

"I'm thinking right away this could be exotic. Lots of scientists here, doctors, PhDs. This was everything that was racing through my mind. And that's when I said to Sorenson, 'Let's get him back on ice, right away.' She was pretty shocked. And the fastest way to do it? Not by the book, but pretty effective. We lugged him naked out into the snow—Sorenson, me, Pritchard, and Dolan, who were still there with us, ready to be useful. We all chipped and packed ice around him, while we jury-rigged a container."

Which they did. And the body stayed frozen. Although at some point in those intervening months the refrigeration unit had malfunctioned, and the temperature had fluctuated, but it was not detected because, this being Antarctica, it was cold within cold, and no indicator had been triggered. The equipment and the notification systems were commercial grade and not built specifically for the extreme weather of Antarctica—nothing was. No indicator had flashed, no alarm had sounded, and the forensic damage, if there was any, was done. In addition to the temperature fluctuation, it was hard to say whether the doctor, quick acting though he was, had screwed up or tainted something anyway. Because a full toxicology report showed only trace elements of toxic materials, which could have been environmental, naturally occurring, or else the vestigial remainder of the purposeful dose that had killed Lazo-Wasum.

Something Heller knows. Something Heller knows the doctor knows.

"I might have done the exact right thing, Mr. Heller. Or I might have done the exact wrong thing. I'll never know."

Heller doesn't want Calloway to brood about it. What's done is done. Better to make him feel useful—and perhaps actually be useful. "You've had lots of time to think about all this, Doctor. About how they found Sandy, where they found him, how they got him in here, what you saw, physically and psychologically. Any theories? Any thoughts about what may have happened that you're even only half-inclined to share? I'd be interested. You've been living with this, after all."

Calloway sighs deeply. "Unfortunately, Mr. Heller, I'm a short-timer here. Nurse Sorenson has been here a long time. A number of people have done ten, twelve years here. But the doctors have all rotated off after two-year stints. So none of us get to know the health patterns, the patients, and their medical needs all that well. We're just not in the culture here like some others are. And I have a feeling that it's someone who's in the culture who's going to be most helpful to you."

6.

Next are Dolan and Pritchard, the communications techs who brought the body in. Hobbes has found Heller an office to use—really just a small empty desk and two chairs behind a partition in a corner of an administration building. Two locking drawers—that's all he'll have for private storage of any notes. But Heller is thinking that the formality of the little office may constrict the comfort of some people, so for initial interviews, he'll try to meet people in more neutral places—and, at the same time, get to know the rhythms of McMurdo a little.

So he meets Dolan and Pritchard in the canteen late morning for a coffee, after their daily communications-equipment inspection. Last June, of course, they were among the lean winter crew of scientists and technicians and support staff. But right now, in season, McMurdo Station is bustling with close to a thousand people in residence, and the canteen is lively and loud. Aromas of fresh coffee and baked goods pervade the room. Music pumps from hanging speakers—Springsteen, Coldplay, Mumford & Sons. Dolan and Pritchard lean toward Heller to make themselves heard.

Pritchard is the burlier of the two, but both seem solid and substantial beneath their parkas and snow pants. Dolan is from Vancouver; Pritchard's from Minnesota. Both move with a comical slowness in their outdoor gear, Heller notices—like they're on the moon.

They're both veterans of Antarctica. Permanent workforce.

"I've wintered over eight years now," says Pritchard. Beard reddish, unkempt, hair curly, eyes wide with childlike wonder.

"Year seven for me," says Dolan. Straight black hair, and black-framed eyeglasses devoid of style.

"Pays real good," Pritchard offers, as if anticipating and heading off the inevitable tiresome question of *why*, thinks Heller.

And despite their roustabout looks, they're plenty smart, Heller can tell.

"Tell me about that morning."

Dolan shrugs. "We head out as usual . . ."

"What time?"

"Six a.m." Dolan shrugs. "Arbitrary. In winter here, it's not like we're waiting for the morning light."

"Yeah, when we say morning, we don't mean sun or daylight, or any of the ways you normally think of morning." Pritchard smiles. "No birds or roosters or pink light or nothing. You gotta adjust your thinking."

"We make inspections once every twenty-four hours in high season and switch to an as-possible basis during winter."

Clearly, they want to be helpful. Eager to please, to be explanatory. *Probably the first two people I can eliminate as suspects.*

Then again, *you gotta adjust your thinking.*

"Ok. Go on."

"Totally dark, remember. So Dolan here practically trips over the body."

"Didn't actually trip over it or touch it," Dolan clarifies. "Did not make accidental contact with the body." *I followed the rules, sir, so don't penalize me.*

"Wind is blowing pretty stiff that morning too, so it's dark and there's snow swirling around. Typical of six a.m. that time of year."

"Typical, and no fun at all," adds Dolan.

Pritchard takes a breath. "At first, I couldn't see it was Sandy. I only realized it later as we were carrying him."

"Wait. How'd you know it then?" asks Heller. "You could see his face?"

Pritchard shakes his head. "No, I still couldn't see. But he was wearing the parka I'd always seen him in, with the duct tape at the zipper . . . I didn't consciously think about knowing him by his parka zipper, you know? . . . I just had a sudden sense it was Lazo-Wasum. What can I tell you?"

Too honest and weird to be anything but true, thinks Heller.

But Dolan adds in a little logic. "You know, there's not that many of us here in winter. We all know each other. See each other every day."

"Did you realize it was Lazo-Wasum?" Heller asks Dolan.

"I only realized when Pritchard said it."

"Said what?"

"Said, 'Hey, it's Lazo-Wasum.'"

"Okay, go back to when you first saw the body. What did you do?"

"Sprang into action. Walkie'd to the base doctor right away. That's what we're instructed to do in a medical emergency. Two-one-zero."

"Two-one-zero?"

"Base doc's code. We both know it 'cause of our inspection walks."

"We figured if there was any chance at all for this person, whoever it is, we need to get him inside. Seconds count. Didn't even have to discuss it, there in the wind. We both just picked him up."

"Him, not her?"

"Oh, by weight, you knew it was a him right off."

"And where'd you carry the body?"

"Straight to Med. The infirmary. About a three-hundred-yard carry."

"He was stiff and heavy, wasn't easy in the cold and blow."

"Plus it's pitch black, don't forget."

"But my adrenaline was pumping. I didn't even notice."

"No surprise it was slow going. So Sorenson, the base nurse, and Calloway, the doctor, were at Med by the time we got there. We helped them get the body up onto the exam table. Then they both waved us off, I guess afraid we couldn't take what was gonna happen next in there, heroic measures or whatnot . . . ," says Pritchard.

"I was happy enough not to see it," says Dolan.

"So we backed off like they wanted," says Pritchard.

"They needed to close the door to get the heat cranked."

"And then what?"

"We waited in case they needed us."

"Turns out they did."

Heller lets them describe the impromptu icing of Lazo-Wasum's body—just to make sure their version matches Calloway's.

"And then?" Heller asks.

Pritchard shrugs. "Then, we did our comm rounds."

"Comm. Communications?"

"That's right."

Heller thinks suddenly of the gravediggers in *Hamlet*. Just doing their jobs.

"Tell me about your comm rounds." Heller is pretty sure it isn't relevant, but he might as well learn a little more about McMurdo. He notices how Pritchard and Dolan light up at the opportunity. Clearly no one ever asks. And this is a lot more of a comfort zone than talking about a frozen dead body. This is a chance to talk skills and success, not failure.

"We need to regularly inspect the communications towers, for damage, for connections, for security."

The comm towers—two scaffolded structures, about four stories each—stand in unobstructed spots: one a few hundred yards from McMurdo, the other almost a mile further.

"That's our communications lifeline. How we connect to the world. See, telecom here is pretty limited, for a couple of reasons. You can't have a satellite in geosynchronous orbit over Antarctica. Earth doesn't rotate enough at its poles for that." Dolan demonstrates roughly with his hands, circling an index finger over his fist. "And telecom providers won't upgrade service for just five thousand people across a whole continent. Hell, less than five *hundred* people for almost half the year. Just not economically feasible. But hey, our towers work great. As long as they keep working. And we keep 'em working."

"All our communications. All our Internet and Wi-Fi and connection to the rest of the planet. Entrusted to a couple of IT dudes."

They laugh.

But Pritchard adds, reflectively: "It's weird, Detective Heller, these old towers for all our comm systems. Sophisticated but primitive, you know?"

"Sophisticated but primitive," says Heller. "You're not the first one to tell me that about Antarctica."

And as they're getting up to go, shaking hands, Heller asks them: "What's that duct tape about? On Sandy's zipper?"

A shrug. "So's he can get a better grip on the zipper in the cold, I guess. Not a bad idea."

Did he need a better grip than the next guy for some reason? Did it make him more identifiable to someone who wanted to identify him quickly? The questions expand. They always do in the beginning. It's part of Heller's love-hate relationship with police work.

"Hey, where do I find Sorenson?" asks Heller. "She's not on the clinic schedule today."

Pritchard and Dolan shoot each other a quick smile. Pritchard slides on his sunglasses, still smiling. "Oh, you'll find her, don't worry. She's pretty hard to miss."

7.

Next: the scientists in Lazo-Wasum's lab. His fellow researchers.

Heller makes his way to the botany laboratory. A sleek, gleaming steel-skinned building that stands out like an alien ship amid much older, grimier neighboring structures. Inside, the walls are brushed aluminum, the floor is a bright porcelain tile, and Heller immediately and intuitively understands that this is the point, the value, the real and central business of McMurdo Station: funded research, commercial applications, bottom-line potential.

Sandy's colleagues are still stunned, upset, six months later. They are glad to meet Heller—finally, the chance for some resolution—and unhappy to meet him, opening up the old wounds, the old questions, the old suspicions about one another. Heller knows this before he even enters the room with them.

A new botany lab director, who was not here last winter, who is untainted, who didn't know Lazo-Wasum, introduces Heller to the team—three men and two women—who worked with Sandy every day. Who knew him either passingly or very well. Who loved him. Who hated him. Who were indifferent. Heller would soon get a sense.

He sits with them at a conference table in one corner of the lab. The botany director offers him coffee. Gathers the researchers around.

"This is Detective Heller. He's here formally investigating Sandy's death. He's got some questions for you. For all of you, and for each of you." He nods to Heller.

As Heller starts to explain, he gets the sense these are classic bench scientists. Quiet. Introverted. *Weenies,* they were called with easy derision at his working-class high school in Northern Vermont—and at every high school in America, he's sure. This could just as easily be a lab on Route 128 in Boston or on the outskirts of Palo Alto or in the gentle hills of Northern Virginia, any of the research corridors—except for the endless snow and ice and brutal cold surrounding it.

Tell me about Lazo-Wasum, he's about to ask. *You were with him every day. Who was he? What was he like? Who did he hang with? Who did he like? Dislike?* But he has the sense that they will be mute. Respectful of their old colleague, as they see it. Eager to cooperate, but not really sure how.

"The first thing I'm wondering," says Heller, "is how you do botany in Antarctica? Plants versus extreme cold and dark—in my mind, they don't really go together, do they?"

Well, this is why it's important, Mr. Heller, this is why it makes a difference—and suddenly the little circle of botanists is looser, more animated, explaining about limited resources, about the fascinating reality and interesting effects of extreme cold, and the concept and practice of adaptive photosynthesis, and its possible applications and the adaptation of the findings to other, more populous places on the planet, and their eyes are lit up, and they are eager to correct his conventional misconceptions, to educate him, which is exactly what he intended.

He chats with all of them together for a few minutes. Then interviews each of them separately for ten minutes or so.

The scientist who was closest to Lazo-Wasum turns out to be a botanist named Theo Cohen. They worked next to each other in the lab. And as conventionally if abstractly good-looking as Lazo-Wasum seems to have been from his photos, Cohen is contrastingly not. Wide ears. No chin. All forehead. The kind of scientist who may have been drawn to the lab as a kid because he felt rejected or dismissed everywhere else.

"Good scientist," says Cohen. "Very capable. I have to admit I admired his basic bench skills. You don't get that in a lot of highfalutin Stanford and MIT types, but Sandy had, I guess, a kind of modesty and steadiness and, I don't know, decency that maybe comes from growing up in Europe." Heller can hear that Theo Cohen was ready to not like his colleague but couldn't help himself. "He had an interesting working theory on nonnative species transadaptation. I had my doubts, but I've been wrong before."

"So you two discussed your work."

"Absolutely. He was very curious about my hydroponics and forced-growing experiments."

"Ever discuss anything besides work with him? Girlfriends? His private life?"

Cohen looks at him horrified. "That's just not . . . just not what you do in the lab, Mr. Heller."

Or not what *you* do in the lab, thinks Heller.

Heller hears, from Theo Cohen and the others, all the respectful mythmaking of a colleague suddenly gone. A kind of hushed, laudatory impulse. A classic response for those unaccustomed to dealing with sudden death. A response he has seen so often, recognizes so well.

His thoughts wander, as he dutifully interviews them all, but wander to the same place. To how cut off, isolated, the five of them are—individually and collectively. Educated, privileged, coddled researchers, living on university or government grants, in an endless series of clean bright labs, long cut off from messier life. These botanical researchers, in their white lab coats and black-framed glasses—hothouse flowers

themselves. As scientists, they have a rarefied existence to begin with—
a life of the mind, of research papers, of conferences, and a shared
language of arcane academic terminology—but these five, sealed into
a lab at the end of the earth, are doubly insulated from the messiness
of life. He can't help noticing, smiling a little, at such a contrast to his
own life. Knowing the streets and alleys and dirt and filth. Inhabiting
the messiness. They are not fully alive, a part of him thinks. Or, at least,
not alive in the same way. And in that way they can't really, fully process
their colleague's death.

Couple that with other, more conventional signs and clues—alibis,
personality tics and traits, nervousness, all of which he sees and inter-
prets with the instant accuracy of long experience—and Heller realizes,
knows in his gut, that Sandy Lazo-Wasum's lab colleagues are, individually and collectively, not only innocent of any crime but useless to him.

• • •

As he is putting on his parka to exit, he asks the group of them, offhand-
edly, "Hey, where can I find Nurse Sorenson?"

He notices one of the two women get a little hard-edged, bristle
a little.

He sees Theo Cohen go a little dreamy. And another researcher
narrows his eyes with what Heller detects as a little jealousy.

Huh.

• • •

He looks for Anita Sorenson at the cafeteria at lunch. "She's usually
here about now." "She was just here." But he always just misses her.
McMurdo does have a thousand residents in high season, but he still
gets the distinct impression she is avoiding him. Which is absurd on

her part, because she will have to talk to him at some point. There is no hiding. This is Antarctica.

A more logical explanation of such behavior would be that she is trying to get something done—take care of something, talk to someone, arrange something—*before* they meet. What could she be trying to handle, or arrange or hide, before she meets him?

• • •

In the vestibule of the base canteen a few days later, he happens to see the name tag on a parka of someone just coming in. "Ms. Sorenson?"

The parka turns. Hooded tightly in the cold. Sunglasses.

"You've been a little tough to find."

She slides her hood off. Pulls the sunglasses off her eyes.

Suddenly he understands what Pritchard and Dolan's smirks were about.

And the woman researcher's prickliness, and the male researcher's dreaminess, and the other one's jealousy.

What nobody said, but everybody was thinking; what Heller had picked up a little bit from all of them.

Sorenson is beautiful. Ridiculously, almost laughably beautiful. The conventional heart-stopping version, the textbook case. Scandinavian blonde. Flaxen hair. Swimming blue eyes. Beauty hidden and revealed in two quick, fluid motions of her hood pulled back and her parka unzipped, like a Bond-movie heroine. Beauty amplified by her slightly flushed skin coming out of the cold. Perfect smile, which she deploys now, seeing, Heller supposes, how he is a little startled.

Almost a thousand people at McMurdo. Some percentage is going to be pretty desirable.

Even more desirable than usual in the long, cutoff, isolated winter?

Heller's mental gears suddenly spin a little more quickly.

One little gear has already been spinning for a while. Something that bothered him right away that he's been waiting to ask her about: how quickly Sorenson got to the infirmary when Calloway called her at 6:00 a.m. In less time, apparently, than it took Pritchard and Dolan to drag Lazo-Wasum's body there. How? Why?

8.

Suddenly, in a cognitive flash, Heller understands "winter-over."

Or, at least, one unspoken aspect of it.

Obviously, the high-toned conversation about reading mystery series and botany texts and the DSM psychiatric manual distracted him.

Obviously, the scientists' pristine lab coats and earnest conversations have misled him.

Or, at least, aren't the whole winter-over story.

"You've been avoiding me."

Sorenson doesn't say anything. Looks away.

"It's going to be better for you if you talk to me. No matter what your role in Sandy's death is."

She turns to him, anger and hurt sudden and pulsing in her eyes, but then tears begin to well in them and run down her cheeks.

"My *role?*" she says quietly. Bitterly.

Heller can tell by her response that she feels she has one. And he can guess by the emotion attached to it that it is not a role in killing Lazo-Wasum. That it is a more nuanced role. And that perhaps more than anything else—or anyone else—she misses him.

So Heller takes a chance. Since Antarctica seems to operate by its own rules, maybe his approach here will too. Maybe he won't do things by the book, since he doesn't really have to, since there is no book.

He looks around. No one's within earshot. "I have to tell you, Ms. Sorenson, something bugged me right away. How did you get dressed so fast? How were you at the clinic so fast, ready to receive the body so fast when Dolan and Pritchard called about finding it? I've walked it. I've timed it. You must have been awake and dressed already. From being with Mr. Lazo-Wasum earlier?" *In fact, just minutes earlier?*

He stares at her quietly. Waits. She says nothing back. Serving up her beauty cold, unadorned.

"I think we're talking about some specialized knowledge here, when it comes to that neck. A mark so small, Dr. Calloway pretty much admits he wouldn't have noticed it otherwise." He narrows his eyes, to watch, hawklike, for any reaction. "I think you saw that mark on his neck because you knew that neck," says Heller.

She looks up at Heller, expressionlessly, before the blue eyes moisten again. "I knew every inch of him," she says quietly.

They both know how much it tells him.

How compressed and efficient. How demure yet explicit.

An affair, thinks Heller. Ongoing. Not some quick fling, some sudden, impulsive coupling in the dark. *I knew every inch of him.*

And he realizes—with sympathetic revulsion, with horror—that as she was looking at Lazo-Wasum's body with the doctor, closely examining every inch of it inert in front of her, she had been examining it live, lovingly, affectionately, laughingly, just a few hours before.

That's what her avoidance was about. An extra wound, much wider and deeper and more evident than a pinprick at the base of the neck. Much bloodier.

That's what the fresh tears might be about as well. An extra bit of torture, of memory that will never go away.

"How long had you been seeing him?" Heller asks quietly.

"Just that winter."

"Did people generally know?"

"That's the thing," she says. "I don't think anyone knew. These winter liaisons. They come in two basic styles, Mr. Heller." They are sitting now, off by themselves, at the end of the dark little vestibule hallway off the main canteen area. A space even long-time residents might not notice. Some boxes of unidentified supplies are stacked around them. "The first style is 'everybody knows.' You're acknowledged as a couple. It's as if to say to everyone else, don't touch, don't mess, hands off, we're together. Like a temporary marriage that other people here witness and accept, even if it is temporary. The second kind of liaison, it's a secret. Some of the energy and thrill of it, frankly, is that no one knows. It's just between the two of you. So it lets you maintain your independence, your identity, your separate self in the eyes of your coworkers. Ours was the second kind. As far as I knew. As far as I could tell."

"Would you characterize this as casual? Or something more."

She smiles sadly. Her eyes well up again. "Something more." Her emotions are close to the surface. They have been waiting, frozen, for someone to thaw them, give them permission to melt, to spread, to show themselves. No wonder she avoided him. She didn't want this. She knew it about herself.

An affair—but not one anyone else knows about, she doesn't think.

She could easily be wrong about that, of course. Or, she could know she is wrong about that and is choosing not to say who she thinks might have known. Choosing not to say for some reason Heller doesn't know yet.

And whoever may have known could have been motivated by jealousy, by hostility, by who knows what.

"Ms. Sorenson, who had you been seeing or been involved with here before your relationship with Sandy?"

She shakes her head.

Does it mean no one? Or does it mean *I'm not going to say*?

"No one?"

"No one of consequence."

"That's for me to decide, Ms. Sorenson."

She shrugs. "Allan Seward. He's in transport."

He writes it down.

"Paulson. Ben Paulson."

He writes it down.

"Covington. Sarah Covington."

He holds his pen still, hovering, before he writes it.

She sees his pen pause. Smiles a little.

He recognizes that he has stepped into a new reality. One that had not occurred to him.

He realizes suddenly that he has to ask. Ask the obvious. So obvious he had dismissed it out of hand. Too obvious, too self-incriminating, too crazy for them to have so openly put themselves at the scene of their own crime. To have committed the crime, in tandem—a camaraderie of jealousy? Of retribution?—and then pretended to "discover" the body. So arrogantly, absurdly, bluntly stupid that he had rejected it immediately. But now, whether merely for due diligence, or because in the strange slanted light of this new reality there might be something he hadn't seen, he has to ask. Not knowing, of course, if she'll give an honest answer.

"Pritchard? Dolan?"

Sorenson looks at him evenly. "Not at the same time," she says.

Good Christ.

"You've got to understand the culture here, Mr. Heller," she says. "Or try to."

Like Pritchard said, *You gotta adjust your thinking.*

● ● ●

He sees Hobbes in the canteen at dinnertime. He gets his tray, walks by him, and Hobbes, as Heller assumed, motions Heller to the empty chair across from him.

"Settling in okay? So far so good?"

"Sure."

"You'll find the food surprisingly good, I think. Our head cook, Robert Manafort, is a genius with mass ingredients. Unless we all just lose our sense of taste after a while. Which is a mild version of what arctic explorers have experienced for centuries—that when you're hungry enough, at the edges of starvation, even beef jerky tastes as good as sirloin steak." Heller senses that Hobbes enjoys educating him about the continent. Hobbes has the teacher gene—for better or worse.

Heller digs in. Hobbes is right. Not bad.

"Manafort is self-taught, but he takes the limitations as a personal challenge, and he's got a couple of full-time assistants he's also trained." He chews for a moment. "The basic communal pleasure of meals becomes more intense, almost overwhelming, during the winter-over. For some of us. Others lose interest in food and socializing entirely." He shrugs.

Heller looks around. They are momentarily out of earshot of anyone.

"Manny, you're on my suspect list, same as anyone, but I do need to ask you about something."

"Sure."

Heller smiles. "Manny Hobbes, we need to talk about sex."

Hobbes looks up, smiles, nods. "This'll be a livelier dinner than I thought." But then pauses. "Wait. Not *my* sex life!"

"Maybe. I don't know."

"That's going to be a very short conversation, I'm afraid." Hobbes smiles. "And *not* a very lively one, I assure you. Try not to fall asleep during it." Then, smiling again: "Which basically is all I do in the bunk room."

"No, not your sex life. I mean McMurdo sex life. Sex life here, particularly during the winter." Heller stabs a bite of chicken on his tray, shovels it in, swallows, continues. "There's a different winter-over culture here. And I need you to tell me about it. And don't sugarcoat it, and don't bullshit me. This is not to disseminate to the world. This is only to inform a homicide investigation."

Manny sighs. Leans back, indicating with body language to Heller that he should perhaps do the same. That they're going to be here awhile. Heller is pleased to get the sense that Manny already knows there is much to say. That he doesn't resist at all.

"You know how the rules are different here? No countries? No borders? You're going to see how that applies to sex here too. Different rules. Undefined boundaries. It's a few factors. The cold—people can't get warm. The aloneness during the day, the aloneness of the land-scape—people want to connect. Want companionship. Lots of young, healthy, physically fit people—that's who gets this assignment. People who are unattached enough, independent enough, to be able to come here. They're here for a few months, then back to their previous lives. This is a different time and place, a time-out from their other lives. And then the old classic problem—nothing else to do at night. And half the year, it becomes one long, long night with nothing to do. No bars, no restaurants, no movie theater, no place to gather. The old "caveman" problem. Got to entertain yourself. Lots of alcohol and drugs available, to pave the way. And these are scientists. Pushing the bounds of the known. They like to experiment." A smile.

But Heller is already thinking. Sex doesn't come unattached. It comes with feelings, territoriality, unleashed passion, and unleashed fury, even genuine love, whatever that is. Ninety percent of homicides are between people who knew each other well. People emotionally involved. He has the sense that this wild, unspoken sex life is where things will lead him.

"No kids, no pets allowed at McMurdo. That's because we don't want animals to bring new pathogens to the continent or kids to be subjected to any. But the result is no pet to snuggle with on a cold night.

No child to hug. Or to model adult behavior for. So of course there's sex. The only companionship. The only comfort. The only warmth."

Maybe it's time for some kids and pets, thinks Heller.

Maybe it's time to normalize things a little.

But Heller suddenly understands much more about winter-over. It's not just mystery books and botany texts.

"I'm pretty sure, Manny, that if I were to check all the caches on personal computers during the winter, I'd find plenty of porn, wouldn't I? Round-the-clock porn, for any number of these guys."

"Women too, no?" says Manny.

"Of course."

Manny shrugs. "I'm sure you'd find plenty of it. But so what?"

"It's what else I might find in the caches, Manny. Maybe sites that tilt from porno to outright violence. Or sites describing homemade poisons."

Hobbes looks stricken. Lowers his eyes, as if in shame. "It wouldn't do you much good to check the computer caches, because we clean them as a matter of course once a year, when the new crew arrives with the warmer weather around October."

"That's gonna make investigating this tougher." Heller figures he can check current caches that haven't yet been wiped. If someone's got an obsession or fixation, it doesn't disappear with the season. Of course, he can't systematically check every cache for no reason. McMurdo operates by US laws. He needs cause.

Hobbes looks at him. "Sorry about the caches. We did not anticipate this. This is unexplored territory." He smiles thinly. "You're at the frontier, Joe . . . of geography, climate . . . and homicide investigation."

9.

Pritchard and Dolan.

Besides the botany lab scientists and Calloway, they're the only two people he's already spoken to.

Who never volunteered that they'd each slept with Sorenson.

Either because they'd had no idea that she'd been seeing Lazo-Wasum. So it would be entirely irrelevant to mention. *Oh, by the way, I once had a fling with a nurse here. The same nurse who came to receive Lazo-Wasum when we found him, because she is the only nurse.*

Or because they *did* know she was seeing Lazo-Wasum, and knew it had turned into something, where theirs had been one-night stands, and being jealous, annoyed, for whatever reason, they poisoned him. The radio guys, who would never be suspected—particularly since they were the do-gooders who found the body.

Or the third possibility, the one that Heller's instincts are calling out to him already, the one that he is almost certain, by long experience, will turn out to be the case: because they knew of the ongoing affair, and also knew the other had slept with Sorenson . . . and while they had nothing to do with the murder, they were sure that, because of their respective previous one-night stands with her and discovery of the body, an investigation not only would lead to them but might somehow—circumstantially or by inference or by mere convenience—actually convict them, and terrified of that prospect, they made the idiotic decision to say nothing.

Pritchard and Dolan. Great.

He's barely been here, and it's already getting screwed up.

The first witnesses he talked to already haven't told the whole story.

Antarctica's clean, white, blank slate is already muddy and rutted, like a dirty alley in McMurdo.

His neat, clean list of 157 names already has asterisks, question marks, scribbles, and he's barely started on it.

He'll have to check back with Pritchard and Dolan. In some less direct way.

Maybe talk them into taking him on a radio-tower inspection.

His investigation. Dammit. The engine is just pulling out of the station and already there are parts rumbling and rattling and threatening to fall off.

And knowing himself, maybe most dangerous of all—Heller is already a little pissed off.

• • •

There is a little more to these sexual liaisons, Heller realizes. A little more than the loneliness and cold that explains the night activity during the winter-over. Something more important behind the coupling. Because what kind of a person comes to Antarctica to begin with? As Hobbes said, someone who can go. Someone with no ties. It's both kinds of pioneer spirit. Both kinds of pioneer personalities. Meaning, someone who wants to seize new opportunity, conquer new worlds and challenges. But also, it's someone who wants to escape. To cut ties. Both kinds of settlers had headed to America, to Australia, west to California. Yes, to experience new, expanded possibility. But also to start over in some way. Erase the past by creating a new future. To put whatever they had screwed up behind them.

He realizes it isn't necessarily so black and white, of course. For most people, it's a mixture of the two: fresh start and escape. Some of our best human impulses, and some of our most covert and shameful ones.

He smiles a little sadly, staring up at the ceiling above his bunk. Because he knows it is a person like him. In the analysis of what kind of person comes to Antarctica, to the end of the earth, he is Exhibit A. Because while he was asked by the US Marshal's Service on the basis of his skills, his résumé, his availability, he said yes because he wanted the fresh start. Nothing was holding him. He was leaving nothing important behind. Or nothing that couldn't wait. Or that might be better if it waited—getting distance, actual and psychological and emotional.

It's people without ties who are willing to come to Antarctica. People without the strong and normal ties of family life, of marriage, of child rearing, of convention. And others for whom life is adventure, life is risk and possibility, who see life's richness and shortness clearly.

So Antarctica naturally draws some of the psychologically healthiest people on the planet, he realizes—and arguably some of the psychologically sickest.

And here both types are thrown in together. Getting to know each other. Working with each other. Sleeping with each other.

And when the two types commingle—when the sick entwine with the healthy, psychologically speaking—some "virus" may get created and pass between them. A dangerous virus. A lethal bug.

• • •

People without ties. People willing to turn their backs on life. To pretend there's nothing in the rearview mirror. He lies there thinking about his ex-wife, Ann. His daughter, Amy. Eighteen now. He should be in her life. And while it would seem, on the surface, that he is the one not looking in the rearview mirror—that he is the one who's torn the mirror off completely—it is actually Ann who turns out to have a surprising aptitude for forgetting, for going forward, for ignoring the past. And yet she is the one who stayed, so she is the one who to the outside world looks steady, remaining in her job, raising her daughter, but psychologically is the one who cut her losses, more easily erased the past, and while he looks to be trying to escape it, he is only traveling to new places to continue to stew in it. He is the one in Antarctica, but he is the one stuck in the past, overly loyal, an unchanging fool. Tonight, he doesn't want to go there. He needs to shut off this line of thinking in the dark. He turns over in his bunk, as if to face away from such thoughts.

Would he be one of those who slept with Sorenson, or someone like her, if he was wintering over? Learning, with the power of desire, to be one of the cut off? One of the isolated? Willing to live in the present, to assume, or pretend, there are no consequences?

And a bigger question comes to him—as if unbidden, from his unconscious—before he rolls into sleep.

Can anyone really start fresh?

Is there really such a thing as starting over?

He realizes—smiles a little to notice, in these moments before sleep—that it is shifting in his mind from a psychological to a philosophical question.

In the weeks ahead, he will remember lying here thinking this thought—and his head will pound at the irony of it, at the prescience of it, at the unpredictably deep and terrifying reverberations of that innocent philosophical question.

Is there really such a thing as starting over?

10.

While he pursues the *who,* he simultaneously explores the *how:*

Poisoning.

He starts to look into the possibilities, and they multiply almost immediately. Go exponential on him every time he turns his thoughts toward them.

The pinprick at the back of the neck. That Sorenson saw immediately, knowing the downy back of that neck so well.

Poisoning isn't just poisoning. It falls into subsets—of materials, technique, delivery system.

One subset it falls into that people don't generally consider: Is it slow or fast? Each has its advantages and disadvantages.

Slow has the advantage of the perpetrator being able to create distance between the deed and him- or herself. You can be in another place, another city, on another continent before it takes effect. The victim might mistake it for sickness, because certain poisons can simply feel like a bad flu or the creep of disease, and a young Antarctic employee might not even bother the doctor with such common symptoms. Or their worsening might be so gradual, so subtle, that the victim hardly notices, until it is suddenly, mortally, too late.

Slow has the advantage of many subtle and undetectable delivery methods. Air, food, water, even a powder or residue against the skin. Alcohol, recreational drugs, even one's daily toiletries—cologne, antiperspirant, toothpaste. Even the skin moisturizer for the face or hands to defend against the Antarctic cold. All potential delivery systems. Each a creepy way to invade the personal, to violate the presumed inviolate. Slow has the advantage of looking for something that works in unique conjunction with the cold. Maybe a lethal chemical reaction that the extreme cold disguises especially well.

Or fast. Fast poisoning being almost a contradiction in terms. Fast can have the advantage of greater certainty. No chance of recovery, of reversal, of accidental antidote. No time to introduce an antidote.

But fast is inherently riskier because the perpetrator cannot get distance of time and place. The only "distance" will be in the exoticism and stealth of the materials. Fast requires, in general, a greater degree of facility with poisons, to disguise the poison adequately, so that it's not just a chemical version of, say, an evidence-laden gunshot wound. Though it is, Heller realizes, a *silent* version of a gunshot wound. And it can be a *guaranteed* version of a gunshot wound, reducing the chance of surviving it, as you might a gunshot wound. And there aren't firearms allowed or available at McMurdo, by order of the National Science Foundation, and because there's no rational need for them—a place of science, no polar bears or other natural predators, no military presence because none of the other countries' research stations allow them either, by international agreement—so the fast poisoning to some degree *replaces* out of necessity the gunshot wound, and it requires less force, produces less mess, no muss, no fuss, and is more lethal, depending on the poison. It doesn't require you to overpower the victim. It takes the physicality out of it. The perpetrator can be small. Which means the perpetrator can be anyone.

With fast poisoning, the big disadvantage is you have to be there. Which perhaps means you have to witness it. Which also perhaps means you *want* to witness it. That you have chosen fast poisoning, you take on its risks, because you really want to be there.

Heller shudders.

Either someone *had* to take the risk. Suddenly. Because something had suddenly changed, something had suddenly been discovered, a sudden, desperate, anxious reaction—the clock was suddenly ticking.

Or someone *wanted* to take the risk. Or doesn't care about the risk. The poison is merely a convenient, unconventional stand-in for a knife or gun. A sudden, furious, vengeful response—in chemical form.

The prick at the back of the neck definitely says fast. Risky and fast.

And the winter-over nightlife—the sexual mores and escapades, the drinking and drugs—definitely points to something passionate, impulsive, vengeful.

Or points to an environment of passionate, impulsive, vengeful people, which would be a perfect cover, a perfect diversion, a perfect misdirection for something—and someone—more cunning.

Poisoning seems exotic, at first. But thinking of all the available chemical ingredients from ongoing experiments, of the collegial atmosphere of science and research, of the lack of conventional weaponry, of the quiet, collaborative, close-knit community, he realizes that it is, on the contrary, the least exotic and most reasonable way to murder someone on Antarctica, and the odds of getting away with it are very high. If you have it in for someone, and you're on Antarctica, there are no guns, and knife wounds leave lots of blood and clues, so poisoning is the way to go.

The prick mark at the back of the neck?

The handiwork of a needle, presumably.

But finding that needle? There is already a useful, knowing expression about that, the haystack in this case being the pile of medical waste, or even general waste, that the needle has undoubtedly been tossed into, and all that waste, medical and general, already transported out aboard one of the previous year's flights, with every other ounce of Antarctic trash, in the cargo section of a 747.

Unless whoever was clever enough to administer this poison was careful and smart enough *not* to want to risk tossing the needle in with other waste, where someone investigating might naturally begin looking for it, because every ounce of trash *is* transported out, doesn't stay put, can possibly be seen and intercepted, so the killer didn't take that risk but put it somewhere else, and that needle and plunger of evidence are still here. Just beneath the frozen surface somewhere? A square couple of inches of evidence amid five million square miles of identical landscape? Not recoverable.

Or in the bottom drawer of a bedside table, the perpetrator still trying to figure out what to do with it? Recoverable, maybe.

Heller, sitting at the little desk in his little room, continues his Internet research into poisoning.

Cross-references it with cold. What does well in the cold? What's untraceable in the cold? When it comes to poisons, is there a cold-weather superstar? Heller searches.

His career has served up countless gunshots, stabbings, beatings, even lethal martial-arts holds—even the proverbial fireplace poker and tire iron—but if there was a poisoning, he can't remember it. Which makes him an odd choice for this case, he thinks.

He has everything to learn.

But this research need not be lonely, isolated. Quite the opposite.

He has dozens of experts to call on, to explain the science, to propose how *they* would do it.

And maybe one or two of them will prove a little too knowledgeable or finally notice some compound missing from the lab, or something.

And he still hasn't quite gotten past the initial question about that pinprick at the back of the neck.

What are the circumstances under which Lazo-Wasum's neck could have been punctured so easily, so perfectly? Commingling with the fluid of the spinal column at such an optimal point?

So far, his imagination is failing him there.

He dutifully researches everything he can about poisoning.

But part of him knows he isn't going to learn anything new.

Because tapping at the back of his brain—tapping there since he first read the file, since the long flight down—is a little drumbeat of knowledge and instinct and experience that tells him he already knows everything he needs to about the poisoning.

Which is that a poison can be concocted pretty easily out of all kinds of common, readily available chemical materials. Anything under the sink will work, in all sorts of combinations. To say nothing of what's in the labs. Which he'd bet the killer knew.

He would also bet that the killer knew the limits of the infirmary here. That they weren't really equipped to do an autopsy and certainly didn't have the tools or knowledge to successfully isolate what the poison actually was.

He'd further bet the killer knew that sending the body elsewhere for a full autopsy was going to be time consuming and impractical, that there wouldn't be a decent weather window to ship the body out in winter, that the evidence would likely be compromised in transit, so any eventual, actual autopsy would prove in the end inconclusive—and knowing all this, the McMurdo authorities might not even bother with an autopsy at all.

All leading to Heller's biggest fear: that knowing all this—with all this working in his or her favor—a killer might just as easily, just as brazenly, just as heedlessly and comfortably do it again.

• • •

He also realizes that some typical investigative tools aren't going to apply.

In a normal investigation, you can call on cell-phone records, but there are no cell phones, because there is no cell service. There had been spotty and intermittent satellite phone service for several years, but only the administrators and key personnel had the cumbersome handsets, because of the expense. Now that Internet service has become increasingly reliable, they've recently abandoned the satellite phones altogether. Some of the McMurdo residents manage to make phone calls over the Internet. Getting those records from Internet providers won't be easy—it will be a first such request from Antarctica, he's sure, and it will be coming from a US Marshal subcontractor and will require lots of patient explanation and perseverance—but Heller has begun that process and that paperwork.

And of course, it's all contingent on having specific records to request.

Police work on the seventh continent doesn't have much in common with the other six.

11.

Exactly 995 miles down the road from Mac Station (as Heller has already learned the locals call it) is the other American base, Amundsen-Scott Station. McMurdo is coastal; Amundsen-Scott is a thousand miles inland, within a hundred yards of the South Pole itself. In high summer, it's accessible by C-130 transport and smaller cargo aircraft, in nearly daily cargo airlifts and exchanges between the two stations, and by Traverse Highway—a 995-mile road of densely packed snow marked by flags, for tractors and sleds, which nevertheless must watch for crevices the whole way there, because the snow and snowpack shifts. In winter, there is no air access—and land access is risky, not recommended except for emergencies, and for several months impossible.

Amundsen-Scott makes McMurdo look positively civilized. It's two hundred people in summer, fewer than fifty in winter, when it is completely isolated, and experiences one long six-month night each year—absolute night, with no hint or glimmer of sun on the horizon.

Originally a geodesic dome, the base is now composed of ingenious curved structures on pillars that allow the snow to blow around and beneath the living quarters to prevent being completely covered after a storm. The pillars can adjust independently to the snow beneath them, which condenses gradually and unevenly and would otherwise cause the structure to tilt one way or the other.

But people do winter over in Amundsen-Scott, and there are on record winter trips between the bases via tractor and motorized sled within weeks of Lazo-Wasum's murder—extremely arduous, only occasional—but for that reason, Heller is including Amundsen-Scott in his investigation.

Hobbes arranges a ride for both of them on the C-130 that goes the next morning.

• • •

Ice. Snow. As far as the eye can see. The drone of the C-130 engines. A primitive workhorse, plying the sky.

All the way there, the Traverse Highway is below him, like a map coordinate. The road to nowhere. A highway with only one entrance and one exit.

They pass a yellow snow tractor below them, making the all-day journey.

On the C-130, it's a couple of hours. The unchanging drone of the four engines matches the unchanging landscape. There are no reference points. No way to judge whether you're moving forward or simply sitting stationary in the air.

The landing is quick, unceremonious, jarring, designed first for actual cargo, only secondarily for human cargo.

As he descends the cargo ramp, the air temperature is noticeably colder than at McMurdo. And though he is correctly defended against it, with goggle shades, balaclava, thermal gloves and socks, this cold is a different thing. McMurdo is plenty cold—laughably or terrifyingly or stunningly cold, depending on your mood—but this is something outside human experience. It is eerie, otherworldly.

It is Mars. He is stepping onto Mars. A human outpost. A fragile human colony—in a small cluster of buildings, each compact and unconventional—amid an unthinkable vastness.

Unlike McMurdo, with its engines, activities, movement, bustle, Amundsen-Scott is still—and silent, once the C-130 engines recede. (The plane takes off immediately once unloaded; they don't risk turning the engines off, in case they don't turn back on, because it's too cold to make engine repairs.)

A silence unlike any he has heard. Because previous silence, he notices now, has presence, has sound to it. A silence that is usually a pause, a noticeable suspension of sound, sound waiting to rush back in again.

But this silence is enormous, oceanic. A silence that feels like it belongs to the cosmos.

Hobbes leads them into the structure. Its door is thick, its edges rounded, like a decompression lock from a science-fiction spaceship.

A bearded Texan named Kevin Morton greets them on the other side of the door.

In contrast to the haphazard, ramshackle spread of McMurdo, everything is packed together here. Kitchen, quarters, meeting area, laboratories, all kept neatly, immaculately. Thick glass windows to the outside. A space vessel.

They sit with Morton in a window bay as Hobbes elaborates further on what he has alerted Morton to before they arrived. Lazo-Wasum. Homicide investigation. Wouldn't involve Amundsen-Scott at all, except that there was overland travel between the stations on a few of the milder days of that winter, around the time of the murder.

"I'm assuming all intrastation travel is logged somewhere, yes?"

Morton nods cooperatively. "Every trip."

"So Heller here will need to check those logs."

"On computer. Can't print them, we're paperless here, but I can e-mail them to you," Morton says to Heller. "There won't be many. Just a handful of trips that time of year. Only something absolutely necessary. Repair work that can't wait, that kind of thing. But even though there aren't that many trips, there's still gonna be an issue with accuracy." Morton starts rubbing the side of his beard, as if trying to rub a solution into being. "The driver is always logged in—every vehicle trip has that in its manifest notes. But we don't bother with a record of the passengers."

Heller raises his eyebrows, registering a little surprise.

"I mean, Mac and Amundsen-Scott. Same team. This is no border crossing. There's a lot of back and forth in general, Mr. Heller, particularly in the busy summer. And the driver is like a ferry captain, I guess—in charge of passenger safety but not so concerned about who's on what vehicle at what time. Truth is, we encourage everyone to think of it as one base, so the culture kinda goes against tracking who's where and when."

"You'll send the trip logs anyway?"

"Don't know what good it'll do you, but absolutely, happy to."

The Traverse Highway is impassible during most of winter. Heller has already checked the Amundsen-Scott Station weather on the days before and after the murder. The weather had been typical for that time of winter—ungodly, seventy below, eighty-mile-an-hour gusts, zero visibility. If some crazy soul or souls tried and somehow made it over the Traverse Highway, it would have been the talk of McMurdo. If someone had tried it and failed, that would be the talk of McMurdo too. Meaning, Heller is already fairly certain there was no relevant trip close to the time of Lazo-Wasum's murder. He was fairly certain of it before they boarded the C-130. But he didn't know if he might learn something different, something entirely unexpected at Amundsen-Scott that has nothing to do with travel between the bases. He needs to be open to anything, to everything. He needs to be thorough. Lazo-Wasum deserves it.

"Is it typically one driver?" Heller asks Kevin Morton.

"Yes. Nick Logan. He's the guy who usually makes those runs."

"Is he here? Can I talk to him?"

Morton disappears farther into the structure for a few minutes, then reappears with Logan. Long hair, sunglasses, big smile, a kind of ski-instructor type.

When Logan slides off his sunglasses to shake hands, Heller the cop notices right away. Instantly learns a little more about Antarctic culture.

"So, Nick, are you just coming off a highway drive?" Heller asks him.

Logan shakes his head. "No, sir."

Heller turns to Morton. "Hey, could I interview Nick for a few minutes, just to see what he might remember from any trips around that time last winter?"

"Sure, go ahead," says Morton.

When they're out of earshot of everyone else, Heller says quietly to Logan, "I thought maybe your eyes were red from driving. But now I know your eyes are red like that 'cause you're high as a kite. If you don't want me saying anything to your boss, Morton, about it, I just need you to answer some questions honestly."

Logan nods quietly, obediently, his big smile gone.

"That pot you're so enjoying, Nick, I figure you sometimes shuttle ounces of it between Amundsen-Scott and McMurdo, am I right?"

Logan nods, startled at how quickly Heller has picked this up.

"What about anything else? Remember our deal, Nick."

Logan looks back nervously at his boss, Morton, then back to Heller. "Some mushrooms. A few tabs of acid. You know, for winter, when people have downtime. I only get paid in 'shrooms and joints. You gotta understand. It's just a little favor for folks at both bases."

"Anything else?"

"Like what?"

"Like lab chemicals?"

Logan looks at him, confused. "That's stealing," he says, clearly unnerved by the idea. "I'm not about to steal official shit from the scientists."

Rodney Marks, the astrophysicist who might have been poisoned years before, was stationed here at Amundsen-Scott. He saw the base doctor several times in the days before he died, but the doctor could find nothing wrong. The doctor certainly wasn't looking for an exotic poison. They found traces of methanol in his system during the autopsy, so they guessed at methanol poisoning but admitted the methanol might have been there simply by postmortem contamination. They could have missed the actual poison entirely. An exotic poison that might have made its way, in the intervening years, from Amundsen-Scott to McMurdo, across the Traverse Highway or aboard a C-130.

It didn't seem like Nick Logan was shuttling poison between the stations—not intentionally, anyway. Could it be someone else?

Another possibility. In an ever-expanding array of them.

Incomplete transportation records. Unavailable Internet phone-call records. Infinitely possible poisons. All in a mocking dance together in Joe Heller's head.

12.

Dinner the next night.

"Manny, can I join you?"

Another of their impromptu meetings in the cafeteria.

"Manny, one hundred fifty-seven names. And twenty-five of them, as you know, people who were here last winter but moved on at the end of the season, to new jobs, new places, and need to be tracked down and interviewed, wherever on earth they are today. Plus, I'm expecting to have Internet phone records to go through. I'm going to need some help."

"Like . . . an assistant."

"Yes. And soon. I'm starting to worry about getting through all these names and all the logistics before the winter-over." *When the weather turns. When I can't fly out.*

Hobbes nods sagely. And then does something extremely unscientific and surprising to Heller.

Hobbes looks around the cafeteria for close to a minute.

Then calls out: "Hey, Trish."

A slender woman of Asian extraction looks over.

Hobbes gestures her over. Gestures to a chair to join them.

"Trish Wong, this is Joe Heller."

"Hi, Mr. Heller." She is fresh faced, smooth skinned, in her midtwenties at most. Her momentary Asian aura—of austere reserve, preternatural inner calm—melts away immediately. In less than a minute, Heller understands her as the Southern California girl she is, through and through. San Diego? Long Beach? Palos Verdes Peninsula? Heller would be willing to bet big.

"Trish does administration and is involved with our hydroponic growing project. We grow our own melons and asparagus."

"Very few. Very slowly," Trish says with an apologetic smile.

"Trish wintered over here last year for the first time. She loved it, didn't you?"

She smiles. "Didn't mind at all."

"She's bright. She's the best of Antarctica. And one other wonderful thing about her. She's your new assistant."

They both look startled—at each other, and at Hobbes.

"Assistant?" asks Trish—that smooth, soft brow wrinkling a little. "On what?"

"He'll tell you," says Hobbes, pointing to Heller.

"But . . . ," Heller says, and looks at Hobbes, hoping his expression reads *But she's on the list.*

Hobbes looks back at him with a sardonic smile. *Come on, Heller. Trish Wong did not commit a homicide. Your list is officially one person shorter. And you've got the help you need.*

She turns to Heller.

"So what is this about?" she says cheerfully. "What do you do here at McMurdo? I haven't seen you before." Chipper. Upbeat. Ready to pitch in.

Oh boy, thinks Heller.

"Sandy Lazo-Wasum's death . . . ," he says. Working up to it.

"It was terrible," says Trish.

"Well, it's now a . . . it's now a homicide investigation."

He watches her expression crumble. Her cheerfulness collapses in front of him.

But as he talks, he sees her take it in. He sees her resolve. A sense of importance and mission and purpose crosses her face. A sense of right and wrong.

He can tell already, without much talk between them, that Hobbes has chosen well.

Heller had a need, and Hobbes has improvised on the spot. Was flexible and lightning fast with a solution. Heller is impressed. He takes it as a lesson in Antarctic life, of which Hobbes is a veteran. Be flexible. Improvise. Jury-rig it if you have to.

In Antarctica, he suddenly has a partner. Young, Asian, female, cheerful, extremely well educated—his polar opposite, so to speak, in many ways.

It has been decades since he's had a partner, of course.

It will either pull him out of his shell, he thinks, or fold him deeper into it. He will know very soon.

13.

Decades since he's had a partner.

Decades since Paul.

Brilliant Paul. Idiotic Paul. Wonderful Paul. Infuriating Paul.

Paul who made him. Paul who ruined him.

Paul who made him joyful, giddy. Paul who enraged him, humiliated him.

For Heller, the jury was still out on Paul D'Agostino.

The actual jury wasn't still out. The actual jury had returned a verdict of guilty on a series of serious drug charges against Paul. Dealing, distribution, smuggling, theft of evidence, on a grand scale.

His partner for years. Doing it all for years successfully behind Heller's back, without Heller even suspecting. And then when Heller found out, he carefully, stealthily gathered the evidence, being sure the evidence was irrefutable, before turning Paul in.

The case of course getting all the unavoidable notoriety of partner against partner.

Not just partners. Partners who had the most stellar arrest record in the department. Department all-stars. Making the case all the more notorious.

He surprised, alienated, and polarized the rest of the department, everyone around him—other detectives, administrative captains, assistant DAs, everyone—by turning his partner in.

And the outcome everyone expected, of course, upon Paul's conviction, when the twenty-year sentence was pronounced, was that Heller, under the pressure of the aggressive silence, the unspoken freeze-out around him, the generalized distaste for him, the glare of publicity, would simply resign.

But he surprised them again. He stayed on. No one would partner with him, and he didn't want to try to replace Paul anyway, so he worked alone. Stayed on, worked cases on his own, and pretty effectively, for years more.

The most universally despised cop in the department.

His divorce from Ann had been part of the fallout. It's hard to live with a man who is universally despised. Whose circle of friends simply falls away.

His other life partner—his wife—lost to him at the same time as Paul. From two partners to none. From double love to double emptiness.

Heller is sure that in the process of his recruitment for the McMurdo assignment, the US Marshal's office, and maybe even Hobbes and the other administrators, saw much of the press coverage. He wonders, deep down, if his being their "first choice" was really about that. Not primarily about his police skills, which are unimpeachable, though arguably out-of-date. Not even primarily about being able to work alone, which he did successfully for years after Paul's arrest.

Is it more about his being incorruptible? Willing to go where the evidence leads. No matter where. No matter to whom. Even someone you care for. Even someone you love.

Putting justice above anything else—and anyone else.

Hobbes and company didn't know what they would find in a full investigation of Lazo-Wasum's death. And didn't know, if something was found, what the judicial process after that would be.

So did they ask for someone particularly dogged? Someone who'd proven a willingness to keep the blinders of justice on forever, wherever? Someone who would stay on it, see it through, no matter what?

He never asked the US Marshal's office how they chose him. Or how much Hobbes and his team had to do with the decision. He doesn't really want to know, so clearly, so bluntly, if this is the reason. Let them—and him—live with the convenient lie of a stellar police record. And put aside that it is actually his commitment—his arguably inhuman commitment—to the rule of law. A rule-of-law robot. Willing to put everything else, even his own humanity and relationships, aside. That's our guy.

Oh, Paul.

Paul who betrayed him.

Paul whom he betrayed.

Paul who has shaped his life. And whose life he has shaped.

Trish Wong will be a great help to him. But she will not be a partner, exactly. No one can be a partner.

Paul died of colon cancer in prison, only halfway through his sentence.

Heller will never have another partner.

Not really.

Not like Paul.

14.

"Heller, huh? Joe Heller?" says Trish Wong, and Heller knows the line of questioning that is coming. "Any relation to the writer Joseph Heller?"

"None at all. My parents were both high school dropouts. They liked the name Joe. They had no idea."

Trish smiles. "Have you read it? *Catch-22*?"

Heller smiles back, shakes his head no.

"Your name is Joseph Heller, and you've never read it?"

He shrugs. He doesn't mention that he's brought a paperback copy with him. That he was thinking he might have the time here to finally read it.

"I'm not a big fiction reader," Heller says, "but I know the premise. That the only way to get out of fighting the war is to be declared insane, but if you want to get out of fighting the war, you're obviously sane, so you have to keep fighting, right? Isn't that it? Something like that?"

"Yes. That the rules, the situation, makes no sense. There's no logic, or an absurd logic." Her smile has a playful slyness, he notices, as she says, "Like, to get a job in Antarctica, you need appropriate references. But you can only get the references if you've already worked in Antarctica. That's Catch-22. You run into it all the time."

She pushes her straight black hair back, keeping it out of her way, to take a hearty bite of her spaghetti. A lean girl with a big, unthinking appetite. He likes that.

"I majored in American literature before switching to science for grad school, to earn a living," she says. "Heller wrote other novels besides *Catch-22*, but that's the one he's remembered for. And he'll be remembered for a long time. As long as it's part of the high school reading list. Although I guess it wasn't on yours."

"Oh, it was on ours," he admits with a smile. "But I was more interested in being a defensive end."

She looks at him and delivers a polite version of *Hey, your loss.* "It's where high school kids first learn the idea of irony. And absurdity. And the fallibility of institutions—like the US military, but all institutions. Governments. Scientific organizations." She smiles. "It's where you learn the craziness of bureaucracy. It's really a good book. Too bad you never read it, Joseph Heller."

He didn't have to. Because he experienced it repeatedly, acutely, in his professional life—more acutely as a cop, as an officer of the law, he would argue, than others in their own lives. The inherent insanities of bureaucracy that he was nevertheless sworn to uphold. The insane murderers, who you would catch by coolly, sanely channeling their particular insanity. Rules that the criminals he chased were flouting, but the rules themselves were often insane, so did that make the criminal sane?

"All my life, when people are introduced to me, it brings back memories of the term "Catch-22" for them, and all the absurdity and irony you're talking about. I wish it *would* get taken off the reading list." He smiles.

She smiles back. "The fact that you're named Joseph Heller, and you've never read it . . . I guess that's good Catch-22 irony right there." She cocks her head. "Are you sure your parents didn't know what they were doing?"

Heller smiles. "That's the catch. They definitely didn't."

She laughs.

He likes this Trish already.

15.

Heller enters Robert Trebor's room. He notices the differences immediately. Most of the sleeping quarters are haphazard, slapdash, random, unkempt spaces; clothes are flung over the backs of chairs and onto beds; beds are cozy, personalized centers of occupancy—books and laptops and phone chargers and more toys and puzzles and games than you'd think for purported adults, all spread around the rumpled bedcovers.

But Trebor's room is immaculate. More than that. Hospital corners on the bed. Books (at least a hundred) neat on the shelves—but more than neat—arranged precisely on the shelves not by author but by size and color. On the tiny desk, the desktop items line up with one another, Heller notices. Their edges make an orderly grid. The cell phone charging cord is wound neatly. The laptop cord is pinned behind the laptop, folded so as to be invisible, creating no clutter. The closet door is closed—but Heller knows the order he would find in the closet, or in the drawers. No photos. No trinkets.

"Welcome, welcome," says Trebor, and Heller can hear the strained effort at friendly normalcy, the constriction in the man's throat. "Here, have a seat." Heller notices that when Trebor pulls the chair out for him, he sets it perfectly perpendicular and, in fact, checks it by eye, before gesturing to Heller to sit.

Whoa. A level of obsessive-compulsive behavior that Heller is not sure he's seen in real life.

"Very shipshape in here," say Heller.

"You mean obsessive-compulsive"—Trebor smiles—"but you don't want to say it because you don't know me well enough yet."

Heller smiles too.

"Look, what can I say?" says Trebor. "It's who I am. Who I've always been. Long as I can remember, anyway." He glances at his desktop—double-checking one more time, Heller senses, to make sure nothing is out of place. "I know it's overboard, but this kind of orderliness is how I feel comfortable in the world. It gives me, I don't know, a sense of control. And independent of that, by the way, I do think the rest of them are just slobs." He shakes his head in disapproval. "Don't you?"

"Oh, they're pretty sloppy, most of them," Heller acknowledges. Without adding *So what's wrong with that?* "Look, I don't want to interrupt your day here too much . . . ," Heller says as he opens his notebook.

"No problem. I welcome the interruption."

"Great, well, I just want to take a few minutes and go over a couple of things with you, Robert. You prefer Robert to Bob, don't you?"

Trebor looks alertly at him. "I'm Robert. Not Bob."

"I thought so. Because I noticed that your last name, Trebor, is actually Robert backwards. Nice and orderly. A nice clear mirror of itself. No letters out of place. I'm assuming your first name was always Robert, and Trebor is a last name you adopted at some point as an adult. Is that right?"

"That's correct," says Trebor, flatly, offering no further explanation.

And then Heller, as if casually and unthinking but very consciously, turns his chair a little—the chair Trebor had placed so carefully—ostensibly to face Trebor a little more, but in truth to see his reaction.

Trebor winces. Doesn't like it. Is clearly uncomfortable. Seems to want to reach out to the chair and "correct" it but manages to contain himself. Takes a slow, deep breath, Heller notices.

74

Heller doesn't know if Trebor realizes his own discomfort about it, or is his reaction totally unconscious? Yes, the man knows he's obsessive. But may not realize he's *this* obsessive.

And then Heller does something sympathetic, generous—and calculated. Perhaps the ultimate helpful thing he could do to put Trebor at ease, take down his guard.

As if just as unthinking, as if casually, Heller shifts the chair back into alignment.

Trebor looks at him. But Heller gives no acknowledgment of what he has done. Pretends not to notice.

But now he has a baseline for his next question.

"Obviously, I want to ask you about Sandy Lazo-Wasum."

No reaction.

A slight shift of a chair creates a wince. A murder causes no response at all.

"Ask you about the night he died."

"Sure. Ask away."

Either Trebor had nothing to do with it—Heller's instinct—or Trebor has prepared himself very well for this moment, rehearsed it, practiced for it—something that, of course, you would not put past such an obsessive personality.

"I've heard you knew him pretty well," says Heller. He hasn't heard any such thing.

Trebor blinks. Confused by the question. One the obsessive-compulsive could not have prepared for. "Well, that's just not . . . not the case. I . . . I'm not really that close to anybody here."

"Ever sit with him in the cafeteria?"

"Sure, at the same table." Silence. Followed by "Fourteen or fifteen times." Heller has the impression that Trebor has actually just added up the occasions. "But not next to him."

"Meaning, no conversation?"

"Just an exchange of pleasantries."

"Give me your own whereabouts that night. Sketch out your own evening."

"Sure," says Trebor brightly. "I was here, reading." He smiles, gesturing to the book-laden shelves. "No surprise, I guess. I was three quarters of the way through *Hunter's Delight*," gesturing to it.

On the one hand, how could he remember that? On the other hand, of course he would.

"*Hunter's Delight*. Is that a mystery? I think of scientists as reading a lot of nonfiction and science texts."

"Yes. It's a mystery. During the winter, I only read mysteries."

"Locked-room mysteries," says Heller.

"So someone told you," says Trebor. "Yes, I'll pick a series or two and read the whole thing. Immerse myself in the personality of the detective, in the puzzles of the case. I love it."

"Locked-room mysteries. Tell me about that."

"It's when the guilty party and all the relevant clues are there from the outset. It's when there's nothing extraneous that can explain it. The clues are all there. It's just up to the detective to unravel them." He looks at Heller. "I have to admit I was kind of excited to have you stopping by today. I was looking forward to it. Because in all my reading of these things, I never imagined that I would be involved in a locked-room mystery. That it would occur in my own life. Ironic, given my eccentric reading predilections." He tilts his head. "Detective, I know it hasn't escaped your notice . . . that Sandy Lazo-Wasum's death is a classic locked-room mystery."

"What do you like about them so much, do you think?"

"The sense of control. The sense of order. It's an orderly puzzle. And you know, they do all get solved."

"So I better solve it, yes? You'll be more comfortable when it's solved?"

A loaded question for a killer. Heller is looking for some reaction. Any reaction. He doesn't know exactly what.

But there is none. "We'll all be more comfortable when it's solved," says Trebor blandly. As if by rote.

"All right, let's talk about that evening."

Trebor sketches his uneventful evening—for which he has no alibi or backup, of course—right through hearing the commotion the next morning. "I ate at seven, in my regular spot at the second-to-last table. People are kind enough to leave that chair for me. I finished at seven fifteen. I came back here at seven twenty-five. I washed my face, brushed my teeth."

"This was months ago. How could you possibly remember that so precisely?"

"That's the beauty of it," says Trebor, with a kind of elation and sense of victory, a sense of relief. "I don't *have* to remember it. Because I do it exactly that way, at exactly that time, every night."

"Do you have any kind of verification of that?" asks Heller. "I mean, did anyone see you?"

Trebor brightens. "Well, no one saw me, but that *is* my verification. It proves I was in here the whole night."

Heller looks at him inquisitively, waiting for him to explain.

"Stadler and Matthews keep their door open. They're always in the galley. They would have seen me go in or out at some point. But they didn't. Check with them. They should be able to verify that. That's your proof. There's no window, right?"

"So you didn't leave your room—not even to go to the john?"

Trebor's look darkens. He looks down. Doesn't answer.

Something there. "These interviews remain confidential," Heller assures him. "Unless there's something material that surfaces."

Trebor looks up at Heller, as if from an underground place.

He goes to the dresser. Opens it. The dresser that Heller knew was so neat. But out of a drawer that Heller figured was socks and underwear in an orderly row, Trebor removes a sealed bottle, three-quarters full of liquid. Yellow-tinted liquid. He holds it out to Heller, who recoils a little, quickly realizing it is urine.

"I don't like to leave here once I'm in for the night," Trebor says. "I pee at ten forty-five, before I nod off, and again at five fifteen in the morning. That's my routine. That's when I go. To the minute. I check the clock." He looks at Heller. "I presume this helps prove my whereabouts."

Locked-room mystery. A little more locked-room and a little more mysterious than Heller expected.

16.

Conducting interviews, learning about poisons, and, at the same time, the third, subtler element of his Antarctic acclimation and exploration: understanding McMurdo.

Getting the feel of it. Its rhythm. Its subtleties that one would never notice at first.

For instance, as he gets to know the scientists and their experiments a little, he learns that, while some experiments are frivolous commercial ventures—testing new flavors in the cold (taste receptors alter in extreme temperatures), trying new cold-weather designs for clothing manufacturers (so they can claim they're "Antarctic tested")—other experiments are significant. Creating hardier crops amid extreme growing conditions. Testing new pharmaceuticals in an environment free of hundreds of trace airborne microbes and chemicals that contaminate the other six continents—pharmaceuticals that hold the potential to treat and even eradicate certain global diseases. These experiments are about improving humanity. Giving people a better chance. These scientists have come to the end of the earth, cut themselves off from humanity, out of their commitment to humanity. Turning their backs on it in order to save it. Hidden in their puffy parkas, behind their glasses, beneath their complex mathematics and papers and scientific language, these are quiet heroes. Extraordinary people, whose default character traits are generosity, care, making life better. Who never question that this is their purpose and, more than that, *life's* purpose.

But of course, they share McMurdo—its barracks and cafeteria, its rutted roadways and canteen and noisy ATVs and disorganized street plan and pop-up seasonal bar—with a very different kind of person. The person who is just here for the job, for the better-than-decent wage. The electrician and IT support staff and logistics monkeys and administrative personnel and blue-collar maintenance and food-prep teams, who could be working anywhere. Who would prefer that Antarctica was somewhere in the Caribbean, on a sunny beach, but, hell, this is where the job is, this is where the paycheck is, so what are you gonna do?

Heller knows that the intersection of those two kinds of people, and those two outlooks, must create some tensions, even some unconscious hostility. Heller suspects that those groups, unfamiliar with each other, at such close quarters, may rub together in unfamiliar ways that could, very occasionally, turn lethal.

He notices that there is a third group. A special subset that draws a little from the first two groups but has members all its own. This third group is not really a group at all—it's outliers, odd types, special cases, who actually *like*—seek out—the isolation. Who *like* the time and light extremes. The kind of people who like the temporal changes of pot or powerful pharmaceuticals, who like Ferris wheels and roller coasters, who like disruption from normality, who like disorientation. Who have some deep trouble with normal, with stasis. This environment, these living conditions, catch their attention, this kind of person. He has the feeling that this person—this personality—can thrive fully, bloom fully during winter-over. Can safely shed their skin. Undetected. Unobserved. Undiscovered. He has a sense, here and there, of that kind of personality, waiting, patiently—or impatiently. And he notices it makes the hairs stand up on the back of his neck. When not much else does.

He notices, for all three groups, for everyone here, the constant contrast of isolation and community. Both experienced in the extreme. You are on top of one another, thrown together, inseparable from and reliant on one another. Yet you are cut off, isolated from the rest of the planet, certainly, but, as if in a planetary echo, from one another too. He notices there is *not* a compensating sense of camaraderie. A sense of isolation surrounds you every day, burrows deep into your bones. There is a built-in distance between people here, a sense of privacy that is respected, an invisible but impermeable wall, maybe because of living on top of one another.

Intense connection. But intense isolation. A little laboratory of those polarities knocking up against one another.

He heard someone singing a Billy Joel song he'd forgotten about. A hit, but one that people rarely remembered, "I Go to Extremes." He heard the guy singing it over and over—a burly cafeteria worker behind the counter. Certainly aware of its ironic content. *"I don't know why I go to extremes . . ."*

He'd forgotten that song. What a good song. And now it is in his head.

17.

With the help of Trish Wong, he's making better progress.

He quickly realizes that many of the people here don't really know what many of the other people do, how exactly they spend their days, what their specialty or work actually is. The scientific work is atomized, even from one science team to another. That's sometimes by necessity, he learns—different teams are working for, and are funded by, competing pharmaceutical companies, so they don't share their experiments or results. He's a little surprised that Hobbes hasn't ever mentioned that, but on second thought, he understands. It's contrary to the collegial nature, the Antarctic spirit of sharing and camaraderie that Hobbes seems so invested in. It doesn't fit Hobbes's vision of Antarctica, so he conveniently chooses to forget about it. But Heller has been around long enough to know, and is hardly shocked to realize, that even science—noble, soaring science—is, in the end, about competition and the bottom line.

Trish proves skilled and adept. She's an excellent choice. She works up and prints out his postinterview notes for him, and they're thorough and clear. She's following up for him on the phone calls and paperwork for obtaining Internet-provider records. Heller shows up one morning and finds a series of colored folders, neatly labeled, where he can organize his increasingly unruly stack of investigative paperwork and data.

"Am I living up to the stereotype of the prim, superorganized Asian girl?" she asks him with a smile.

"Am I living up to the stereotype of the brusque, brooding, disorganized old white detective?" he responds.

Her smile turns easily into a laugh.

But in a moment, her face goes serious, and she hands him a folded note. "This was here this morning, slipped under the door."

He opens it.

Just one line on it, but lettered carefully. No signature.

Talk to Seth Breen.

He looks up at Trish. "What do you think?"

"I think it's from someone at McMurdo trying to be helpful. Someone who obviously doesn't want to be involved."

"And someone who knows something?"

She shrugs.

"And who's Seth Breen?"

She smiles. Opens the folder already in her lap and reads to him:

"Breen. Texan. Single. Biochemist. Multiple tours in Antarctica. On a grant funded by Rice University's Department of Graduate Studies."

She closes the folder, looks up at him. "He's working on something extremely technical that apparently could have applications not only for long space missions but for battlefield survival. His funding keeps getting renewed, so someone somewhere must see it as important work."

"You've been busy this morning," Heller says, smiling, appreciative. He's totally impressed. "Nice work, Detective Wong."

• • •

He sees Hobbes at breakfast. "What can you tell me about Seth Breen?" Heller decides not to tell him about the note slipped under his door. Not just yet.

"Why do you ask? What have you heard?"

Heller shrugs. Doesn't answer.

"Person of interest?" Hobbes asks, looking a little perplexed, however.

"Everyone's a person of interest," says Heller, avoiding an answer.

"Well, there is his odd hobby, I guess, but we all pass the time here somehow. There's plenty odder." Hobbes shrugs. "He's a very reputable scientist, you know," says Hobbes. "Some consider him a genius. And his hobby . . . well, that's just the Texan in him."

Heller doesn't reveal that he has no idea what Hobbes is talking about.

Why let Hobbes think his lead investigator is clueless?

• • •

"Come in," says Seth Breen, welcoming him into his sleeping quarters, though Heller has the feeling he is not welcome here at all. Breen had suggested meeting in his lab. Heller had said he wanted to do it in his personal quarters.

Heller takes a quick, unobtrusive, orienting look around and immediately sees and understands Hobbes's oblique comments—and the note.

There are wood carvings, whittlings—all over the living space. Intricate, careful.

They immediately seize Heller's attention.

Because at first he can't tell what they are.

And then, in another beat, he can.

One is a human heart. Intricate. The arteries and veins in bas-relief. Exactly life-size, Heller would guess.

The next one is a liver. A human liver.

There's a kidney.

A couple he doesn't recognize. A pancreas? A thyroid?

"I used to do portraits," says Breen in his slow, deep Texas drawl. "But this is more useful and interesting, and a way to keep learning."

He gestures to Heller to take a seat—it's a substantially beat-up, low-slung leather chair, so Heller figures it's his "carving" seat. "I know, it's not heads," says Breen. "It looks a little disconcerting. But as I'm doing it, I'm learning so much about the organ. I'm reading about and pondering its interactions. It's relaxing . . . so much more relaxing than doing a face. What can I tell you?"

Heller understands the anonymous informant's note. The instinctive alarm about this little hobby. The oddness of it. But there is no evidence of any knife, of any knife injury, to Sandy Lazo-Wasum—or to Rodney Marks before him, for that matter. No cuts. No marks. No signs of struggle. In fact, that is one of the more remarkable things about both victims.

Which obviously the note's anonymous author didn't know.

"Grew up whittling and carving. My daddy taught me in West Texas. He was wonderful at it. It's a family tradition.

"Every season I take on a new organ. They're very involved." He picks one up, shows the intricacy of it. "Look at this thyroid, for instance. Like a red-veined butterfly, right? Or a glandular starfighter with Luke Skywalker at the controls. Almost delicate. It regulates heart rate, central and peripheral nervous systems, muscle strength, menstrual cycles, body weight, body temperature, cholesterol, respiration—our breathing, for Chrissake! But no one really knows how it does any of those. Nobody understands the damn thing at all. The red butterfly flies just out of our reach." He puts down his carved model with more than a hint of frustration.

Heller understands the frustration. He knows what this season's carving is really about. The thyroid is the culprit—the mysterious culprit—of Polar T3 syndrome.

Polar T3 syndrome. Compromised thyroid function from 24-7 sunshine for months on end, then 24-7 dark for months on end, combined with isolation, extremely cold temperatures, etcetera. Symptoms of the syndrome: forgetfulness, irritability, in some cases a fugue state. Commonly known as "Antarctic stare." A condition observed for more than a century of polar exploration and habitation, from the pioneers to the present. Amundsen, Scott, and Richard Byrd all reported it. And there are plenty of extreme cases documented and even self-reported. Heller has by now read as deeply about it as possible on the Internet. A host of common additional symptoms: depression, severe headaches, sleep disturbances, derangement in thought patterns. And yet, despite the disconcerting severity of the symptoms, they subside almost immediately with the advent of sunshine and normalized daylight hours.

"I'm guessing you chose the thyroid because of T3," says Heller.

"I suppose. Although my whittling a nice thyroid ain't gonna tell us much about it," Breen says. "So, Mr. Heller, what can I help you with?"

Heller interviews him further, but he already knows. Seth Breen is not the guy.

18.

Trish reminds him of his daughter, Amy, of course. Close in age, though Trish is almost ten years older, thank God. But the same youthful outlook. It is a curative relationship with Trish, he's already noticed. One where he gets to do it right—listening, supporting, affirming. Qualities he feels—he knows—he shortchanged Amy on.

They look and sound completely different. Trish has black hair, that beautiful olive Asian skin (dark, flawless, no visible pores), and California all the way—that California liveliness and loud direct voice and love of the outdoors and natural happy lack of too much self-examination. Amy is blonde, white skin, freckles, fragile looking, translucent, willowy, soft, ultrafeminine somehow—a reflection and restatement of her mother's classic Irish looks. But he notices how their physical difference only highlights their sameness. Their inquisitiveness, their hyperconnection to events around them, big and small, their sense of being so deeply and fully "in" the world, where he is not, has never been.

Her California optimism. Her bright-eyed upbeatness. "My grandparents came from mainland China in the 1920s, started a laundry in Sacramento, raised six kids, and California's tuition-free university system arose right about then."

"So let me guess. Within a generation the Wong clan are doctors, scientists, engineers, professors, am I right?"

"More fulfillment of the stereotype, huh?"

"But am I right?"

She smiles. "Yes, mostly right."

This was the California—educated, sophisticated, accomplished, well-off—that Trish was raised in. And global travel is now part of that upbringing—to expand horizons both physical and intellectual—a thoroughly ingrained value, he could tell, that was part of her spirit and her family's spirit, a family that had risked the journey to California to begin with. Antarctica was just a stop, one stop, on a lifetime tour of growth and expansion and deepening experience.

It was in such contrast to his own formative experience. Crusty, depressing Northern Vermont. Hardship and cynicism part of the land-scape, and no less part of the Heller ethos. Dairy farmers and tinkerers, laconic dad and uncles. A beer-and-whiskey culture. So for him, the fabled, oft-cited attraction of opposites was more than just that. More than just opposite American geographies. More than just her youth. It was her very outlook that could lift Heller up even here in the cold and ice and dark. Lift them both.

During the course of the interviews, he is becoming more attuned to the highly charged sexual nature of wintering-over. He is starting to gather that it is a self-fulfilling prophecy, that people are expecting it, looking forward to it, that it is almost cultural now. And he finds himself thinking of Trish—single, attractive, and seemingly attracted to him. This must be what older guys who date younger women face. But millions of older guys get past it somehow. Are very happy to get past it. There may be something almost biological, he thinks, in the prospect of coupling up for the winter. It may go back to the cave. It may be hardwired into the amygdala. Unconscious signals about hibernation. And he is somewhat relieved at Trish's and Amy's complete physical differentness from each other.

Why all the interviews? That's what Hobbes has asked, a little mys-tified and perturbed. And Heller has had to tell him. Because it has become apparent to Heller—unfortunately, depressingly, but more and more clearly—that Sandy Lazo-Wasum, despite how it first seemed, is increasingly likely to have been a completely random victim. That someone picked him not because of his relationships but because they were not involved in those relationships at all. Chose him because he was at such a distance.

He dutifully circled back to Pritchard and Dolan, but it was as he suspected, as his instincts told him—they knew that Sorenson was involved with Lazo-Wasum, they knew they had each had a night with her, they felt guilty, anxious, withholding that from Heller, but they thought Heller would never understand, wouldn't get the culture here. During the busy summer season at McMurdo, Pritchard and Dolan had their own casual girlfriends at the base, apparently. The pickings are slimmer during the winter, they explained, and Sorenson and others are casually accommodating. As for the night of the murder, they cheerfully and cooperatively provided each other's alibis. Pritchard woke Dolan (as always, apparently, a running joke between them—they were suitemates), they got dressed together for the morning inspection, were first in line for coffee and donuts at the canteen, et cetera, et cetera. Heller had interviewed them separately, looking for inconsistencies, but all the details matched up. They were what they seemed.

• • •

The problem is (and this he has not yet mentioned to Hobbes) it is looking more and more to Heller like this is the work—the MO, the style, the care and cautiousness and resulting lack of clues—of (he hates to even form the phrase in his mind) a serial killer.

All the hallmarks: Seemingly random victim. Tracks covered perfectly. Not a crime of passion, or, if so, an eccentric weird passion that no one could understand or relate to except the killer him- or herself.

A serial killer who, as it happens, has only just begun.

A killer who, this being Antarctica, with its limits and frustrations, has managed to freeze or limit his (or her) temptation and proclivity and disease. But now, Heller is afraid, it has been awakened.

He's afraid the genie may have gotten out of the bottle.

He's afraid the taste may now be in the killer's mouth.

•   •   •

It's something he started to realize fairly quickly, as the clues didn't come. As the prospect of clues shut down tight.

It's something that long experience has told him. A knowledge that crept in at the base of his cerebellum, that tapped at his preconscious.

He began to suspect it, to feel it in his bones, even on the flight down. He kept it to himself, though, figuring he had to do his due diligence. At least start the conventional investigative process.

But the neatness of it, the immaculateness, the perfection of it that he was already sensing, pointed strongly to the possibility.

Someone whose extreme care and caution is already projecting the decision, the temptation, to try it again.

A serial killer. Just getting started.

Serial killer . . . not a term he wants to use with Hobbes.

Serial killer . . . not a term he likes to say even to himself.

A serial killer. Typically, by the profile, a loner.

Who has only killed one. So far.

Something hard to explain right off to a roomful of administrators you've just met for the first time. So he kept his mouth shut.

Amid all the prospective law-enforcement candidates, they hired Joe Heller. There were younger, more technologically savvy candidates, no doubt. Maybe more up to speed on the latest techniques. On the latest white papers. They couldn't know if Heller's long experience would make any difference. But this is what his experience gives them. This is what it buys. The creep at the back of the neck. The institutional knowledge. Unfortunately, he has seen this movie before.

So he flew down to Antarctica, in fact, with a different understanding of his role.

He figured he might serve as a deterrent.

Whoever did it, Heller's presence at McMurdo might be enough to prevent another crime. Might be frightening enough—deterrent enough—to be worried about getting caught for the first one.

Even though Heller also knows in his bones that they aren't going to find this murderer, if the murderer does manage to stop at one.

But he also knows the reverse possibility—that his presence at McMurdo might provide incitement. Might provide a challenge. Often a compelling, irresistible element for a serial killer. The thrill of getting away with it, amplified exponentially by the joy of fooling law enforcement, tangoing with the police, stumping the authorities. Heller knows that his mere presence might provide excitement, a renewed determination to try it again.

As he knows that his daily inability to solve the problem might only embolden the perpetrator to act again. That observing Heller's impotence up close, firsthand, might be bringing daily joy to the perpetrator—and fresh inspiration, fresh creativity.

There is a small piece of Heller that wants his presence to provide that challenge, to motivate, to tempt the killer again. Even at the risk of another victim.

Heller is acutely aware of the double knife edge of his presence:

A possible deterrent.

Or the very opposite: A possible motivator.

Heller's presence might be just enough to keep the killer from striking again.

Or just enough to make the killer strike again.

There's a "Catch" for you, Trish.

Heller also knows the corollary.

Knew it, suspected it, on the plane down, just as deeply in his bones.

That whether he's serving as a deterrent, who would keep the perpetrator from striking again, or whether he's serving as a motivator, who would ultimately draw the perpetrator out, either way, he's going to have to winter over.

As a deterrent, to keep the perpetrator from striking again during the ideal "striking time"—when he or she understandably struck last—when no one is watching, when they can get away with it.

Or to be here, when the perpetrator attempts to strike again.

To attempt to stop it.

Be smart enough. Alert enough. One step ahead.

Either way, he is wintering over.

He will be seeing and experiencing the weird, eerie, ineffable Antarctic winter for himself.

A thought—an experience—he's not relishing.

Wintering-over.

Returning to the scene of the crime.

Restaging it in a way. In time, mood, temperament, surrounding players, surrounding personalities. Creating the circumstances for it to be reenacted. And comprehended.

Experience tells him that's what's required.

That's the problem with experience. That's the bear, the burden of it, thinks Heller. You just know too damn much. Way more than a person should have to.

• • •

A serial killer, just getting started. Heller tries to tell himself otherwise, but he knows it in his bones.

He does not look forward to the second body that will prove his thesis right.

Please, please make me wrong.

19.

After the interviews, before dinner, he always compares notes with Trish. It's always disappointing, because he has found nothing, accomplished nothing, and he can tell that she feels the same way. They are doing it to be dutiful and thorough and also, he can tell, to be with each other, and to let the conversation drift naturally away from the interviews themselves, to how Trish, the Southern Californian, the girl of freeways and malls and sunshine and bright concrete and urban sprawl, finds something so soothing, so powerful in Antarctica's stark, natural beauty. And how Joe Heller, the Northern Vermonter, a *real* Vermonter, finds something of his love of Northern Vermont rekindled here, something of his youth, although he has not been back there in, well, a lifetime.

One night, after their debriefing, as Trish puts on her puffy red parka, Heller finally notices.

The observer, the detective.

"Hey," he says, startled by it.

"Hey what?"

"That parka."

"Yeah?"

He pauses. He smiles. A warmth of recognition runs through him. A sense of fate. "It was you I saw the first day I came here. You were a tiny figure way out at the edge of McMurdo, standing at the ocean looking out."

She looks up at him. Surprised, flattered that he recalls.

"I wondered what you were thinking about. Whether you were happy or sad or distraught or contemplative. I couldn't tell from that distance."

She smiles, teases. "You can't tell from this distance either, Heller."

"Do you remember?"

"Yes, I remember."

"So what was it? Happy? Sad? Contemplative? Awestruck?"

"All of the above," she says.

Looking at him harder, and then smiling, she adds, "But accent on the happy, Joe. Right now, accent on the happy."

And she zips up her parka and heads to the cafeteria.

20.

"Manny?"

"Yes, come on in. How's it going?"

"Well . . . it's going . . ."

"Well, if it's *going*, then I guess it's not going as well as you or I want, is it? 'Going well' would mean done with going. 'Going well' would mean coming to an end, not just going."

Heller is silent in the face of this.

"Manny . . ."

And Heller then shares his intuition. His experience. He sees Manny Hobbes flinch at the first use of the term "serial killer" and look at him dismissively and skeptically, and then, as Heller continues to speak, to explain, he sees Manny Hobbes listening more intently—a scientist, endemically curious, open. He sees the bureaucrat, the administrator give way to the scientist . . .

"It's going to require returning to the scene of the crime," says Heller finally.

"But this is the scene of the crime."

"No, the scene of the crime is wintering-over. The scene of the crime is the conditions of the crime."

Reconstructing the scene of the crime. Following in the criminal's footsteps.

"Ah, the conditions of the crime." Manny Hobbes, the scientist, leans back, as if to literally settle into the idea of the scientific experiment, creating the control conditions for the experiment.

"And speaking of the conditions of the crime, I want to ask you a little about T3," says Heller.

Hobbes smiles. "Of course. I figured. A fascinating topic."

"I know the basics. What the Internet says. But anything more you can tell me about it?"

"Initially NASA was here researching T3," says Hobbes. "They were very interested in studying it because of planning manned flights to Mars. The isolation, the sameness and invariability of vision and routine and sensory deprivation and social disengagement—a lot was analogous. They had a whole team here. Monitoring almost all of us over a couple of winters. But then funding for the manned space program was cut, and there was no reason to do the research, and they abandoned it." He shakes his head in a mix of frustration and resignation that Heller has seen in Hobbes before. "So no one else was doing it 'cause NASA was doing it, and then NASA suddenly abandons it with budget cuts, so as a result, we don't really know anything about it. No findings available. No suggestions on what to be looking for as far as susceptibility, or how to diagnose or treat it. It remains as weird as ever."

"Can you give me, I don't know, a flavor of how you've seen it manifest itself?"

"Oh, anecdotal evidence galore. Look around online. You'll see lots of people writing it up in their blogs, their online journals, because its effect can be so wacky—and so individualized. A guy puts one earbud in one ear, puts the other in his mouth and swallows it. A woman reads an entire novel cover to cover and realizes only later she has read it backwards." He pauses. "Or, you're standing talking to someone, and suddenly you have no idea who it is." And it is clear, with this last anecdote, Hobbes is talking about himself.

Heller knows the possible corollary. The eerie possible ancillary fact. That in some way, the killer doesn't know he or she is a killer. That the murder took place in a fugue state, an altered condition of consciousness. Through some mental filter that may prove impenetrable. If the criminal at some level doesn't know, then confession is pretty unlikely. (And if the criminal doesn't know, maybe he or she won't strike again. Leaving the community safe—and leaving the killer beyond justice forever.) And if T3 is a factor, who will determine—how will it be determined—how much personal and or legal responsibility there will be?

T3. Short for triiodothyronine. The complex, poorly understood chemical compound in the thyroid that just goes suddenly crazy. An organ Heller has never thought about for a moment, before his trip to Antarctica. The brain, the heart—these are the organs of center stage, where we live or die, succeed or fail. But now, he muses, the thyroid—strange, mysterious, opaque—will take center stage for the season.

For those who winter over, time bends, sunrise and sunset deform. He has asked Pritchard and Dolan about Polar T3. Pritchard had pretty good analogies. Like smoking pot, he said, or, better yet, like riding a rollercoaster or some other amusement park ride. Some people can't get used to it, fight it, are ill. Others love it, relish it, swim in its effects, look forward to it. Earth's high. The cosmos's high. God fooling with night and day on you.

He's even looked into getting hold of the NASA studies, as far as they go, but the space agency bureaucrats he reached were unwilling and unapproved to release partial findings, sorry. Typical government bullshit and runaround and ass covering. So his knowledge is stuck in anecdotal.

T3. Antarctic stare. And what would be his own susceptibility to it? Who knows? Everyone is different. Before seeing the Texan's carvings, he couldn't have told you the first thing about the thyroid. No idea about its size or weight or where it is in the body, and certainly not its function. The strange, misunderstood, mysterious organ. After an existence as an unknown, most misunderstood, least glamorous human gland, in Antarctica it takes center stage.

21.

The last of the summer crew boards the last supply plane of the season.

Joe Heller, Manny Hobbes, and Trish Wong stand together and watch. Waving goodbye, raising a beer or a shot of vodka or a glass of champagne, along with roughly 150 others. The toast, the send-off, is a McMurdo tradition.

The last of the summer crew scrambles up the cargo ramp, scurrying like tiny fleas into the butt of the plane, thinks Heller, as the cargo ramp is raised. The huge gray beast, its engines singing in gleeful harmony, lumbers across the ice to the beginning of the landing strip and takes off.

It is a perfectly clear day. Heller, nevertheless, feels the darkness begin to close around him. Feels the darkness at the edges of his consciousness. Sees it begin to rise from behind the distant mountains, come up from beneath the sea. An anticipatory darkness. Not literally there yet, but quite inevitably coming. An encompassing darkness. Because the literal darkness will overlap, interact with the psychological darkness. They are cut off, isolated; there are no two ways about it now. It is already echoing for him with loss, with confinement, with narrowness, with a sense of imprisonment. Reverberating with a sense of isolation that he has always felt, that is part of his nature. That he has always fought for fear of where it will take him. He has a vague, passing sense that T3 may prove especially troublesome for him.

Jonathan Stone

Trish raises her glass after the plane and smiles, bright eyed, with a sense of approaching adventure, it seems.

Heller and Hobbes do not raise their glasses. They merely exchange a brief, sober, wordless look. Hobbes too, perhaps, has a foreboding sense of the darkness, of the long night, already beginning its creep toward their existence and, more than that, into their consciousness.

They watch the takeoff of the last supply plane of the season.

They could hardly have guessed that it might be the last supply plane, ever.

BOOK TWO: NIGHT

22.

Joe Heller hunkers down.

Settles in for the long night.

On April 24, the sun sets at McMurdo and won't rise again until August 20. A slight residual halo of light for a week or so—an echo, a memory—and then nothing. A night of several months. A night of more than a hundred days. Heller wonders: All the comforts and all the discomforts of night writ large? Elongated, expanded, in some disorienting way? A slumber, a hibernation, a time of dreams unleashed beyond previous borders? And what of the typical tremors of 2:00 a.m. and 4:00 a.m., the acute anxious questions that keep you up before you are able to fall back asleep on a regular night. Do those get stretched? Exaggerated? Do they take hold of your soul even more? Unshakably? Since you can't say *at least it will be morning soon.* It will not be morning soon.

But wintering over in this season soon becomes something entirely different.

The darkness soon enough becomes something else altogether. A different kind of night.

Every year the long night progresses from literal to psychological.

This year it will progress from psychological to existential.

Life always becomes different, wintering over in Antarctica. But in a predictable way. In a way that has rhythm, memory, from previous winters.

That is not what happens to Heller or Hobbes or any of the 155 others at McMurdo station.

This winter-over's head count remains, coincidentally, at 157 people. "How 'bout that?" Hobbes says. "Same as last winter." Hobbes shrugs at the coincidence. But Heller takes it more to heart. As if the number *157* is taunting him, haunting him, for his not yet being able to solve the murder. Taunting him with the fact that nothing has changed. That the murderer is still here, still hidden among 157 people.

One hundred fifty-seven suddenly very special people. One hundred fifty-seven suddenly very special existences.

A murder investigation in Antarctica. Antarctica's first. Something seemingly unusual. Seemingly noteworthy.

It soon comes to seem like nothing. Tertiary. Distant. Forgotten.

Like nothing at all, in comparison.

23.

"Hey, wait a second," says Trish. "You said you're into astronomy, right?"

Heller nods, smiles. "You remember."

His little hobby. That he'd started to distract himself from the earthly turmoil with Paul. Lift his mind, his attention, as far from it as possible. A hobby he was soon sharing with Amy as a little girl. The telescope on the back deck. Something they had had in common, did together. Until they no longer spent any time together.

Trish frowns, checks the notebooks. "But you haven't been over to the observatory yet?"

Heller smiles, confesses. "I was saving it. I was told to wait. That viewing is the most dramatic in the winter dark. That's when they do most of their experiments. That's when the observatory is at its best."

Many of McMurdo's science experiments revolve around the extreme temperatures and conditions, but most of the important astronomy experiments proceeded—full speed—only when the Antarctic night sky finally enveloped them.

"Along with the telescope at Amundsen-Scott, it's the only uncontaminated viewing on the planet," Trish tells him. "There's light and atmospheric distortion everywhere else on the globe. The observatory is just amazing," she says. "Since you have to interview Dr. Green and his assistants anyway, I'll make sure they give you the royal treatment."

She smiles. "They'll give it to you anyway. They don't get streams of visitors."

"Want to come with me?" Heller asks.

Her answer is her wide smile.

• • •

The observatory is several hundred yards away, set off by itself. Trish arranges an ATV for them. Dr. Green greets them at the door. Like an elf or gremlin welcoming Heller and Trish to his magical dome-shaped home. Green fits the part perfectly. He has a white beard, he's rotund, cherubic, but there's something street tough about him too. A Southie Boston accent. Brains that elevated him from his circumstances. Astrophysics—a jet pack out of the Boston ghetto.

"Come in, come in." As if he's about to offer them a cup of chamomile tea.

Green's eyes sparkle.

You, you with the stars in your eyes.

Astrophysics PhD, MIT labs, California Institute of Technology, hadron collider advisory team. Trish read Heller the bio binder before coming.

"For months, it's calculations, computer modeling, simulations, discussion with colleagues all over the world via e-mail and Skype," says Green, leading them down a short, low metal-and-riveted corridor—a tube really—something from a space station in a space movie. "But it's all preparatory, all countdown. Really just a way of marking time, until we can get to the real business. Of looking. That's all we're doing here. A very advanced form of it. But in the end, just looking. Looking around us, to see what we see."

The tube opens onto the amphitheater of the observatory. The big telescope sits at its center, its interlocking, stupendously wide white-and-silver cylinders gleaming, and gradually narrowing, to a reverse focal point—a scuffed leather seat.

A kind of throne, thinks Heller. A throne of science. A throne of observation. The universe, out one end of this impressive, gleaming device, and at its other end, a single human, a single set of eyes, and a single humming brain—at the nexus of all this technology.

Green motions Heller silently toward the telescope seat. He suddenly stops talking, and it seems symbolic, meaningful, in conscious deference to what is about to be experienced by his guest.

Heller ducks into and settles onto the throne. In fact, a beat-up jump seat. Green slides the viewing assembly—about a four-foot square—into place in front of Heller. Like preparing for a massive eye test. Green adjusts some dials, pushes some buttons, and there are faint accompanying whirs from elsewhere in the otherwise silent observatory.

"Light and atmospheric contamination are a factor everywhere else on the planet. It took mankind getting to Antarctica to finally see clearly. Like we had to be good girls and boys for several thousand years, to develop enough and not kill each other off or blow ourselves up, to earn the privilege of reaching this special vantage point. Like the gods were testing us, or thought we needed a little more seasoning, before they could bestow this gift." He giggles loosely.

The eyepiece that Heller has settled his eye against suddenly bursts alive—like a movie screen in a dark theater suddenly igniting. It is a stunning, startling density of stars, thick as stew, bright as fireworks, not the white of the Vermont night sky of Heller's youth but a dazzle of blue, red, green, violet, orange, pink, and yellow, in a range of hues. There is hardly any black between the stars. It's a night sky, yet night is effectively banished. The sky is alive is all Heller can think, all that occurs to him. The sky is alive. He is aware of his own startled intake of breath only after he inhales. Only as he recovers a little, grabs the edges of the seat to stabilize a little, after that first view.

"That's our sky, Mr. Heller. The sky that's out there every moment, above us, around us, has always been and will always be, and it's just we haven't been able to see it. Like the millions of microbes inside us, like the millions of atoms hanging around us."

Heller says nothing. Words are immaterial and inadequate and interruptive at this particular moment. A little later. Not right now.

Green lets him look a little more in silence.

Before saying: "Strange thing to be at the very tip of our planet, searching for other ones. Trying to peer into the beginning and end of time, among other modest pursuits. Nothing but ice for a thousand miles in every direction and infinite space above you, and you're nothing but a big eye, a huge eye, humanity's appointed representative of pure observation and infinite sight. I sit here, and for minutes, hours, days, weeks, there is nothing else. There is no planet behind me or around me, there is no past or history, there is no technology, even, in a way—there's just me and my highly advanced eye and the universe. That's all. All focus. All forward. All possibility. A powerful Zen present. It's a strange experience, Mr. Heller. As you can readily see."

This is what Antarctica is about, Heller suddenly feels. Not the cold, grim task of survival. But reaching beyond us, for knowledge, for understanding, a way to know, to ascend to, aspire to something beyond the muck of ourselves.

This is what the schedule of ships and planes—what all the supplies, what all the activity, all the systems and organization—are really about.

They are about Dr. Green sliding into his jump seat to the universe. They are about *forgetting* Antarctica, forgetting the cold and the complexity, and the national fiefdoms and the treaties and alliances and competing territorial claims, and seeing into the beyond. And only by sitting in this seat, having his breath momentarily sucked away in startled awe, glancing at the universe from a unique vantage, does Heller experience this meaning of Antarctica, of this frozen and otherwise useless continent. Useless to man. Everything to mankind.

"Your turn, young lady."

Heller looks up at Trish. Smiling warmly at him. Waiting patiently, but eagerly.

He slides out of the seat.

She touches her hand to his—affectionately, in the magic of the moment—as she slides lithely into the seat.

Trish. Her sense of wonder. Her eagerness. Her own keen observation of the world. Magnified here, somehow. She belongs here, somehow. Part of this breathtaking moment.

He watches Trish watching the universe.

The old cliché, thinks Heller, about feeling your own insignificance, looking at the countless—literally countless—stars. That we, on our planet, are a mere dot, so much smaller and less than even a single star. If anything, sitting in that chair, he felt the opposite—at the center and crux of things, the universe focused, for a moment, down to the pupil and brain and mind of the lucky occupant in the telescope's jump seat.

Trish, holding her long black hair behind her, leaning in, transported.

For a moment, the crusty cop finds he can think nothing but good. He can think of nothing but the poetry of not just what Green has said but of the poetry of what Green *is*, what he does, what he represents of humanity's best impulses. As he can think of nothing but the surprising, breathtaking poetry of Trish Wong in that jump seat to the universe.

He knows better, of course. He knows the elfin, smiling, gentle white-bearded man with the poetic soul must be looked into like anyone else. He knows that there could be a hidden darkness, like some black hole, an explosive supernova violence, hiding behind one of those gloriously glinting star clusters.

But for just a moment, Heller puts that aside. For just a moment, Dr. Green is everything we hope, everything we dream, everything we can be. All our human possibility. All our sparkling-eyed Dr. Greens. All our eager, coruscating Trish Wongs.

• • •

It's a moment that will soon seem wildly ironic, immeasurably absurd.

Another "Catch" for you, Trish.

This "Catch," a monster.

24.

It begins, on May 7, with a sudden loss of communications.

The comm system that Pritchard and Dolan are charged with maintaining is fairly reliable, secured with multiple backup systems. But temporary comm failures are hardly unprecedented. Every year sees two or three—it's Antarctica, after all. Annoying, to be sure. Several hours of frustration. Of rolled eyes, of computer reboots, of calls to McMurdo admin services. Before the communication is restored, as if by spontaneous magic, and the failure is all but forgotten.

On May 7—two weeks into total darkness, McMurdo's official "winter-over" period—at precisely 2:44 a.m., the communications system goes down. Across the board. No Internet. No transmission. No detectible signal. Nothing.

At 2:44 a.m., of course, the loss of communications isn't creating much annoyance. McMurdo Station is generally asleep.

But by 6:00 a.m., there have been some questions sent, some complaints to admin, from a few early risers.

By 7:00 a.m., there is an expanding annoyance—awakening as if with the day.

• • •

As the morning proceeds, as 7:00 a.m. becomes 8:00 a.m. and turns into 9:00 a.m., the frustration spreads. To be cut off like this? Yes, they are always cut off. They are used to being cut off physically, generally—it's in their wintering-over DNA—but for the past twenty years, they've always had some fairly consistent form of communications with the rest of the world, at first extremely glitchy and unreliable compared with the rest of the planet north of them. This has happened before—they're used to it—but every further minute amplifies the annoyance. They are waiting—waiting for the repairs that have always come. Like all other IT repairs. Out of their hands. But well in hand, they are sure.

The weather has already turned treacherous, making it extremely difficult for Pritchard and Dolan or anyone else to go out to physically trace the problem. Extreme temperatures of fifty below, steady Category 3 and 4 gust equivalents have already set in. One communications tower is a few hundred yards away, and the other one almost a mile. But the observation cameras—installed specifically for just this weather and just this contingency, when onsite observation is problematic—are functioning and show the communications equipment is intact.

McMurdo veterans know that Dolan and Pritchard are checking everything closely via instrumentation. It is unenviably technical work. But Pritchard is a communications whiz, and Dolan, according to Pritchard, is a genuine communications genius. Could rebuild everything alone by hand, if necessary.

The internal McMurdo comm system, which runs on batteries and local electricity, works fine. The messages trickle in to admin:

Hey, Admiral Byrd here. (A reference to the first human to winter over, in a hut with only his cairn terrier for company. Feeling that same isolation.) What gives, gents?

And Get it up, Dolan. Get it up, Pritchard. What's wrong, you guys can't get it up?

And Anything we can do to help? Bring you cookies? Bourbon? Anything to motivate you guys, say the word.

Pritchard and Dolan are—as anyone who has observed the process knows—running their diagnostics. As they have every time before—and every time before have brought the system back to life.

This time, they don't bring it back to life.

This time, there seems to be something different to contend with.

• • •

Heller happens to be in Hobbes's office late that morning, giving his update on the homicide investigation, when Pritchard and Dolan come to report to Hobbes—and to Simmons and Bramlett—after ten straight hours of intensive work.

Heller can see that Pritchard and Dolan look particularly anxious, shuffling, nervous—and uncharacteristically silent.

He catches Hobbes's expression on seeing them. Surprised to have them in his doorway. Heller picks up that this isn't how it's been before. That it's been the two of them at their radio panels, tuning, adjusting, checking, and the systems have always come back, as if magically, without Pritchard or Dolan leaving their eccentric communications lair—the Comm Cave, as it's known.

"So?"

Pritchard looks pale.

"So here's the thing," he says, "and we're not happy having to say this, because you're going to think it's our failing somehow, that we're missing something, but unfortunately, we're not."

"Go on," says Hobbes, but he is already feeling it—feeling the weight of what his comm team is about to tell him—whatever it turns out to be.

Pritchard mumbles it. He's having a hard time conveying it, processing it—and, Heller will come to feel, even believing it. "It's, um, not on our end," Pritchard says.

"What!"

"It's not on our end. Everything is working."

"What are you saying?" Hobbes's elfin features wrinkle in genuine confusion, as if literally struggling to process the thought.

"There's . . . no transmission. Nothing."

"But that can't be. The problem *has* to be on our end."

Pritchard shifts uncomfortably. "That's of course normally what happens. Normally it's us. Our equipment. Our somewhat shaky infrastructure, which we've always asked you for upgrades on." He looks up with a flash of accusation but immediately abandons the moment of defiance, of blame. "But we've been over it. It's not rocket science. We know this stuff inside and out, Dolan and me. And"—he twists his hands awkwardly in front of him, an unusual motion of free-floating, generalized discomfort—"it's not on our end."

He looks desperately, sheepishly, at Hobbes. "Believe me, I know how that sounds."

"Well, look again. Keep trying."

"We will, sir. Of course. We won't stop working on it, not for a minute. But that's not the worst part of it." He glances at Dolan, seemingly for support, but Dolan simply stares at the floor. "Thing is"—and here Pritchard pauses and mumbles again—"as of now, there doesn't seem to be any transmission from anywhere."

"Wait. What?"

"See, we've been trying to ping everywhere. Australia. New Zealand. Argentina. South Africa. And we're getting nothing."

"Well, that just *proves* it's on our end, doesn't it?"

"I wish it did." Pritchard and Dolan, while they've been working furiously, intently, have had a chance to absorb the possible meanings. Heller can already see that—in their looks of bewilderment, of desperation, of ambient gloom.

Dolan speaks up. He's normally the much quieter one, nearly silent, Heller has noticed, unless addressed directly, but he steps in with his expertise. "Sir, just FYI here, at 2:44 a.m., there was no temperature event, no microburst that registered on our communications equipment. We're set up to detect that kind of thing."

"You mean like a sunburst? A solar event? Could that have disrupted communications worldwide? Could it be that strong?"

Dolan lights up at the chance to explain. "Well, yes it could, a substantial one, so that's why I double-checked. But no," says Dolan, more quietly again, "that didn't happen." He looks around the room as if noticing the others in it for the first time. "A nuclear event—a nuclear accident or exchange—would have registered on our equipment too. A nuclear detonation can cause massive signal disruption. What's called an EMP, an electromagnetic pulse. Especially if the detonation takes place miles up in the atmosphere. Our equipment would capture that kind of disruption too. But there's nothing nuclear indicated by the data either."

"Jesus, Dolan." Nobody wants to even hear about—contemplate—such a possibility.

On the other hand, he's saying these are all the things that *didn't* occur.

There's silence in the room.

"Sir—I . . . I feel like something has happened. But if it was geological or nuclear, we'd know about it."

"If it was geological or nuclear, it wouldn't affect everyone, for Chrissake," Simmons interjects—indignantly, Heller notices. Unable to accept—lashing out at the very notion. The long arms of his lanky frame whipping in the air.

"No," concedes Dolan, "but it could—*could*—affect all communications. At least with us. At least for a time."

"But you're saying you think, based on your seismic equipment and other readouts, that it's not either of those things," Hobbes says.

Heller regards the two radio techs. Dolan's downcast eyes. Pritchard's hands shaking. They alone have spent the last ten hours wrestling with the equipment and, while doing so, inhabiting the possibilities. Their information is new to everyone else here. But they've been living with it. Focusing on the data, or lack of it. For Dolan, it's a version of the scientific method—a process of eliminating what it can't be to leave something it could.

"Look, whatever the nature of the event or events, if it even *is* an event, it's affected communications operations substantially," says Hobbes. "That's all we really know at this point. Let's not speculate on more than that. It would be just that—speculation."

• • •

Pritchard and Dolan keep checking for the next few hours, for the rest of the day. The backup systems have now all been triple-checked and are technically working. Backup systems that have never even been called into play.

"Are you sure?" ask Hobbes, Simmons, and Stanford, separately, each in his own way—skeptical, persistent, anxious.

"Yeah, we're sure," says Pritchard. "We're using every analytic device. We know this stuff. For whatever reason, there is no signal coming, of any kind."

"The problem is on the other end," says Dolan, shaking his head, repeating the mantra gloomily, like a fact that he can't escape. "I don't know what it is or why it is, and we know how crazy it sounds, but the problem is at the other end."

"I'm sure it'll get worked out," says Bramlett.

A sentence—a sentiment—that is greeted with silence.

Because they're starting to think it won't.

• • •

The next morning, Dolan does report a seismic disturbance to them, and accompanying temperature irregularities consistent with nuclear blasts or an EMP or a geological event at least. But he also explains, gloomily, that this occurred *after* the communications breakdown, which is why he never noticed it in his data until last night. He was originally checking for data linked to 2:44 a.m., the moment the comm system went down. The seismic disturbance occurred at least some minutes after, he said. Maybe some part of a chain reaction to whatever was the precipitating event? Maybe some horribly miscalculated nuclear overresponse, or full-on series of infrastructure attacks, by some government or other? That could explain the communications blackout. But it is pure conjecture. Conjecture running wild.

There is silence, before Dolan asks quietly, "Sir, could it . . . could it be some kind of pathogenic event? That we're insulated from here?"

Insulated from, for now.

"T3 setting in early, eh, Dolan?" says Hobbes. But he's just trying to deflect his own incipient anxiety. Heller can see it's because Hobbes doesn't know what else to say, how else to answer. Heller pictures Dolan sitting in the Comm Cave, the sparse data points in front of him, trying to figure it out. Do his hours of silent concentration—his anxious focus—lead him to ponder the possibilities too much? Or too clearly?

• • •

Heller thinks again about those screaming newspaper headlines in the seat next to him on the airplane down. The headlines he wanted to escape. The news streaming in to them via Internet until yesterday, counteracting their isolation, connecting them, reminding them. The breathless articles. The alarmed editorials. The sudden acceleration of chest-thumping threats from Russia, the increasingly vocal attacks from China, the heightened readiness of warships and nuclear-equipped air fleets of all three superpowers. The discovery of Russia's microbial experiments, as long-standing and institutionalized as their computer network hacking—and wouldn't America be doing it as well? The infrastructure infiltration that every intelligence agency knows its enemies are capable of. The weaponized chemical capabilities that go undiscussed. All the alarmist reports that Heller had previously dismissed as the hyperventilating of the press during past administrations, trying to create news, highlight friction, peddle it for profit. But this administration has proved different from the start. Prided itself on its unpredictability. Thrived on disruption and take-no-prisoners bluster. His instincts told him from the outset that these people were genuinely different. Genuinely dangerous. What if something *did* happen, thinks Heller. Is *happening*? Something nuclear, solar, environmental, microbial, meteorological? Some unforeseen interaction between them? But Heller knows enough to know that he knows nothing. That amid any half-valid scientific speculation, his own visions of calamity are the most speculative, the least informed, the least competent of all. He takes Hobbes's advice. He pushes his personal speculation aside. As much as he can. Because of course you speculate a little. You fill the unnerving radio silence with the noise of your own thoughts. You can't help it. You're human.

But what if something did happen? *Is happening?*

• • •

A few scientists do begin to speculate, in the days that follow, more carefully and scientifically than Dolan did, that judging by the speed and thoroughness of the silence, if you provisionally accept as fact such speed and such silence, then it could indeed be a microbe. Maybe unleashed too fast, too complex, or too multiform and mutationally adept for science to get a handle on it to craft a defense. The possibility has always been there, apparently, Heller learns from Hobbes and the others. A prospect far more alive, far more conceivable, and therefore more terrifying to the scientific community than to the general public. Microbiologists and epidemiologists, the CDC, and similar watchdog organizations across the globe have been only too aware of it. The possibilities and scenarios have long troubled science's sleep.

Bred in the warming oceans—the warming oceans not yet decimating cities but harboring and spreading with alarming global efficiency something much deadlier, as it turns out—a pandemic.

What happened? What *is happening*? Hobbes, Simmons, Bramlett—the leadership—do their best to quash any speculation. Trying to continue to function normally. But, at the same time, starting to process the possibility. Trying to think clearly.

And unsaid, at the back of all their minds, Heller can sense, by their circumspect silence, by their closed conference room door: beginning to think about survival. Collectively, individually. To cobble it together. Trying to plan for the short term, for the medium term. Too petrified, too undone to think too much beyond that, pushing away the unthinkable idea—momentarily unthinkable—that they might be what's left of mankind. That their isolation, by a quirk of geographic and meteorological circumstance, is going to save them. Save them in the short term. Save them from instant annihilation. Would it consequently subject them to a slower, more painful annihilation—starvation, say, or some new plague or disease—all the same?

And the subsequent nuclear or microburst events that Dolan's equipment indicates—he admits he can't be sure which it is—either way, the resulting microwaves could wipe out communications and modestly but sufficiently disrupt comm satellite orbits. If it wasn't winter, if it wasn't so goddamn windy and extreme, they could set some geological instruments out on the surface that could detect the whiff, the faint fallout, of atomic or hydrogen explosions. But the instruments they have available, or can reasonably assemble, can't handle the winter conditions.

So what is it? What's happening?

Is it, as science has long projected, not one cause but a combination of things working detrimentally together?

And though unplanned for and unpredictable, it seems that it could have happened, be happening, in exactly the ways that have always been predicted. That science has long warned of. The scientists around him understand the possibilities perfectly. Are cursed, in a way, by their advanced degrees, by their highly informed imaginations, to so quickly and thoroughly and intuitively entertain the possibilities.

In the way that Heller has predicted—feels, knows, based on his vast and ingrained experience—that he is dealing with a serial murderer (held at bay for whatever reasons) about to be either unleashed or contained, some of the scientists feel, know, based on their vast and ingrained experience, based on even the scant information gleaned by the radio silence, the information of no information, what the dark scenario might be.

It would be God's irony, wouldn't it, thinks Heller, or perhaps proof of God (he is starting to have such odd thoughts, right off, right away, he notices) that it is scientists who are left to witness it. But also *not* to witness it—not to scientifically observe, which would be at least some consolation, something to do, instead of mere speculation from afar. From very afar. Useless. Unhelpful. Probably dangerous.

"We don't know anything" Hobbes needs to remind them almost hourly.

But we know it's something. That's the problem. We know it's something.

25.

"Sir?" It's Dolan and Pritchard.

Heller is standing near Hobbes in the cafeteria, when Pritchard and Dolan approach.

Pritchard, the more talkative one, moves closer. A bounce of hopefulness in him.

"Listen, Manny, we had a thought. Well, actually, Dolan had the thought. Tell him."

"Sir," says Dolan, shifting a little sheepishly, "you know how being cut off, isolated like this, sort of sends us back to the old days of Antarctica? Well, it got me thinking. We'll keep trying to figure out if anything's wrong with the equipment, recheck every connection, but at the same time, we can assemble a simple Morse code device—and I think even cobble together a ham radio."

"Morse code? Really? Why?"

"Communications students all over the world still start by learning Morse code," says Pritchard, jumping in. "Some of those radio systems must still be up—unreplaced, still operable."

"Plus, Morse code SOS is still the default method in an emergency at sea. If this is a catastrophe, like it appears it might be, people may be using it right now," says Dolan. "And there are still amateur ham radio operators all over the globe. Including New Zealand and Argentina. Not a lot left, I know. Lost art. But enough to reach."

Heller hasn't ever heard Dolan say so much. There's an odd formality to his speaking style—a private person, a voracious reader, a quiet but excitable nerd.

"You can do that? Build it from scratch?"

"Hey, Dolan's a genius," says Pritchard. "My partner's modest, but he's a genius. He taught me everything I know."

Dolan smiles a little, aw-shucks shuffles his left foot a little, and elaborates: "It'll mean cannibalizing some other equipment for parts, some music components and a computer or two, to jury-rig a transmitter, but we've got components to spare."

"Go to it," says Hobbes. Unable to fully hide his enthusiasm.

Heller is more cautious. He worries that what they may learn from a successful communication could turn out to be more harmful than what they don't yet know.

26.

"What do you think?" Trish asks him.

They are sitting together in the office Hobbes gave Heller. They jammed a second desk into it when Trish joined him. The two small desks face each other, lamps on each, their interview transcripts spread out. A miniaturized precinct.

"Really. What do you think?" she asks again. Inquiring of a colleague, asking a friend. Asking him out of his wisdom, but mostly out of his honesty.

He shrugs. He doesn't know if the shrug—a short, noncommittal nonanswer answer—is meant to try to protect her. She doesn't know either.

"I'm thinking about my family," says Trish. Eyes tearing, but unblinking. Looking at all the facts. But allowing all the emotion. "You're thinking about your family too, Joe. I know you are. Everyone here is thinking about their family. How can you not?"

"We don't know anything, Trish," Heller says gently.

They look at each other. Each one of them knowing by now that each will find a warmth and connection awaiting in the other's eyes across the tiny closet of an office.

"We all hope it was quick, uneventful, mercifully instantaneous," says Trish. "Like a pinprick to the back of the neck . . ."

"Trish, you're getting ahead of yourself . . ."

She holds up her hand, to stop the blandishments, the appeasement. "Won't I be pleasantly surprised, then. Won't we all be pleasantly surprised when it all turns out to be okay. A big, silly mistake. A mass hallucination." She narrows her eyes. She stares wordlessly. *We know it's not a mistake. Or a mass hallucination. Don't we, Joe?*

They have grown close to each other. A natural closeness from working together, on a life-or-death matter, on something consequential, meaningful. But also a surprising closeness in spirit, a camaraderie that both are completely surprised by and pleased to discover between a Southern California Asian girl and a crusty Northern Vermont cop. They have discovered a capacity for laughter, for lightness in one another that Heller, for one, would never have suspected of himself—and that is still a kind of secret between them, which makes it even more special. An affection that springs from the situation, from the cold, from the loneliness, from the boredom—but equally springs from nowhere, is mysterious, unpredicted, magical.

But that laughter is now hidden, tucked away. Maybe, Heller thinks, forever.

Maybe the closeness is inevitable, given the hours together, discussing the case, going over the interviews, projecting possibilities for each other. The working relationship turned quickly into something more than respectful and cooperative, polite and collegial. Her bubbly intellect and upbeat spirit probably pushed away the big drinkers, the professional roustabouts, the temperamentally cynical and experienced Antarctica hands who are more her own age. They have grown close working side by side, but closer for how each offers the other an instant sense of connection, of stability and security, out of cold, thin air.

"I think about my sisters. All their potential. The boyfriends they won't have. The experiences they won't have. I think about my grandmother . . . thinking she is leaving the world to a new generation, thinking her sacrifice has always been worth it for the future . . ."

He holds up his finger to cut her off. He can't take this pain. "Trish," he says, trying to calm her, distract her, reason with her, "what do we do here? What's our job, the two of us? We gather evidence, right? Well, is there any real evidence about what's happened? No, there isn't. Radio silence is not evidence." He wants to say *Be a cop, Trish*. But he knows that would be harsh, wrong.

She seems to only half hear him. "I know I'm doing this, thinking about my family," she says, more hushed now, "to avoid thinking about anything broader. I know that in a way I *can't* think about anything broader. That none of us can."

Her intuitions are probably right, he thinks: one probably can't fully see it, can't get adequate perspective. It makes sense that our mental capacities have subconscious self-protective limits in a situation like this. She is so smart, which doesn't, however, stanch or compress or divert any of her raw emotion.

"What do you think?" she asks him again. Her tone of upbeat curiosity not hiding the sense of terror forming, lurking, just beneath. Balancing, tentatively, above confusion, above despair. Stretching her long, beautiful neck to peer over the edge into the abyss. Needing an answer.

He has none. And, of course, she knows he has none. He has only a partial answer, a nonverbal one. Because in answer, he extends both hands to take, to hold, both of hers, and she looks at their hands together, and then up at him, as he draws her in to him, and it is suddenly, clearly, to both of them at once, exactly what she has been waiting for from him.

They hold each other, silently. A moment of knowing and not knowing. A moment of comfort, solace that they knew would be there, and a moment of surprise to discover it, to feel it. A moment of both focus and necessary distraction. Of being alone in the world. Of being together in the world. Of hanging on for dear life. Of plunging into dear life head-on.

27.

The news goes around McMurdo quickly when Pritchard and Dolan succeed in configuring a Morse code device that, they say confidently, can broadcast up to fifteen hundred miles. This will give them the Argentine mainland, the South Island of New Zealand, the western edges of Australia, and—most promising of all, according to Pritchard and Dolan—several shipping lanes, whose ships still maintain Morse code capability, more out of tradition than necessity. Suddenly, tradition has become necessity. Suddenly, the primitive is back—and is a lifeline. How appropriate for Antarctica, thinks Heller.

Pritchard spreads the news about the Morse code key. Reports it to Hobbes. Dolan doesn't take the time to stop. He keeps working on the ham radio components. Pritchard says they are getting closer on that too.

• • •

According to Pritchard, Dolan tapped the Morse code key every three minutes, hour after hour. They started with the international dots and dashes of SOS. Three dots, three dashes, three dots. The original international signal of distress.

For the first thirty-six hours, there were no responses at all. Pritchard asked Dolan how they could be sure the signal was projecting. Dolan assured him it was. Showed him on the graph, on the dial, where its reach was, where its signal was reflecting.

Pritchard described how they traded off. Dolan showed him how to work the key. How to minutely direct and redirect the transmission.

They decided to switch from a simple SOS to an actual message.

They debated it a little. They crafted it. Needed it short but specific, for practicality and because of their limited skills. They theorized that the SOS might have been too general, might seem like a residual signal mistake.

They settled on MCMURDO STATION—SEEKING ANY SIGN OF LIFE.

Again, Dolan taught the code to Pritchard, and Pritchard, a quick study, picked it up almost instantly.

Again, they traded off. Kept awake, kept going, with coffee. Kept at it, hour after hour. With a little amphetamine too, well, more than a little, they confess, when they relate all of this in detail to Hobbes and Stanford and the rest of the leadership.

Relating first, of course, what has just happened. What they have just heard.

• • •

Nothing. No responses.

An ocean, a planet, a drifting marble of silence.

And then.

A flurry of dots and dashes.

Dolan jotting them down furiously.

YES, MCMURDO, RECEIVING YOU.

Pritchard describes the feeling to Hobbes. A dizziness. A dizzying dopamine release.

They show Hobbes and the senior staff the text of the full communication, in Dolan's hand.

FIRE STATION #4 RANGER POSTED AT MOUNT USBORNE, FALKLAND ISLANDS.
HAVE LOST ALL RADIO COMMUNICATIONS. NO OTHER CONTACT.
AFRAID TO GO BELOW 2500 FEET INTO TOWN.
NOT SURE WHAT'S HAPPENED.

"Not sure what's happened."

In the meeting room, they feel an inextricable mix of elation and gloom.

At the success of the communication, at Pritchard and Dolan's efforts, at life—some proof of life, at least—across hundreds of miles.

But confirmation, it would seem, of a catastrophic event of apparently broad proportion.

The ranger's name is Winslow, Pritchard tells them. They continued to reach out to him, Pritchard says. Explained McMurdo's communications isolation. The senior staff would pore over Dolan's transcriptions.

Ranger Winslow said his supply situation was not critical.

Pritchard and Dolan agreed with Winslow's judgment to not venture forth. To shelter in his current location, for the short term, at least. Until there is some indication of safety in descending to a lower elevation.

Had Winslow had any other communication from anyone else, in any form at all?

No, he had told Dolan and Pritchard. He had been trying, reaching out, exactly as they had on McMurdo, but he'd had no response.

HANG IN THERE. KEEP LOOKING.
YOU TOO.

• • •

In two days, Morse code responses from Station #4 Ranger Winslow
suddenly stop.

The presumption is inevitable. Hard to escape.

Whatever "happened" has now happened to him.

28.

They are crammed into the cafeteria, shoulder to shoulder. One hundred fifty-seven people. From what Heller can tell, everyone at McMurdo.

The cafeteria is the only place that can hold them all. They have gathered together here before only for parties, for special events. A couple of weddings. And the time-honored annual New Year's Eve tradition of screening *The Thing*, John Carpenter's horror film set in Antarctica, a reliably raucous evening. All occurring during the busy, upbeat, productive high season. When McMurdo brims and bustles with close to a thousand people.

Occasions of predictable happiness. This is neither happy nor predictable. One hundred fifty-seven people, gathering together amid the darkness. Against the darkness.

In the room there is silence. The speculation has already spread, and there is a strong, shared undercurrent of fear and panic and confusion that everyone in the room is trying collaboratively to keep at bay. They are scientists. They will turn to science. They will immerse themselves in science, in the currency of facts, to keep other considerations, other terrors, at least for the moment, in check. To "lock themselves in the lab." They are essentially locked in the lab now anyway. A big laboratory, a big experiment that no one applied for.

"First of all, we have enough food and rations for well over a year," Hobbes says to them, right off. His voice, his manner, poised between authoritative and familiar, Heller notices. Part leader, part friendly neighbor. "And we've already begun discussing the expansion of our hydroponic growing experiments. Expanded hydroponics can be up and running in eight months. We have the seed stock we need. In spring, we can convert and configure the extra growing space. Our sense is that if necessary, we can be self-sustaining."

The subtext: *we can survive.*

"What about fuel?" someone calls out.

"We have fuel for ten months, and we have the materials to expand our solar. I'm told we can increase our natural-gas efficiency easily by twenty-five percent, and we actually have extra solar panels in storage for two new buildings that we haven't yet constructed, so we can deploy those, and we have the manpower. If we limit ourselves to the main barracks by next winter, our energy situation is sustainable."

We can survive.

"We have plenty of antibiotics, sulfa drugs, and essential medical supplies. I'm going to have Doctor Calloway and Nurse Sorenson train two more of you in nursing and medical intervention."

We can survive.

"Of course, this is without knowing the status or the supplies of our Russian and Argentinian counterpart stations. We're not going to know those until winter subsides enough to get to them, or for them to get to us, or as soon as we get any kind of weather window." In deep winter, the other stations are effectively as inaccessible as the rest of the globe. And any communication with the Russian or Argentinian stations normally routes digitally through Russia or Argentina, which seem to be part of the same communications outage, so for now there is no contact.

And left unsaid: This is without knowing if the Russian and Argentine stations are going to be our allies in this experiment of survival, or if they are going to see us as enemies and come after our supplies. Or if any interaction with them poses a threat of infection for us.

Or if we will have to actually turn them away. Fight them off. Or if they are even there. And in what condition. All unsaid. But not unthought.

"What about our colleagues down at Amundsen-Scott?" someone else calls out. "Any contact with them?"

Hobbes swallows, pauses before answering. He knows it's been on everyone's mind. The tiny sister outpost at the South Pole, reduced to their forty-person winter-over contingent. "No, no contact. But there's every reason to believe they're in the same situation as us. Meaning plenty of supplies, plenty of food and medicine, no immediate peril. They—and we—will just have to wait until the weather changes enough for the Traverse Highway to be passable.

"Look, everybody, we are in very good shape here, until we get to a seasonal point or position where we can better ascertain the extent of what's happened or is happening north of us. And it seems unlikely that whatever has happened is universal. It still seems that this is largely a combined effect of some major event, natural or pathogenic or even radioactive, coupled with, primarily, its immediate effect on communication."

First and foremost, a communications event. That is still indeed most likely. What Heller can't tell, what he can't process, and suspects that no one can adequately process or calculate either, is whether this is just as likely a total global event or whether they simply can't clearly conceive, as humans, a total global event.

"And speaking of communication, where are we on that?"

"Pritchard and Dolan are still on it. They've set up an automatic search-out/reach-out system to try to connect with anyone, scanning extant satellite systems, low orbit and high orbit. They're working around the clock on this. Am I right?"

Pritchard and Dolan nod solemnly. They know there's some doubt and irritation with them over the communications failure—rational or not. It is so sudden, so disconcerting, so unprecedented and complete. They're the only two experts. No one can contribute anything to their arena. And no one can fully judge the adequacy of their efforts. Heller feels bad for them. That's a level of annoyance you don't want against you as T3 tempers and attitudes settle in.

"We can obviously amend the rules about pregnancy and procreation. We can establish a neonatal unit. We can begin construction of an unmanned exploratory watercraft, to remotely inspect the New Zealand and Argentinian harbors. We can design and deploy air-quality sensors, to detect radioactive fallout and airborne pathogens." Hobbes doesn't say any of that. Not just yet. Way too soon. Way too much. But he's thinking it. They're all thinking it. He would say it only to be reassuring, and its effect right now would not be reassuring.

"For the winter, we're on our own. But we're always on our own in winter. Nothing has changed in that regard, except our ability to know anything about the rest of the world. In that way, we're temporarily like our predecessor explorers here in Antarctica, right? And look, it's scientifically reasonable to assume there *is* still a rest of the world. Science tells us to await the facts. Not to jump to conclusions. Not to speculate uselessly."

Heller knows Hobbes is trying to establish an assuring, sturdy, natural authority. He knows other people know it too. An implied chain of command that is like any other winter's. Because if people think that no longer exists, that it is called into question, then who knows what would happen? They have to pretend things are largely the same, except for communications. If it's a group delusion, it's a useful and adaptive one. For now.

"Look, we really don't know what's happened. Our communications are down. Remember—we just don't know," Hobbes says, once again. Like a campaign theme, to be drummed into the heads of the voters. Of the undecided.

No, we don't know, thinks Heller.

But the problem is, we can imagine.

29.

"There would still be pockets," says Hobbes, at dinner with Heller, both of them hunched over their trays, "in mountains, preoccupied with battling disease, being smart about it, taking it on. Climbing parties up there for days, those living above fifteen thousand feet—Lima, Peru . . . Quito, Ecuador. Maybe. The thin air—the microbe may have had trouble. People in those kinds of areas maybe have a fighting chance. If no one carries it into their midst. If they closed their gates. Responded immediately to the emergency." Hobbes stares blankly. "There's no way to know. Pure speculation. Pure hope." And in those last two words, uttered more quietly—*pure hope*—Heller hears, for the first time, true feelings Hobbes has been hiding from everyone else. *Pure hope.* That mere hope may be at this point the appropriate response.

So then what? Scavenger societies? Dystopias, postapocalyptic primitive communities?

Earth would regenerate, thinks Heller, no problem; some species would adapt, but not in the needed amount of time. Not in a human lifetime. That was the problem. The fragility of human life—not the welcoming, adaptable Earth itself. Time itself was the problem.

And this nationless 157 of them—scientists and support personnel, who happened to be here. They couldn't leave. They would never leave.

Pure speculation. Pure imagination. But speculation and imagination now bleeding into assumption.

• • •

Back in his room, Heller looks down at his spreadsheet. At his list. Originally it was a list of all the people who had wintered over—all of them possible suspects.

Heller's list is now, strangely, potentially, a list of all people alive. In his hands. As if he is playing God.

He would no longer be just a murder investigator. He would be, quite possibly, the planet's peace officer. Its unappointed, unofficial arbiter of justice. If life here headed in certain quite conceivable directions, he could be all that stands between civilization and barbarism.

No longer just a homicide investigator?

The lone law officer on Earth?

The puzzle has been simple. Who did it, and how. Simple enough to state, though complex enough to solve, because he has gotten nowhere.

Now it would be a new puzzle. The puzzle of survival.

He hasn't solved the first puzzle. And has trouble even grasping this new one.

People are weeping already. Pounding the walls of their dorm rooms. Stunned into silence. He—Joe Heller—would be dealing with that. And the moments—inevitable, increasingly frequent moments—when it boils over.

He will be responsible. Responsibility itself will take on a new meaning.

Hobbes remains outwardly calm, but he sees the panic in Hobbes's eyes. A sense that this is too much for their logic, for their education, for their brains. A sense of numb incomprehension already pervades everything, everyone. They don't know anything yet. They know they don't. But it doesn't stop them from "knowing"—imagining, articulating, envisioning the possible scenarios quietly with one another, silently to themselves.

Is he in any way up to the task?

He knows he is not. He knows his limits, and he knows they are severe.

He is forced to think again about Paul. A line of thinking, of brooding, of haunting that some part of him hoped to escape by taking this assignment, by coming to Antarctica. But the prospect of unfathomable responsibility suddenly thrust upon him reignites, amplifies these never-dead issues, makes them echo in the late and endless night . . .

How could he not know what his partner was doing?

Working side by side with him. Filling out reports. Interviewing witnesses. Covering cases. On all-night stakeouts together. How could he not know? How could he have no clue to his partner's other life?

How could he have been so blind for twenty years?

A detective? How could he call himself a detective? How could you trust yourself to observe human nature?

It was what he had asked himself then, over and over.

And it was no mere private question.

It was what they had asked him, what Paul's union representatives and defense lawyer had asked, with their puzzled, befuddled looks, in the hearings. Asking for the sake of their client, a way to make a point about calling all of Heller's testimony into question. How can we even begin to believe a guy who never noticed anything for all those years? But also, it seemed to Heller, asking genuinely as well.

How could you not know?

What does it say about you?

What kind of a partner could you be? Not much of a partner at all. That was the clear implication.

Paul had been slippery. Paul had been adept, it was true. But Heller had thought there was a connection between them. Camaraderie.

It indicated such naïveté, despite the profession. The exact wrong choice of profession, where alertness, suspicion, powers of observation were essential currency. Heller's departmental record indicated that he had plenty of those abilities. But his blindness to Paul told him he had none.

And Ann ambushing him, announcing her long dissatisfaction in the marriage, grabbing Amy and loading her into the car and heading to her sister's in Michigan. His other partner of years—equally misconstrued, misunderstood by him.

These questions, this history, never really buried, stirred up again by his partnership with Trish. Is he incompetent, blind, unseeing in some fundamental way in this new partnership too? Is there already something going on that he is missing? He doesn't want to screw this one up. There's so much so quickly that's so meaningful to him, to both of them, he doesn't want to mess up this partnership too. And now, the old questions, his old history are stirred up even more by what's happened, or seems to be happening, on the planet north of them. By the stunning, haunting prospect that his eyes, and his instincts, may be the only cop eyes and cop instincts.

And—beating at the back of his brain, a kind of summation and bottom line of all this brooding speculation, focusing it all down to one point, like all the stars of the universe converging in the eye of a beholder behind a telescope—

What will this do to the murder rate?

To the serial killer who Heller knows, just knows, is here?

This is not what he signed on for.

30.

Pritchard shows up breathless.

"He got somebody."

"What?"

"Dolan. He got it working!"

"What are you saying?"

"His ham radio. He rigged a ham radio and finally got it to work, and we were broadcasting, systematically adjusting frequency, and finally we got a hit." Pritchard is smiling. Breathing heavily with elation. Chest puffed out in victory. "A farmer in Australia. Guy in the outback. Heavy Aussie accent. But we were talking to him! Before we lost the connection."

"Can we get him back?"

"Hope so. Dolan thinks so."

"What's he saying? Did he tell us anything?"

Pritchard smiles, giddy. "You can hear for yourself, Manny. Dolan was smart enough to record it."

• • •

Hobbes, Simmons, Bramlett, and Heller huddle around the radio in the Comm Cave, along with Pritchard and Dolan. Heller's been invited in order to listen to the voice, to help hear its stresses, to help assess its psychological state.

The ham radio that Dolan and Pritchard have cobbled together certainly doesn't resemble any image of a ham radio from the past. No wooden case. No big dials. An assembly, instead, of colored wires, diodes, potentiometers from inside clock radios and audio equipment and computers, or the guts of a computer exploded, turned inside out. And, of course, a remote computer speaker that they all lean toward.

Wordlessly, Dolan hits a computer key. The recording begins to play. Dolan's voice. And, opposite it, another voice. The farmer's voice—sounding heavily filtered, the filter of a thousand miles or more, but no matter. Yes, a farmer, but no mere outback rube, as it turns out: a sophisticated agriculturalist, it becomes quickly apparent. The man is clearly, acutely alert and recognizes very quickly the situation at McMurdo station. Miraculously responding to Pritchard and Dolan's blind call into the darkness.

"Hey, blokes, this is Aussie 2094, broadcasting from the Brindabella Range. Anyone out there? Anyone know what's happened? Our grid is down. We've been operating on generator plus batteries and flashlights here since Monday . . ."

"Aussie 2094, this is Patrick Dolan, McMurdo Station Antarctica, please come back."

"Back at you, McMurdo. This is Andrew Donovan, ham license 2094."

"Donovan. You can hear us?"

"Clear enough. And you?"

"Yes, you're coming in okay."

"McMurdo. Wow. Wouldn't have taken anyone there for having a ham license."

"We just built it, actually. All other communication has been cut off. We're trying to figure out what's going on."

"Me too."

"Tell us whatever you can."

"Here's what I know, blokes. We've had no communication. No cell service, no satellite radio, none of the systems we count on out here. We normally get daily deliveries of supplies from a hundred miles away. Feed, grain. This is a huge operation. But no delivery trucks since Monday. No calls. I've got staff of about fifteen people that commute out here daily. No one since Monday. No cars. No word. It's just me and me mum and me daughter, Maggie. Was about to head into town and see what's going on, but I'm a mite frightened to. More than a mite."

"Do not head into town" they hear Dolan say to the farmer on the recording. "Repeat, do not. There may have been a massive pandemic or other event. Please wait till you know more." Dolan looks up now at Hobbes and Simmons, seeking their approval for the instructions he gave the farmer. They nod agreement.

"Please stay in touch, Aussie 2094" they hear Dolan say. "Let's check in, in twelve hours, same frequency, code 90954ST. Is that good for you?"

"Righto. Talk then."

• • •

"And then what happened? Let's hear the next recording," says Hobbes.

Dolan hits a computer button, turns to Hobbes behind him. "There is no more, Manny. He didn't make the twelve-hour rendezvous. That was the last communication."

Hobbes stands silent, looking at the little speaker. They all do.

It goes without saying that Pritchard and Dolan will stay on it. Will keep trying to raise Andrew Donovan, the farmer, and keep searching for anyone else. Search what seems to be—is increasingly feeling like—a gravely attenuated universe of possibilities to the north of them. Individual beacons of survival.

"Keep looking." Hobbes says it anyway. With no feeling behind it, Heller notices. Blank-eyed. Empty-hearted. "Keep looking."

31.

It doesn't take long.

Just a week.

A week of anxious isolation, of eerie quiet, of routine. The very concept of days evaporating, disappearing, as the night extends, as its strength and depth grow.

Heller and Trish continuing their interviews, dutiful, systematic. A routine to follow. A steadying connection, a link of the before with the after.

When it happens, it is exactly as Heller predicted.

Exactly as he knew.

And more so.

As if whoever it is, is mocking him for his foreknowledge.

For knowing that whoever it is would strike again.

Mocking him for not yet knowing who the killer is, of course.

But mocking him too for not knowing, not foreseeing who the next victim might be.

And with that next victim, proving they know Heller.

Proving they know more about him than he knows about them.

Making the point with particularly cruel emphasis.

● ● ●

There are still—despite the latest anxieties, the latest sense of uneasiness and fragility at McMurdo—certain strict rules that everyone respects. No one violates them. They still apply.

Certain environmental rules, for instance. An agreement not to interrupt nature, to let it follow its own course. Respecting the indigenous environment. That's why there is the no-pet regulation. Even a little domesticated dog or cat threatens the ecosystem with different microbes, a danger to indigenous species. And it's why recycling is so strict. Zero tolerance on waste. (And it goes both ways—protecting the habitat from mankind's germs, but protecting mankind from the habitat as well. You can't touch or move seal or penguin droppings—no one knew what unique microbes it might contain that could jump accidentally into the McMurdo population. So it's left alone.)

It's why food scraps are sealed off from the terns. And why a thirty-meter perimeter for photos of the various penguin species is respected and enforced.

And it's why when a seal carcass washes up on shore or when a sick or deranged seal wanders close to McMurdo, they don't touch it. They leave it. They can't remove it.

The carcasses of seals—either mortally sick or rejected by the pack, who have struggled in from the beach to the edge of McMurdo—are always sad and disconcerting to see, but not all that uncommon.

And that's why on that dark morning—not actual "morning" at all, morning merely by the clock—no one is at all surprised to see the shadow of a seal carcass, curled in on itself, a hundred yards off. Far enough away to be left alone, as if, in its dying breaths, it knew.

And no one has any reason to venture near it for several hours, in the dark and brutal temperatures, which is why no one sees, for much of the morning, that it is not a dark seal carcass, but—when someone finally passes a flashlight beam over the carcass from a distance—it actually shines back in a reflective red, because it is the red parka of Trish Wong.

Trish curled dead at the side of the road.
Bright-eyed, innocent Trish.

• • •

Mocking me, Heller knows.

Amid his pain, his heartsickness, his dizzying rage and fury and distress, he knows:

Mocking me.

And he knows it has begun.

32.

Hobbes, Simmons, Heller, Sorenson, and the doctor, Calloway, are gathered in the infirmary around the body of Trish Wong.

She is naked on the table.

"We can try to autopsy her here, but it's going to be limited," says Calloway.

"Whoever did this probably knows that," says Simmons, "and if it's the same person, we're not gonna find anything this time either, are we?" He is exasperated, desperate. It's a rhetorical question. No one answers. Everyone knows the answer.

"We've got to decide in about two minutes or so," says Calloway. "Do I cut and we take the chance of my discovering something? Or do we freeze her for the season, for a full and more conclusive autopsy later?"

Left unsaid, but hanging in the little infirmary room:

There may not be a place left on the globe to do a full autopsy.

There may not be any transportation left to get the body there.

There may not be a later.

"Freeze the body," says Hobbes.

A temporary, sidelong, implied vote of hope for the future.

It doesn't require a full autopsy, of course, to check the base of her neck for a tiny red puncture mark.

Calloway and Sorenson bend down to look. Shining the exam light closely at the base of her neck.

There is the red mark. The tiny needle prick. Identical to Sandy Lazo-Wasum's.

Calloway and Sorenson look up at Heller, at Hobbes. All eyes meet silently.

Unsaid. Unnecessary to say *Here is the mark. The mark that told us nothing. The poison we couldn't detect. The mark that mocks us with our lack of understanding. That tells us that an autopsy might reveal nothing anyway.*

• • •

"What the hell is going on?" Hobbes asks Heller, privately, outside the door, as they exit the infirmary, before stepping out into the seventy-mile-per-hour wind and forty-five below together. They will all have to move together, use and enforce the buddy system, from now on.

Heller takes a breath. *Exactly what I feared, Manny. Exactly what I knew.* "Unfortunately, Manny, what's happening is that the killer is stuck in this new situation, same as we are, and this new situation is having its effect on them too—emboldening them because we're preoccupied. And the bigger point—if they're feeling the stress of this like we are, the pressure of it, then they're feeling the need to act, to be themselves, to prove themselves . . ." He doesn't verbalize the rest of what he has been thinking: *before there's no one left to prove it to.*

"And your being here is not a deterrent?"

Heller smiles grimly. "My being here might be an accelerant." He looks at Hobbes. "I think it was Trish Wong because of her association to me."

"So *I* killed her," says Hobbes, in brooding, melancholy realization. "I assigned her to you impulsively there in the cafeteria, and that was her death sentence."

"Don't be ridiculous. You can't blame yourself. We didn't know anything like this would happen."

"We didn't?" Hobbes looks at Heller, the accusation implicit: *Did you know? Should you have known? Did you kill her, the moment you asked for an assistant?*

Heller doesn't answer. He has already wrestled sleeplessly with that question.

He could feel, in the infirmary with Calloway, Simmons, and Sorenson, Hobbes's unspoken frustration with him. Annoyance triggered even with his very presence. *Why haven't you solved this yet? What are you doing? What's taking so long?*

From Hobbes now comes something less accusatory—and more troubling. An expression in Hobbes's eyes of stunned, abject incredulity. *Wait. I may be dealing with the end of the world—and a serial killer?*

Hobbes looks up at him. "So now that you're operating alone again, maybe it'll stop?"

Heller looks at him. "It won't stop."

It's only getting started.

33.

He had adored her laugh, reveled in her intelligence. Liked her eyes, her hands, her strong lean body. He had liked her more than enough, and she had liked him more than enough, here in the strangeness of the months-long night, to slip into bed with each other. And every time they did, it was both comfortable and new.

He didn't know if it was T3 hormonal disruption, for either or both of them—creating a greater sense of ease and companionship, or a greater threat and fear of loneliness—but they had enjoyed each other recreationally, emotionally, thoroughly. It was a good way, a gratifying way, to pass the night. The defined nights of the clock. The ill-defined long night.

He is almost certain no one knew. Someone could suspect or speculate, but Heller doesn't think anyone actually knew.

So how much did the killer sense about the relationship? Anything at all? Did he or she observe something in Heller or Trish, or in the two of them together, that set the killer off?

He thinks about who was close enough to see.

But in these circumstances, in the strange and artificial arrangements of Antarctic winter, everyone is close enough. Everyone can see.

Standing there in the infirmary, with Trish naked in front of him, in front of all of them—the body he had enjoyed on so many nights, the body that had equally enjoyed his—did the killer envision, anticipate such a scene? That Heller would be standing there with her naked, with Calloway, Hobbes, and the rest of them, discussing the autopsy? Was the crazy, disorienting pain of that moment part and parcel of the killer's clever cruelty? This is more than a murder. It is an incidental—or knowing and intentional?—severing of his own soul.

He has thought that at some deeper, unconscious level—deeper than the rational choice of exploring her love of nature, expanding her outlook and education—Trish was seeking opposites. Attracted to the opposite that Antarctica offered. Seeking the opposite of California's gently insistent warmth in Antarctica's relentless cold, the opposite of California's stunning topographical variety in Antarctica's sameness.

Lying there, with typical Trish curiosity and expansiveness and imagination, she had asked Heller to think more deeply about what had made him say yes to the assignment. To talk about his own home, his own upbringing, and whether in some way that home and upbringing had brought him here. Lying there with her, and only because of her, he paused to consider it more—to go beyond the obvious answer of a temporary exit from the cold, muddy trench of his own lonely life. For him, it was not the attraction of an opposite—of an unknown. For him, Antarctica was, in some way, a chance to revise the past by shaping a more useful and meaningful present than his flawed past would have led to.

In contrast to Trish, he thought, lying there with her, he knows winter. Winter is in his Vermont blood. Its harshness. But even in his native Northern Vermont, winter is sometimes merely picturesque. A season, not a permanent condition. Yes, Vermont winters can be tough. He knows the cold, grew up in it. But Vermont winter is about how man conquers winter, rugged farmers and craftsmen and crusty Yankee ingenuity. Antarctica is about how mankind *can't* conquer it. How it's too much. In Vermont, man wins. In Antarctica, man loses.

That little insight comes back to haunt him. How here, you can't conquer it. You can't master it. It masters you. And, now, that is coming to pass. In a way more devastating than he could ever have predicted.

Maybe someone knew of the relationship. Maybe knowing of it, they couldn't resist. So much better than just killing Heller. Killing what he loves and letting him live. Letting him live with the guilty knowledge that she is dead only and purely because of him. If he had chosen someone else, if he had chosen no one, she would still be alive.

And it's worse than that. And maybe whoever did this to her knows it's worse. Because he and Trish would sometimes spend the night together in Heller's private room, but other nights, she would return to the dorm room she shared with a roommate—so if Heller had insisted on that night that she stay, if he had pulled her to him, curled her against him, she might still be alive.

The killer may have been waiting for just this chance, may indeed have known, then, about their nights together, may have waited patiently for Trish to wander out alone, heading back to the dorm.

Why hadn't he pulled her toward him that night?

A knife of guilt, twisting in him . . .

Heller had made the decision to winter over just as he was getting to know Trish. Just at the moment when there was obvious affection—a spark, a flicker of aliveness, of attentiveness, of *something* in the relationship. His decision to winter over—so logically and somberly presented to Hobbes—*"to reconstruct, re-create the conditions of the crime"*—how much was it motivated by the chance to see things through with Trish, see what happened, see where it went?

The knife of guilt . . . twisting deeper . . .

And now, the killer is watching Heller walk around dead. Seeing what he does. An exquisite torture to witness. Who is this? Who is this, drawn out again by the Antarctic night, and now a permanent night? Drawn out under the perfect cover, the perfect distraction, of the prospective end of the world?

34.

What's more unsettling to McMurdo? A second murder or the prospective end of the world?

But the second murder and the end of the world are more interrelated than Heller would have thought.

Both could be poisonings, he realizes. A global poisoning, it seems possible, of some sort, from an unknown, unidentifiable source. And if it is a deadly pathogen, it has poisoned the air, the atmosphere, the planet with an unprecedented lethality.

And his inability to solve the individual poisoning, from a similarly unknown, so-far-unidentifiable, mysterious force—his inability to make any headway—is his personal version of global science's failure.

He begins to wonder vaguely if they're more literally related. Could these murders be similarly microbial? Whatever seems to have afflicted the planet, is this some smaller, individualized version of it? The relationship of the second murder to the prospective global catastrophe is on the surface ridiculous. But is there something to it? Could this murderer have stumbled onto something similarly lethal? Inadvertently or intentionally unleashing something long dormant, suddenly and globally ignited? Part of him knows the thought is absurd . . . so is this his own T3 subtly settling in, starting to talk to him?

There is for now at McMurdo a fragile sheet of cooperation, like a thin layer of ice, of permafrost—brittle, temporary, in danger of cracking suddenly, and certainly of melting slowly. Heller had looked around the room as Hobbes spoke. They were still too stunned, in too much shock, not to listen—blindly following, unthinkingly obedient. They are used to the rules, to organization. But under these stresses, what would happen? What could happen? And he realizes: anything. Anything at all. Their society is tentative. All bets are off. And order, civility, the rule of law, the veneer and maintenance of civilization—is it all going to come down to one lone semiretired subcontractor cop?

Should he continue his investigation? Or is doing so putting his own head in the sand? His own way of not being able to process what is happening to them? Is he simply in shock, in the same way that he has observed everyone around him is? He's presumably no more or less human than anyone around him. Sure, he can have perspective on everyone else—but you can never get enough perspective on yourself.

How much of this is T3 talking?

35.

Simmons and Bramlett institute some systems for tracking food and medicine usage.

Some tighter controls, some more-serious reporting procedures.

The biggest change is the daily briefing.

There isn't much to say at the initial ones.

Heller knows what Hobbes is really doing. It's a way of creating closeness, a bond, a sense of family and mission. Hobbes is sensing they might need that.

It's also a way of keeping an eye on one another. In case certain people indicate that they are heading off in their own psychological directions. Into uncharted psychological terrain. That might need a little help, some redirection, some restraint.

Heller has no illusions. It's what Hobbes can do—the little bit he can do—in the wake of the second murder, and to try to head off a third.

36.

They are thinking about their own families, of course. Their own wives and sons and daughters and parents. Personalizing the global catastrophe in order to absorb it. Or personalizing it because we are human. Because we think about our own lives. Because it's a self-protective way to keep from thinking of it in broader terms. In its broader reality.

Putting human scale on it. Did my wife, my daughter, my mother, my brother experience a fast death? A slow death? Sudden? Painful? Suffering or no suffering at all, instantaneous? But they would never ultimately know, would they? It was therefore the ultimate mystery story. It would have no ending. The lives—life itself—had an ending. Finality. But the story itself, the nature of that ending, the particulars of it—*that* might have no ending. Ever. The ultimate crime story. A massive crime, against humanity, and at McMurdo they might never know if it was humanity's own crime against itself or if humanity was merely an innocent victim, a bystander. The ultimate crime story, the final crime story. And humankind would not be solving it. It would go into the cold-case file. The ultimate cold-case file. How appropriate that it would be here, in Antarctica, the final disposition of the ultimate cold case.

He is thinking about Ann, living outside Toronto, moving up there from Michigan, farther, ever farther away from him. He is thinking about his daughter, Amy, in her freshman dorm at NYU in downtown

Manhattan. *Hey Dad, I'm going to minor in astronomy.* Her sweet little smile. Manhattan—Grand Pathogen Central. Pandemic Ground Zero. Picturing them minutely, obsessively, and then, he notices, his mind reeling back, cutting the images off, something primal and protective going on in the synapses, some special neurological defense, summoned only in extremis. Something temporary. He weeps in the shower. He weeps before sleep. And then tries to push it aside, because he knows—they all know—they must, for the moment anyway, put survival ahead of weeping.

There is an unspoken agreement not to talk about it. Not to bring up relatives and friends. Not just yet. Not right now. An unspoken agreement that they are all in the same position. The exchange of looks suffices for the sharing of suffering. And they don't really know yet. They don't really know. They are scientists. This is a scientific community. They will, with an ingrained scientific skepticism, with the skepticism and detachment of their training, await the weight of evidence.

They are the families gathered in the airport waiting lounge, awaiting word of the flight. The families gathered above the mine, awaiting word of the fates down below. Gathered outside the hospital, awaiting word about the surgeries following the attack.

Which is to say they know, but they don't know.

And the downed flight and the collapsed mine and the busy ER—now it is a planet. Now it is human history. A problem of scale that the mind cannot process.

Multiply this effect—this personal brooding, this profound and impending sense of loss—by each personal reaction. Each one different, each one unpredictable, because for each, it is unprecedented. Some suffering in silence, but some about to scream, about to unleash, about to explode.

And—always, underneath, always the bottom line, the question always lurking, because Heller is Heller—what does this new information, this unprecedented new input, do in the mind of a serial killer?

37.

The ambitious winter projects that Heller heard so much about—learning Latin, reading Proust, constructing a beautiful jewelry box, writing the first draft of a novel—all fall quickly by the wayside. Put aside. Overwhelmed by events. Overwhelmed by preoccupation. Overwhelmed by the imagery, global and personal, assaulting them.

Heller passes Trebor in the mess hall.

"Still reading the locked-room mysteries?"

Trebor looks away from him, shakes his head no.

Heller understands the glum, wordless gesture.

What's the point?

38.

It creates an unusual, and maybe irresistible, opportunity for a serial killer.

Heller knows the profile. Perhaps counterintuitively—given their profound delight and immersion in the gruesome, given their often-extreme exploration of blood and bone and skin—they are, in their typical-surrounding behaviors, essentially cowardly. They gravitate to safe situations, where they can exercise—even perfect—their perversities with impunity. The hitchhiking indigenous populations on Canadian Highway 16 in British Columbia. The sparsely populated Badlands reservations of North Dakota. The unpoliced prostitution streets of Juárez, Mexico. The favelas of Rio de Janeiro. Places where serial murderers have struck repeatedly. And now, counterintuitively, the closed, frozen, isolated borders of McMurdo Station may have just become one of those places. Added itself to that list.

He thinks of that Norwegian kid, armed to the teeth, brazenly taking out an entire island of high school teenagers on retreat. One of the most horrendous and unpredictable cases. This is a little like that. They are now isolated in the same way. A group in the same way that might raise the ire and resentment of a psychopath several notches higher. To the breaking point.

If the murders stop now, they might remain unsolved. So he knows he is hoping for a mistake. Which might mean—might *require*—another murder. A thought, a line of reasoning he would never admit to anyone aloud. Not even to Hobbes. Only barely to himself.

• • •

Hobbes corners him in the cafeteria. "Can you come see me in my office in an hour?"

"Sure. Something we can't talk about here?"

"It's a bigger discussion," says Hobbes.

• • •

"I'm sure you have some sense of why I asked you here."

Yes, Heller does. Heller knows that Hobbes needs to now ask more of him. He knows that the investigation is inevitably going to take a back seat to issues of survival.

Murder is primal. And yet it is now going to be usurped by something even more primal.

Hobbes look glumly at him. "We've got some bigger policing issues ahead of us. People are stunned. We're all stunned. We're all trying to process the possibility of this. And Calloway is a good doctor, but he's not a psychiatrist. We don't have a psychiatrist at McMurdo." He looks at Heller. "And there may not even be such a thing as a psychiatrist anymore."

He leans forward. "And I think you know as well as I do people are still in a state of shock. People are *not* processing this. But, eventually, they are going to. And we can't expect people to take this calmly. They are going to awaken to the horror at some point. They are not going to be orderly. This is an existential terror—unprecedented for any of us. We can't know exactly what to expect of people in this situation, but I think we can assume it will be things we *don't* expect. I guess I'm saying we have to prepare for the unexpected from any of us, from anyone here . . . because we know it's coming. Prepare for it the best we can. And part of that preparation is you . . . a bigger role . . . more expected of you, Joe. And, truthfully, I don't think you even have a choice here."

"But, Manny, we still don't really know what we're dealing with north of us, right? It's still speculation."

Hobbes looks at Heller. "Doesn't matter, Joe. It's what everyone *thinks* we're dealing with. And we have to deal with what people think."

"But couldn't this be . . . some kind of, I don't know, mass T3 hallucination?" Some mass T3 state, Heller thinks vaguely. Some common virus, some shared cognitive poisoning spreading through, infecting McMurdo Station.

"*Now* who has the T3?" says Hobbes, with a sad smile. "Come on, Joe. Whatever it is or isn't, we know it's not that."

He presses on. "I've had these meetings, these organizational talks to give people a feeling, a sense that we have a plan, we have organization, but I . . . have no actual authority for this. You and I know that. And people here know that. Sure, I'm an appointed Special Deputy of the US Marshal's Office. But what's the status of that office now? I'm just worried that we may be in more of a primitive tribal situation than we realize. We're a bunch of scientists and technicians, so the tribal is disguised, but it may not stay disguised.

"Things are extremely fragile. This is uncharted territory. Antarctica has always been that. But now in a way no one could have predicted."

And then he adds—with a sudden glimmer of determination in his eyes—"Still Earth's best hope. Now maybe Earth's only hope."

The old argument, the meeting room discussion of his first days here, comes back to Heller. The two friendly, teasing, but collegial camps. The *utopians* who saw it as a place of hope. The *authoritopians* who saw it as a place of lurking anarchy. Now the two schools will be tested. No longer theoretical or academic.

"Besides my special deputy status, you're the closest thing we have to law authority. So I'm going to need you to take on that role, assume it, grow into it organically, without any formal announcement, which we can't risk. So obviously, yes, your investigation now takes a back seat to the issues of survival. We're going to have policing needs. I can feel it. You're going to have to be McMurdo's cop."

The planet's cop, Heller thinks again. A subcontractor at that. The last human barrier between civilization and end-times anarchy. He sees it, can picture it, both vaguely and sharply.

Hobbes looks at him. "I'll need you to quietly be part of our team. In on and part of all our decisions. You're our law enforcement. I know how absurd that sounds, Joe. But this little proto-nation, this little survival cell—you're the face of law and order. You're the physical and visual representation of rules. You're all we've got. Like it or not."

Hobbes pauses. "Can I count on you, Heller?"

Heller nods.

A noncommittal half response, they both notice.

39.

So the murder investigation takes a back seat to far more pressing concerns. To the business of survival.

The tight little McMurdo community puts aside two murders among its inhabitants.

Heller can remember several times in his career going into similarly tiny communities where there was an unsolved murder. It had consumed the community. It was all the residents could talk about. Theories, suspicions, flew around wildly. Discussions among neighbors took place at all hours of the day and night. It was all the local paper could focus on. And even when it was solved, it was rehashed, reexamined, relived repeatedly. It remained part of the community's identity and personality for years to come. *Monroeville—isn't that where that guy . . . ? Sanders Point—isn't that where that little girl . . . ?*

And here is a similarly small and tight-knit community, and they are putting it aside.

Reasonably.

Of necessity.

You could argue.

But letting it beat at the back of all their brains. Letting it simmer on the back burner, while the matter of the meal—the food for survival—is on all front burners.

It couldn't simply simmer forever. You couldn't just walk away from that back burner. That wasn't safe. That wasn't smart.

40.

The leadership team meets. Hobbes, Simmons, Bramlett, Stanford. It's an emergency session, but they don't call it that; events are too fluid, too opaque, and too big for that old, outmoded designation "emergency." That referred to a world where some things were an emergency, and some things weren't. Here, now, everything is.

"While this has been a scientific community, a research venture of the National Science Foundation, we've been nominally in charge," says Simmons. "But now, if it's not going to be primarily a scientific community anymore . . ."

"But we have to *stay* a scientific community in order to survive," says Stanford, chief of science. "We're going to need our scientific focus more than ever."

"That's true . . ."

"The point is *somebody* has to be in charge, and there has to be some validity behind their authority. Some agreed upon validity."

"So what? We hold elections? Under what system? Like a constitution? I think that kind of fundamental starting from scratch is going to make everyone even more anxious . . ." Simmons shifts his lanky frame uncomfortably, shakes his head.

"Yeah. Like everything is up for grabs. So I better grab mine before someone else does . . ."

"Then look, let's tell people that this is a temporary committee, a temporary arrangement, and that we will figure out a system to reflect the will of the community as soon as we can. What about that?"

"I think people will accept that, for now. They're too stunned—we're all too stunned to do anything else right now."

"This is bizarre," says Simmons. "We're talking about our system of government? Like we're, what, founding fathers or something? This is absurd."

"I think we're going to have to get used to the absurd, Wick."

"So okay, what's the most pressing thing?"

"To me, it's the Russian station. Are they there? Are they in the same situation as us? We've got to somehow find that out."

"Pritchard and Dolan are trying to reach them too. They've gotten nothing yet. The thought is that maybe the Russians, if they're in the same situation, might also be trying an alternative comm system to reach out to us."

"Should we be trying to supplement Pritchard and Dolan with others? I mean, so much depends on communication efforts."

"Nobody else on this base has any similar communications or electronics expertise."

"So should we have them training more people? Assign a couple of smart tech-savvy types to try to help them?"

"That would require Pritchard and Dolan to teach them," says Simmons. "I'm afraid of wasting their time. We need them both focused on this every minute. Not stopping to teach others. Plus, the equipment they've rigged is so eccentric only they can work it."

"And here's the thing," says Hobbes, grimly. "All these efforts at communication? Having more people help? That may not be worth anything. It may not get us anywhere. A waste of resources." Hobbes looks down. Doesn't want to meet anyone's eyes as he says it. "What's the point of finding a few surviving, uninfected—temporarily uninfected?—sheep farmers or ranchers who can't help us? Who can't fuel and man ships and planes to come rescue us. And conversely, we can't fuel up ships or planes to come help them. And if some such hero could be found? To take us back to an infected, contagious, lethal planet?"

There is silence for a long moment, all contemplating it. The narrowing of options, the narrowing of fantasies. Before returning to the practical:

"We'll have to just keep an eye on the weather." They don't know the weather anymore—there's no weather broadcast. The most essential, daily, taken-for-granted thing. They are lost, unmoored without it. "We'll just have to use our judgment for when it's safe to go any distance outside."

"Or safe enough. We're going to have to accept some risk."

"Well, I'd say we want to not accept risk. I think we need to be risk averse, as a philosophy, in order to survive."

Silence. All contemplating risk acceptance versus risk aversion.

All of them seeing, already, the problems of not having a system of authority.

They all know they can't make a physical journey right now, in the wind and extreme winter cold and dark, to the Russian station or anywhere else. It would be literally a suicide mission. But at a certain point, in a month or two, they could. The question will be when, exactly, to attempt it. When, exactly, is that moment?

"Here's the other thing," says Stanford. "What if we don't want to be in contact with the Russian station? What does it gain us for survival? What if we need to share our limited food supply with them?"

"What if they have an abundance of food?" says Bramlett. "What if they can help us, in the short run, or even in the long run?"

The long run. No one jumps on her for that phrase. Nobody jumps on its questionable, fragile meaning. Though plenty around the conference table certainly hear it. Its strange new resonances.

"What if they've been infected? What if the winds have carried this virus or microbe or whatever it is to them and not to us?" Stanford says.

"Maybe we should be letting them reach out to us . . . and if they reach us, then we'll assess. We'll make a judgment," says Hobbes.

"But what if they need us? Our colleagues!" says Bramlett. "What if we have the resources and the capacity to save them? Don't we need to?"

"But if it's going to endanger us, it may be endangering humanity," says Stanford. "Humanity's existence. In which case, we have a responsibility *not* to reach out. To not take the risk. A responsibility to keep them away from us. A responsibility that goes far beyond ourselves. See, it may not be just a matter of *our* survival. It may be a matter of survival, period. Human survival. And that's a much bigger thing than the Russian station *or* McMurdo."

"It's true. We don't know why everyone else seems to be gone. But just as important, we don't know why we're still here."

None of them can quite believe that this is the discussion. The room is quiet. The talk feels somehow holy, religious. Heller feels himself shaking.

"Luckily, it's theoretical for the moment," says Hobbes finally. "Luckily for us, it stays theoretical, until the weather gets good enough to try to reach them or until communication is restored."

"Yeah, we have enough to think about," Stanford adds glumly, shaking his head slowly, so his long white hair moves behind him, like a closing curtain.

41.

His name is Eric Anderson.

He is the first to lose it. To officially and fully freak out, come apart. To have the apparent facts, the situation overwhelm him.

He is holding two steak knives out, sweeping them in wide threatening arcs in the center of the cafeteria, eyes wild, turning in a wary circle, not letting anyone in to disarm him.

It's difficult to tell whether he is threatening to kill himself or whoever comes close, if anyone tries to move toward him to calm him, to dissuade him, to save him.

"Don't you understand? Any of you? The world is ending! We're all going to die! All of us!" He circles, waves his arms and the knives wildly.

The problem being, of course, that what he is saying is not crazy at all. It might be perfectly accurate. Perfectly prophetic.

It seems to Heller—standing toward the back of the cafeteria, out of harm's way, along with two dozen others—that this is just a sudden, overwhelming need in Eric Anderson to take some summary action.

Or bring attention to the problem. Maybe he thinks they're all deluding themselves. Not sufficiently recognizing what's happened.

"Don't you see? We're all going to die!"

Many of them, of course, have been weeping behind closed doors, distraught, shaken, as they go about the long night, talking softly, refusing to talk, each reacting in his or her own private or natural way, but this is a more public display of what they have all been feeling.

"We're all going to die! To die!"

"But slashing someone here? Slashing yourself? How's that going to help?" a tall kitchen assistant named Perry asks, approaching Anderson cautiously, but not getting too close.

"Help? It's *not* going to help! Nothing will help! If I die first, or last, it doesn't matter, don't you see? We're all finished, either way! We're all that's left, and we're stuck on this ice, stuck in this night, and Earth is contaminated and uninhabitable, don't you see that yet? Can't you tell that yet?"

He swipes the knives with new resolve. Perry takes a step back.

"If this knife goes into me, or you, into your heart, my heart, it doesn't matter, don't you see? It doesn't matter! What you or I think, what you or I say, it doesn't matter. It's ended."

It's an existential crisis, Heller sees. Not theoretical. Based on evidence. Scant evidence, at this point, but evidence. Eric Anderson is having a crisis, firmly based on genuine doubts about existence. By that argument, Earth's first truly existential crisis. Heller is certain it won't be Earth's last.

Eric Anderson. Heller knows him from the interview lists. Lab assistant. Grew up on a farm in the Midwest. Ten siblings. Heller makes a little note at the back of his brain, stores a little truth there: those connected the most to life may react the worst to all this.

"Don't you all see? We're doomed! And you're all proceeding like we're not. You're all in a delusion. Well, maybe stabbing you—stabbing myself—will break the delusion for you. For all of you! You'll finally know what we're dealing with!"

Does he need to feel alive as he feels the end approach?

Does he need to express himself? Unleash emotion?

Heller is watching, hoping to help, knowing he is expected to help, but trying at the same time, in the moment, to process, to understand. Because he knows that Eric Anderson is only the first.

"Eric, we know. We know what we're dealing with. And we're trying to deal with it, step by step. We want you with us."

It is Stanford, surprisingly. Heller hadn't seen him. Speaking calmly, moving forward. Stanford, Anderson's lab boss, maybe hoping to make the most of their relationship.

"I'm no pioneer," says Anderson, in tears now. "I'm no traveler into the unknown. I don't want to go with you! I'm just a guy. I don't have the stuff for the journey ahead."

He's been thinking, Eric. He's been brooding. He's overwhelmed.

"Put down the knives, Eric. We need you. We need each other."

"We're all that's left!"

"Eric, we don't know that. Yes, there seems to have been a catastrophe, but we don't know the extent of it. We're . . . we're having a communications problem . . ."

Eric looks at Stanford, smiles, dazed. "A communications problem? That's what you're calling it? You see the delusion? It's T3! You're suffering from T3! Massive T3!"

"Well, Eric, maybe it *is* massive T3, and everyone on Earth is fine. What about that idea?" Hobbes now too is moving cautiously toward him but doesn't get too close.

Doctor Calloway is there as well. Heller can see him moving cautiously, stealthily toward Eric. From this angle, and from the bend in his arm, Heller senses the doctor is holding a hypodermic.

"Put down the knives, Eric. We're a team. We're in this together. You're our brother. You're our son."

Eric slashes the air again. But Heller can see it has no heart. It is defeated. The feeling has been lost. He sees that Eric will not be hurting anyone.

He realizes it's a chance to establish some authority. His helpfulness. To make a deposit in the bank of his trustworthiness. He walks past Stanford, past Hobbes, straight up to Eric. Looks him in the eye and holds his gaze on him.

He figures that if Eric is looking back at him—if there is human connection between them—Eric will not do anything.

You're not going to hurt me, Eric. You're not going to hurt yourself. We're in this together. You're not going to, Eric. Not right now. Not today.

Eric holds out the two steak knives toward Heller. Doesn't move them. They're no longer slashing the air. They're immobile. Held high. Symbolic only, thinks Heller, for an instant. Heller reaches a hand up for each one, like a handoff, and Eric yields them easily, effortlessly. Lets Heller take them. Like passing cutlery at a table.

Eric crumples to the floor.

Doctor Calloway is right there, plunging the hypodermic into him.

42.

Eric Anderson's freak-out only puts everyone further on edge. The anxiety hangs above, hums underneath, every moment. Every meal. Every nonmorning morning. Every nonevening evening. Every bedtime. The night comes to stand for what they can't see. What is lurking, waiting, everywhere to the north of them. The answers that they all sense will only be further questions. Eric Anderson, rather than being crazy, has had a completely sane reaction. His reaction is an unfortunate by-product of thinking perfectly clearly. The perfectly logical extension and expression of a completely reasonable anxiety and fear. Simply given vent. Fully expressed. In a way that is not socially desirable.

It occurs to Heller more than once. It seems perfectly logical, increasingly likely: Maybe they are never going to know what happened up there, across the seas, on the other continents. Maybe they are never going to know the cause.

If they survive—most of them, some of them, a few of them, any of them—and they have no way to learn what has happened, then they might very well never know their own past. They'll be starting over. The slate wiped clean, tabula rasa.

All these highly educated scientists and technicians. Thrown into a situation in which they have most in common with a primitive, ancient tribe. Focused on survival, carving out a functioning society.

Not knowing what happened. Doomed to ceaseless, useless speculation, and soon after, not bothering with speculation at all. Shutting it down, pushing it aside, burying it from consciousness in order to concentrate on the present, on survival only.

It's fascinating, if you could get perspective. If you could somehow step outside yourself for a moment and imagine a forthcoming civilization founded not on knowledge but on a lack of knowledge. On not knowing. Would explanatory myths eventually sprout? Explanations based solely in the imagination—would they come to stand in for facts? For "fate"? For "reality"?

All these scientists, these knowledge seekers, consigned to live in a world of not knowing. Of perpetual ignorance, of question, of rampant speculation, incessant whispering, undergirding every moment. As fascinating as it is unprecedented, and terrifying in being unprecedented, because you don't know where it's going to lead.

Such thoughts are beginning to circle him, circle all of them.

Sleep is fitful. Irregular. Always a challenge during winter-over. But now fractured, jagged, sometimes impossible. For Heller. For all of them. One hundred fifty-six people. Heading into the future together. Or into some final annihilation.

• • •

"Meet us at the infirmary," says Hobbes into the walkie-talkie that Heller now carries at Hobbes's request. "We've got a new situation." Sounding alert, urgent, but tired and resigned at the same time.

"Be there in five minutes."

• • •

"Must have been last night," says Calloway, showing them the empty medicine cabinets, pried open, bottles spilled, contents missing.

"What's gone?" says Heller.

Calloway clicks it off on his fingers. "Xanax. Ativan. Antibiotics. It looks panicked, terrified, hasty. Grabbing everything to sort it out later."

"Maybe whoever it is just wanted to assure their own supply. Their own survival. No supply plane coming. Can you get me a list of who's on these medications currently?"

Calloway looks at Heller. Questioningly to Hobbes. "You know I can't do that. That's against the rules. That information is confidential."

"The rules?" says Hobbes. "What rules? We're living in a new reality. We're in survival mode. And survival mode says that you need those medicines to dispense as you see fit."

Heller is half listening. He is looking at a roomful of clues. A welcome abundance of them, for a change. The fire extinguisher that was used to smash the cabinet. Normally, it would have prints, but since the perpetrator came in from the cold, unfortunately he or she was likely wearing gloves. But his attention quickly shifts: There is the imprint of the sole of a boot. Large. Tread worn down on the left, indicating someone left-footed, and in old boots. That could narrow it very quickly. He squints and sees a thread, caught on the edge of the exam table. He leans in, looks closely, lifts it gingerly in his fingers. Purple thread. Purple gloves, grabbing as they rounded the corner? A purple parka? Either way, not many of those. That could narrow it down even further.

A roomful of clues. An impulsive, panicked perpetrator.

He has no idea who it was, but he knows who it wasn't:

It wasn't the careful, methodical killer.

43.

It doesn't take very long. Three days.

Heller is waiting in line in the cafeteria, when he sees the purple gloves, two people ahead of him in the food line. Steve Goethals. Upstate New York. Maintenance.

He looks down at Goethals's boots. Huge and worn out.

He watches Goethals reach for spaghetti. With his left hand. Left-handed. Left-footed.

Heller stays silent. Ignores Goethals. Gets his food. Sits down with Hobbes.

"It was Goethals," he says quietly. Takes a bite. "He's got the medicines."

"You're sure?"

"Absolutely." Heller continues eating. "I don't think he's had much opportunity to hide them anywhere but his own sleeping quarters. I'm pretty sure you're going to find them there."

Hobbes smiles. "You mean, pretty sure that *you're* going to find them there. This is part of your new job description."

• • •

They surprise him at night. Four men selected by Hobbes to help Heller. They toss the room. The stash is stowed randomly around it.

Goethals, a big man, doesn't resist. Weeps, in fact. "I need those drugs. I need them."

The base is as rattled by the recovery as by the initial theft.

Goethals is reprimanded. In the end, a stern talking to, nothing more. Any further punishment is deemed to be counterproductive, pointlessly disruptive. He is reassured, gently, quietly, that the Xanax that he has relied on will be available for him, as before, from Dr. Calloway, always there as needed.

All the infirmary's medications go into a safe they bring over from Administration. Calloway begins a list of who is on what medication. He divides the medications equally, puts a plan in place for parceling out the medications over the coming months. The list is made public, accessible to all. These are new rules. No privacy; the old conventions are abandoned. This is a new world.

• • •

The resulting new rules of medication dispensing and transparency are disconcerting to Heller, though, in a new way. The list of people on various medications is a lot more extensive than Heller would have ever thought. Almost two dozen people are on serious psychoactive prescriptions. A cornucopia of medicines that Heller knows of, and many new to him, several that he can't even pronounce. Xanax, lithium, Benzedrine, Ambutol, Ativan, duloxetine, citalopram, fluoxetine. And lots of people consistently using heavy sleep aids, of course. Ambien, Lunesta. Understandable in a world of endless, featureless night. But it's well documented that such aids cause disruptions, hallucinations, and he highly doubts that the FDA's clinical trials have ever been conducted in Antarctica's endless-night conditions, so who knows what the local effect might be? Is the killer—only half-aware, or fully delusional—among them?

He's initially shocked that so many of these scientists and support staff, these hardy, pioneering sorts, are reliant on such an array of medications. Day in, day out, part of their body chemistry, part of their lives. Then again, they have fully experienced the stresses of the long night, and Heller has not. It's a community of science, which turns naturally (or unnaturally) to scientific solutions and trusts—feels comfortable with—chemistry and biology. It's like doctors who come to rely on a shelfful (or pocketful) of medications to keep going, keep doing their jobs, keep performing the work of angels, and who simply and privately manage their addictions, for the greater good, until they can't, until something happens . . .

In the short term, according to Calloway, there's enough medication for everyone's specific current needs. He's charting them. But in the long term, they can't manufacture any of this stuff, of course. In the longer term, everyone is coming off their meds. Their Xanax and lithium. But also their asthma and allergy and heart medicines. In the longer term, there's no medicine at all. No antibiotics. It's a reality that beats at the back of Heller's consciousness and of everyone else's too.

44.

Night settles deeper over them. The days and days of Antarctic night, the deep night that the human biometric clock and circadian rhythms are unprepared for, are tested by. Our physical systems, thinks Heller, are geared since time immemorial for a cycle of daylight and night, since the rise of the species in the savanna, at the equator, bred in our blood and bones and DNA, so that nothing could be so deeply unnatural to our senses, to our core, to our physical functioning as the Antarctic night.

The annual deep night—which brings with each return a profound sense of isolation and disconnection that is intense enough every winter at McMurdo—is now compounded, amplified, to an untested, uncharted level. They are all suddenly explorers again. Suddenly all Shackletons and Admiral Byrds. But this time, the uncharted terrain is their own rampant imaginations, a new kind of terror, as they try to see the depth of what they have missed, what catastrophic thing has gone on in the world above them.

Heller realizes that every one of them, in his or her own way, is forced to become a philosopher. Is forced to think about existence. About one's own individual purpose, and the larger human purpose as well. It is an exercise that, in the course of their elite educations, many of them have occasionally, voluntarily chosen to contemplate or found temporarily fascinating. It's also an exercise that many have avoided in life—too uncomfortable, too "soft" for scientists, and now forced upon them. Life's meaning is now front and center, the only topic, in a way.

They're forced suddenly into the incessant consideration of life's biggest questions, of existence, meaning, purpose, and that leads in many cases to desperation, to a defeated search for meaning, a defeated psychological expedition that cannot turn back now—it's too late to turn back, we must dig in, team, and make a stand right here in the snow and ice, right here in the vast cold nothingness of our interior lives—and it is simply too much for some people, and in many cases, he knows, there is a resulting psychological collapse. Some can quietly handle the philosophy, inhabit the metaphysical. But others who go deeper, too deep, into the disorienting whiteness, do not emerge. It's a tenet of mental illness and social adaptation: if you think too clearly about life, you'll go crazy. And this is, unfortunately, a situation in which they're all forced to think. Deeply, individually, alone.

It turns them into philosophers. And Heller senses that if they're all turned into philosophers, there'll be no one left to attend to the business of living. He knows that doesn't make any literal sense, but it's an instinct he has. Put another way: he has the sense that if they think too much, they'll die. Death by thinking.

Heller imagines that they all are doing their own version of what he is. Thinking first about what happened. Imagining every scenario, building every scenario around the scant and no doubt erroneous evidence they have.

And the first question—was it fast or was it slow? Meaning, was it painless or was it painful? Because everyone in a postnuclear and weaponized world has had the thought: Well, okay, if I exist in one moment and am snapped out of existence in the next moment, then what's the big deal? I'm never gonna know; I'm never going to know it or even (hopefully) feel it, and even if I do, so what, if the pain is ended in the next second? So I can live with that (meaning, die with that), if it's so instantaneous and clean and antiseptic, snapped out of existence; that's really okay.

And it's doubly okay if it happens to everyone else too. If we're all snapped out of existence together—instant, presto, painless, one moment here, the next not—why, there's technically no sadness or regret, no memory. There's no feeling at all. It's as if nothing has happened at all.

But if there's pain, foreknowledge, a consciousness of it, well, that is painful to contemplate. If they were not snapped out of existence but dragged out of existence, kicking and screaming. If they saw it coming, even for just a few last seconds—a flash of light, a brightly illuminated, holy meeting with your maker—or saw it for a few hours, the disease rolling like weather toward them, like a storm, unstoppable, a final mysterious, unstoppable gale force, a wall of hail. Or was it a few days? That would be worst of course—all that time to contemplate it, to desperately and uselessly try to fight it—or would it be best to get your affairs in order, to say and do what you needed to, to finish things, round things out, right wrongs, love those you love in a last and fully contemplated act of love and life and existence?

And all of them at McMurdo thinking incessantly about their own families. Their own relationships. The arc of their own lives. What it could mean to be left here. The responsibilities. The purpose. Thinking about beliefs, or lack of them. Doubting God, as always, many outright dismissing the idea, but at least summoning up the God idea now too, for this is what humanity created it for: circumstances like this, when you might have nothing else.

He thinks again, again, again of Ann. Images circling him, incessantly, a loop of memories, spinning, thickening. Of what happened between them, all the good, all the bad, all the petty and foolish and insubstantial, all the substantial and significant framed behind it, all the minutely but profoundly human. He thinks of all the regret, of chances missed. Assuming, knowing, that Ann would have thought of all they had together too. That her memories are different, of course; it's always amazing how you remember events differently; part of your training in police work—the untrustworthiness, the stunning divergence in well-meaning eyewitness accounts—that you rediscover in your own relationships, and there's a part of him that believes that women remember things differently anyway, that their memories work in a different way, driven more by the senses, but nevertheless there is a store of events that you do share, an arc of your lives, and despite the wedges that drove them apart at a certain point, there was so much shared—and is it gone if Ann is gone? Is it snapped away if she is, or is it actually *more* important if she is now gone, because that is what still exists of her? And for now it lives on in Heller, but if something happens to him, is it then gone forever? Or does it still exist, somehow, infinitely, in the universe, as important and unimportant as ever? These are the philosophical questions that surface, inexplicable, inextricable, relentless. And where was she when it happened, if it happened? Where exactly? Doing what? With whom? What did she see? What last earthly image? Thinking what? Is a last moment any different really from a previous moment, in quality or profundity or importance? Not if you don't know it's coming. It's only one in a million moments, indistinguishable, so it means nothing greater, in its quality or essence, but there will be no more experience beyond it, so in that alone, it is unmatched; it stands alone in its content, no matter how mundane the moment or the view.

And Amy. Amy. Amy. The human expression of the love that he and Ann had shared. The very idea of Amy. The idea that she carries the spirit of Joe and Ann, the memory of them and the genetic expression and the proof of their love and union, into the next generation, carries Joe and Ann themselves into the future. Although that was never the idea of Amy for them. For them it was to have a fuller household, a fuller experience with each other, to see what it was like, to see how it expanded their daily experience of life. But once she arrived, he could see how Amy was an echo of each of them literally—in the shape of her eyes and mouth, in her lean limbs and in her uncannily reminiscent movements, and more subtly but unmistakably in her temperament, in her pouty frown, in her slow smile, and soon, more interestingly, she was a changing, *dynamic* echo—becoming more Ann at a certain stage and more Joe at a certain stage, as if they were watching the active interplay of their genes on the stage of life. At the same time, watching Amy draw away from both of them, becoming something of her own, something new entirely, and this was an accidental project for both Ann and Joe, one they didn't ever discuss much, but one they both watched with fascination, and it created if not a deeper love between them (it didn't), then a bond and connection that Heller would argue went beyond love, to something truer and more trustworthy. Truer and more trustworthy than love—he knows how strange that might sound and seem, and yet he honestly feels there is something to it.

So is all that gone, in the teary and disappointed blink of God's eye, in an instantaneous destruction of the species? Joe and Ann's legacy, to say nothing of Amy's unborn children—all six, eight, twelve of them!— and their children too?

Heller thinks again, again, again about Amy's final moments and of course has not the slightest idea who or where or how or what she would have seen or would have thought or would have felt. He has not the slightest picture of it; it is a blank. And lying alone in his McMurdo bunk he weeps, weeps more, as he knows—is already sure—that he will weep continually, until he is not around to weep. As he knows—is already sure—that he will go on and do what he can and function as well and as helpfully and as fully and as focused and as efficiently as he can despite the weeping.

And he multiplies this, of course, by all the survivors on all the bunks in McMurdo, curled into the same brooding thoughts, the same waking nightmares, the same inescapable cursed visions of family, of existentially severed connections . . .

Heller doesn't believe in God, or any version of a hereafter or a beyond—never has, can't see that he ever will, even now—but he can't help but picture a few billion souls, of completely indeterminate size and composition, floating now above Earth, circling the planet, waiting for a safe place to land, to start again. A kind of substitute system of stars, as if the stars have waited for this metaphor for a billion years, have been waiting for these souls, having at last an earthly purpose, as a representation of seven billion circling souls. This would be either the moment to start believing in God or the moment to firmly put any incipient belief to permanent rest, to crush it out of you. But despite his unbelief, Heller can't help seeing the brilliant earthly ring, the shimmering circle of patiently waiting, displaced earthly souls. Taking on some unbodily, spiritual form—of radio waves or frequencies or an advanced form of matter—conveniently, efficiently, only temporarily waiting for safe touchdown, waiting for Earth to cool, for Earth to recover, to welcome them again.

Personal pain. Personal memory. Multiplied by seven billion. Multiplied by humanity.

Yes, he can see how the floating facts of it—the stresses of it—could turn them into philosophers or psychopaths, or some unprecedented combination of the two.

• • •

And thinking always—beginning with, ending with, most humanly, most achingly, most bitterly, and always—about Trish.

Trish, the frame of all this contemplation. Snapped out of existence not as speculation but as reality. Not as an act of imagination but here, a few yards away, a few days ago. *Jesus.* Reminding him that the conditions of existence—and of absence—are in the here and now. In a way that he can exercise some control. In a way that there is profound responsibility. In a way that there is a path forward.

Does he feel some guilt—or some defiance, or some inner truth about himself—in making her equal to Ann and Amy?

But it's more connected, more integrated than that. She is the representation of their loss. She is their stand-in, their nameless sister on the front lines, in the battle of existence versus absence, of life versus death, in all that is versus all that isn't, in light versus darkness. There is no grading, no judgment of one versus the other, of *more* loss versus *less* loss. Trish, Ann, Amy—they are all the same. They are all, equally, everything. And everything he must fight for, continue to think for, continue to reason for, continue to exist for, continue to survive for.

45.

"Should we try to get to the Russian station? Should we just try?" asks Bramlett, blinking, pushing her black glasses quizzically against her pale face. Her voice wavering. The anxious child, always lurking within the opaque career bureaucrat, now emerging.

The Russian question again. Their neighbors. Like checking on the neighbors after a storm.

"Eventually, Antoinette. As soon as humanly possible. We can't make it there now, in this weather," says Hobbes.

The wind and cold could freeze and burst vehicle fuel lines within a few miles. Getting to them would still have to wait. But they are the closest. Just a hundred miles away. They are evidence of life. And if they are there, and if they are okay, they are presumably having the same mirror conversations.

"Wouldn't you think they'd try to get to us?"

"Yes. And if they're more desperate . . . maybe they'll try first."

"If they're there, presumably they're dealing with the same problems."

"And presumably they have the same questions about whether it's safe to reach out to us. Whether we're carriers, contaminated . . ."

"But maybe they've established communication. That would be a big difference."

And presumably they have no serial killer stalking them. That would be a big difference too, thinks Heller.

Simmons is somber. "Look, eventually we'll go to the Russians, or they're going to come to us, but it could be when one or the other of us has run out of supplies and is throwing themselves on the mercy of the other. And whether it's us or them, it could be an ugly confrontation, an ugly moment. So I'm just as happy not hearing from them, for now."

"There could be an out-and-out battle over the last supplies . . . ," says Stanford.

"Or maybe they aren't going to let us in, or we aren't going to let them in."

"Nationalism, tribalism, for the sake of survival."

"Survival for just a short time."

A new cold war, thinks Heller. This time, literally.

Heller is thinking, as they all are, of the previous months' news stories, of the escalating geopolitical tensions between the two countries, tightening, tightening, corkscrewing to a breaking point. Russia meddling in other countries' elections, insinuating itself into other countries' computer and electrical infrastructures, endowing its own nuclear program with new stealth and flexibility, its robust spying, its infiltration of other governments; it's hardly a stretch to imagine their stockpiles of weaponized pathogens. Pathogens they meant to deploy narrowly and strategically, or pathogens that—like their Chernobyl— might have gotten quickly out of their control. His research into poisons reminded him that it takes only a thimbleful of certain toxins to instantly decimate billions.

Rolling their arsenals into place. Strike-first readiness. You could argue about whether it was a defensive response to the newly unstable, unpredictable US administration, or whether it was a long-awaited opportunity they were seizing. On Antarctica, as in outer space, the relationship between the two countries had always been cordial, collaborative, in the interest and advancement of science. Has all that now changed? Are there instructions to the Russian stations from their own government? Is it all returning to tribal? The research stations suddenly rendered medieval fortresses? Turning to the ancient strategies of starvation, invasion, plague?

"Look, we're getting ahead of ourselves," says Hobbes. "It's communicating with them we have to explore first."

"Maybe Pritchard and Dolan should focus on trying to reach them. Forget about the world to the north. Maybe there's some other way with them? Some other kind of signal to rig?" says Bramlett.

"Let's get them on that. Maybe they can figure something out. They jury-rigged a way to at least reach out to Australia and the Falklands, you'd think reaching the Russian station would be a piece of cake."

Heller has no idea. Communications are a black box to him. Communication is taken for granted in the modern world, until it isn't there.

It's a mirror, in a way, the Russian station. A mirror of their own existence. And when there's communications, you can look in the mirror, see and feel a friendly competition and camaraderie, in their own experiments, in their lifestyle, and these days an internationalism that makes them all somewhat the same, brings them all together. Like any mirror, it's reassuring. Reassuringly reflective of each other, proof of each other, like a photograph.

But now, the mirror has gone temporarily black. Unlit. No reflection. In a strange way—like any mirror, he supposes—the absence of the mirror makes it harder to see what's going on in their own world, at McMurdo.

And the thought they share silently: *Is* there a Russian station? Or has whatever befell the latitudes above them already found its way into the Russian station, and are Heller and the 155 around him all that's left, for a few days or weeks or hours until the "event" finds its ceaseless, relentless way to them too? Heller pushes that black thought aside.

• • •

"They'll rescue us, won't they? When winter lifts enough, they'll come rescue us, right?"

Hobbes looks at the young woman who has asked—Pam, a lab assistant in her first winter—and says, surprisingly harshly, "Who is this *they*, Pam? What *they*?"

An existential statement. Said with a harshness showing how Hobbes, upbeat and even-tempered and practical Hobbes, is nearing the end of his existential rope.

There is no they. There is only we. A few we, and that's all.

46.

But amid this transforming, transformed existence, Heller can't help himself:

He is thinking about poisons.

Is it a way of clinging to his identity? Focusing in, because loss of focus will mean loss of self?

But if it is poisoning (and if you can't detect it, that doesn't *necessarily* mean it is, but *probably* means it is—the lack of any other kind of evidence points strongly to it), then as Heller has speculated from the first, given the available exotic chemicals for the wide range of experiments, it is very possibly a *new* poison, a particular chemical combination that forensic databases have no previous familiarity with. And Heller is willing to speculate that the new combination of ingredients—opaque, undetectable—might enjoy an effectiveness that has to do with the extremes here. The temperature extremes, yes, but even more so, he thinks vaguely, the thyroid stresses and changes, another possible secret advantage to this particular designer poison.

Logic and circumstance say it's something new. Something not only new but new and perhaps "tested" here.

He needs the Internet to further explore poisons and temperature extremes, either himself or with the help of a couple of the chemists and biologists here.

But, of course, there is no Internet. An enormous advantage to the killer, who may have made extensive use of Internet data to get to his lethal formula, by a path that Heller and others could pick up and follow. But not anymore. Now the digital drawbridge has been closed, there is no way to follow the perpetrator into the deep recesses of the castle. What a lucky break for a killer.

So to get closer to the truth, he has to fall back on old-fashioned police work. In the proxy "small town" of McMurdo Station, he has to be a small-town cop again. Interviews. Gumshoe instinct.

Like Pritchard and Dolan, falling back on old methods. Having to start over. Rummaging around in the toolbox, looking for old, cast-off pieces and ways of doing things, dusting them off, going back to them. He needs to do the same.

Amid this transforming, transformed existence, still thinking about poisons.

Unlike all the disconsolate readers of locked-room mysteries, botany texts, the DSM, unlike all the disrupted, distraught scientists, he's unwilling to abandon his winter-over project.

Maybe they did pick the right subcontractor.

47.

"I think we need to have a funeral for Trish Wong," says Hobbes.

Heller knew this was coming. The subject has been held in suspension, in light of everything else imploding around them. And, he has thought, in light of her special relationship with Heller, which may have been speculated about, been leaked out by now—nobody has wanted to bring up the prospect of a funeral with him.

"She was well loved here," says Hobbes. "And we have to accept the possibility that we may not be going back, so there's no reason to wait with it."

No indication, in Hobbes's words or expression, of knowing about Heller and Trish's relationship.

A funeral for Trish Wong.

Using death to symbolize life going on.

Or is her death—her funeral—a symbol, a harbinger of what is still to come?

Trish as symbol, as stand-in for them all.

• • •

It will be McMurdo's first funeral. Though not Antarctica's, of course. A history of death goes hand in hand with exploration of the forbidding, inhospitable continent, and makeshift funerals to accompany and acknowledge those deaths. Shackleton had always memorialized each man lost. In that old, proper English explorer tradition, he gave them each their sermon, their send-off, their due, even when the body could not be suitably prepared for the next world. Sandy Lazo-Wasum's remains, of course, were sent home—to family, friends, a proper graveyard.

"But her parents can't even be notified right now. Her siblings. I think it's premature," says Heller.

If there are parents. If there are siblings. No one says it. Everyone thinks it.

"I think it's a way of accepting it. Of symbolizing that we are on our own here. Her funeral could serve a larger purpose for us. Show acceptance, moving on, show that we must build a life and community for ourselves here, with all its attendant tasks and traditions—death, birth . . . ," Hobbes adds. "It's a way of saying that our life is now here."

Memorializing and acknowledging death, to symbolize life. It seems paradoxical, and yet that's what all funerals are actually doing.

"It's so strange to do," says Heller.

"It's too strange not to," says Hobbes.

• • •

The morning of Trish Wong's funeral, Heller bundles up in preparation, as they all do. No one has a suit or a dress in Antarctica, not even the top administrators; nonessential clothing takes up too much space.

There are no flowers, of course. Some plastic ones here and there on the base, all deemed too tacky, thank God, for this occasion. But someone has fashioned a simple lapel pin with her name and her ID photo, with an image of a single orchid, and has run off several dozen copies of it, and as they all gather in the cafeteria, they're united in wearing their simple Trish lapel pins and in their shuffling, respectful silence.

The ceremony is in the cafeteria.

The cremation will be outside. Extremely brief. Fifty-below temperatures dictate and guarantee that. There is no burying a body in ice. They debated keeping the body frozen somewhere, waiting until the spring thaw and burying her then, but that seemed gruesome and open ended. The idea of a funeral is acceptance. Sending the spirit to its next home. Letting—*helping*—a community move on.

"I guess Calloway should still do an autopsy," Hobbes says to Heller uncomfortably. "As much as he's able to, anyway."

Heller shrugs. They both know how limited it will be. That it won't show anything new. An exercise in frustration.

Heller wonders how much everyone recognizes another subtext here: That this funeral is a precedent. A precedent for how they will deal with further death, from here on.

That death will no longer be a matter for the mainland. A matter to be shipped out, to be banished from their previously magical and suspended existence. It's now real and now theirs. A practical matter, like nutrition, like food, like safety.

Cremation is the logical choice, and the only choice right now. No one knows anything about any religious affiliation of Trish or her family. "California scientist" would be most accurate and telling. The Wongs—scientists, doctors, researchers, lawyers, professors—hadn't been in a church in three generations, Heller would guess. Trish was a naturalist, they all know. Cared deeply about the planet and its survival, so cremation seems right. Not to take up ground space, and it doesn't matter, because they can't bury the body anyway because the continent is ice, not ground.

The morning is even colder than usual.

Heller knows he is on display. Everyone at McMurdo knew of the working relationship. Everyone knew she was assigned to the investigation—and she was teased, in fact, because she was such an upbeat, positive California girl, and people were secretly amused or horrified that she'd been given this administrative task, although people understood the rationale too: her careful, meticulous researcher personality, her trustworthiness. Some were undoubtedly amused, he's sure, by this crusty, humorless, colorless, white Vermonter and this bubbly, petite, brown Asian Californian working together. What Heller doesn't know is how many people, if any, knew of the affair. And, specifically, whether the killer did.

So he doesn't know how much he is on display, and to whom.

He holds a vague wish for some clue to emerge, when they're all gathered here like this. The whole base is here, of course, to pay respects. And the killer is here among them. As they all know.

It makes a somber occasion even more so.

The cafeteria chairs and tables are cleared away. They expect everyone. And Heller of course will want to know—will look to see—if anyone is missing. He's enlisted Bramlett and Simmons to help him on that. He can't literally take attendance but wants to know if anyone's not there.

They had all assumed at first that there was no one of any religious authority in this scientific and agnostic community, but they were wrong. In the preparation for the funeral, Robert Manafort came forward. The food services chef Hobbes had raved about. It turns out he was previously a minister in a church near Coeur d'Alene, Idaho—The Life Hereafter Christian Guardians. A small sect that exists in only a few North Idaho towns, Manafort says. A sect that Heller has never heard of. Manafort has volunteered to lead the ceremony, if they want him to. If they are comfortable with that.

"Do you know what to do?" Hobbes asks.

"My father was a minister. My grandfather was the minister who founded the sect. I grew up attending funerals. Helping him with the details. Unfortunately"—a little smile—"I know exactly what to do."

Heller gets the sense that Manafort is here in Antarctica, perhaps in part, to get as far away from that upbringing as possible. A sense he gets from more than a few people who winter over in Antarctica.

And Manafort does know what to do. In fact, recites several prayers by heart. Admits he probably knows hundreds. "Still echoing in my head," he jokes to them. They hand him a Bible. He never opens it. Doesn't need to.

He supervises the construction of the coffin, the bier, and the pyre, shows how and where to add accelerant to make the cremation pyre most efficient.

"But your congregation in Idaho didn't cremate its people, did they?"

"No, everyone is buried. But I know about accelerants independently. My dad was the minister, like I said, but we were both volunteer firemen north of Coeur d'Alene. Small towns—you have to do a little of everything. A lot of everything." Manafort smiles.

Manafort seems to grow into the role, into his authority at the funeral. There's something noticeable about it, thinks Heller. Out of the ordinary. Either a good thing, Heller thinks, an ordinary cook rising to the occasion. Or something more troubling—manipulating, seizing an opportunity.

The coffin sits in the middle of the cafeteria. The mourners have gathered some plants under grow lights around the base—not part of official botanical experiments—surrounding the coffin with them.

They find some photos on Trish's cell phone. Blow them up on the printer. Cut them into frames. Prop them around her coffin. Smiling on a beach somewhere. A picture with a sister and brother, judging by family resemblance, at the Statue of Liberty. Some happy moments, here and there. Snapshots from a life snapped and snuffed. No one knows for sure who the people are, where they were, what the pictures meant to her. There are no relatives here in Antarctica, of course. No long-term friends, no schoolmates. The pictures have no meaning for anyone in the room. They have meaning only for the person in the coffin. And their meaning here is only in that an effort has been made. A normalizing effort to grieve, to acknowledge, and to move on.

Manafort quotes Ecclesiastes. Deuteronomy. Heller hears him suppressing an impulse for grandiloquence. For a little fire and brimstone. For backcountry preaching.

Heads are bowed. There are tears. Heller has never heard such a silence in the normally boisterous and bustling cafeteria.

The tears flow now. And he knows that the grieving is not just for Trish but for all of them. A moment of gathering, a sanctioned moment of release, of grief. A need unleashed.

Heller feels eyes on him.

Trish's best friend at McMurdo, Pam, the research assistant, goes up to speak, stands next to the coffin, unable to look at it, Heller can see, trying to compose herself, but in the end she is too distraught and simply shakes her head, weeping, shoulders heaving, goes back to the crowd, never uttering a word. Allan Harkavy, a scientist Trish worked with, plays an instrumental of his own composition on the acoustic guitar.

And then a moment they have all waited for. Hobbes stepping to the front of the room.

He first says what is expected about Trish. All the right things. About who she was, her energy, her kindness, her absence. And then the part they have waited for. That they have gathered for, whether they understood it or not.

"As everyone here knows, as everyone here senses and feels, this is not just about Trish Wong. This is about something more than Trish. This is, yes, about saying goodbye to her, but about preparing, if need be, to say a larger goodbye too. Learning, preparing, to say goodbye to a way of life. To a point of view. A larger farewell. The voyage of her soul—the voyage of our own souls."

He looks around, examines their faces individually, speaks more quietly. "Does it feel inappropriate to take this moment about Trish and expand on it? Use it? Do something more with it? Make it not about her, but about us? I'm doing it because we seem to be entering a time when our expectations will be challenged. When we will have to rethink everything. When we will have to respect our traditions but make our own new ones.

"We are not keeping her body to send home later. Because we don't really know if we'll be able to do that come spring. We don't know if we'll be able to do it at all. Let's be honest. We are preparing for a new world here. A world that we will do our best to create reasonably and practically and humanely, but a world that will surprise us. That we are unprepared for. That we will do our best to shape but that, more realistically, will be shaping us.

"And part of this new world will be death. Death hopefully for the fewest of us possible, but death nonetheless. Because even if we are successful here, there will be death.

"Trish's came too early. But isn't that how it comes for us all?"

His eyes narrow. "We all know, as we stand here, that Trish's killer is here among us. We will find you. Yes, we are distracted and preoccupied by the needs of survival right now, but trust me, we will find you, and you will pay a price, and I hope that we can discover why you have done this, but even if there is no why, that will not keep us from meting out justice."

And unsaid—which they are realizing, some faster, some slower—Trish Wong's funeral is a kind of funeral for all of them. It is cremating, ending, sending up into ashes a way of life.

• • •

It could be Amy. It feels like watching Amy. Sent into the next life. Or Ann. A little of both. Daughter and lover. Both kinds of love. All kinds of love.

It is a funeral that could represent seven billion funerals. It is an important funeral, Trish Wong's haphazard funeral. Maybe mankind's most significant funeral ever. The funeral that leads mankind into its endgame, or its new start, its new history, depending.

And Heller's speech that he doesn't give.

Heller's speech that he wants to, but that he contains, keeps to himself.

I know you're here. We all know you're here. And make no mistake, I will find you. That is what I do. I don't know whether you chose Trish because of me, to slow me down or derail or frighten me, if she was a targeted victim because of that, or if she was random, if her position assisting me was incidental, but I will find you, either way. I know you may be getting a special perverse joy out of being here right now, hiding in plain sight, "sharing" the grief, pretending to mourn but perhaps in fact snickering, perhaps even hoping to break me in some way, to have me abandon my mission. But knowing you're here gives me a perverse pleasure similar to yours. Because I know, for a certainty, that I will catch you, and whatever international or provisional laws we choose or choose not to apply, I will personally be sure you pay. I see you. It's one of you, and that's good enough for me in this moment. Good enough to motivate me, to keep me going. Your only escape from me might be suicide, and I'll accept that escape, if I have to, but I tell you now: That would probably be your best option. Die now, before I find you. Because who knows what form justice is going to take here now, in this new world we are entering together.

He knows that they are looking at him. Some with pity perhaps, if they somehow know fully about Trish and him. Or regarding him with frustration that he hasn't solved anything, that it's happened again. He feels the stares at the back of his neck. Like he is in some way the next of kin. A proxy for the next of kin.

He doesn't care anymore. He lifts his head, turns around, faces the mourners.

He starts going face-to-face. Hoping, yes, to see something, catch something, pick up on something, but that's not really the point. The point is to say, *I see you. I don't know yet which one of you it is, but I will. I will.*

• • •

The light of the pyre pushes into the inky blackness; the flames lick the darkness. It's the first outside illumination in weeks, carving a small piece of the landscape into a temporary, shimmery visibility. It is a few precious, temporary meters of warmth in the vast cold. They can stand close to it and feel the warmth, the two dozen of them who have ventured outside to attend this last part of the ceremony.

It is freezing cold, literally freezing cold, just beyond the funeral pyre.

A temporary light, a temporary warmth amid the vast cold and black.

A metaphor for human existence, thinks Heller. For the current fragile state of humanity. A good proportion of it, possibly, actually standing right here.

A temporary, merely evanescent heat and light, only made possible, he thinks grimly, by human sacrifice, by human flesh. Too high a sacrifice for heat and warmth? Isn't that always what survival has required, sacrifice? But this is unnecessary sacrifice. Or are the shortcomings of the human species—the jealousies, the sins, the uncontrolled rage—just part of the deal, part of the package, from time immemorial?

The thoughts are vague. He is more absorbed in watching the flames. Seeing the light flicker and dance on the faces of those close around it. In worship. In awe. In stunned, silent observation.

The flames start to die down. The resulting cold rushes in. Heller can feel the temperature's descent. They can feel the dangers of it on their skin, the sensitive thermal instrument, the warning system of their own epidermis. Time to get back inside. The remains of the pyre will stay out here, untouched, until they can clean it up in the warmth of spring.

48.

He can't shake the association, the conflation, the spinning mental dance of the two events:

An unpredictably virulent pathogen—a new *kind* of poison, uncharted, unanticipated, too quick and sinister to concoct a defense.

And an unprecedented, still undetected poison that took Sandy Lazo-Wasum and Trish Wong. Quick and sinister as well.

As if the death of Lazo-Wasum somehow augured the global poisoning, and Trish's death somehow brings it back to Antarctica, closing a loop, tightening a noose.

The rational part of him knows they have nothing to do with each other. One is a catastrophic event, if it is some kind of poison, far beyond the realm and control of science. The other is a personal, highly focused, highly directed effort, a carefully concocted, bespoke poison, with a narrow, specific goal, allowing its creator to murder undetected.

Unless the concoction of the one has inadvertently, unpredictably unleashed the second. The first, say, sitting in Lazo-Wasum's body, dormant, entombed, undisturbed, mercifully inert in the Antarctic cold, until it met with the warmth of a New Zealand or American autopsy lab, or interacted with some chemical agent in the lab.

This is where Heller's mind is going. From the specific to the general. Making a metaphor of poison. Poisoning the world, whether one specific and selected victim at a time or mankind all at once—is it the same impulse? The same evil, different only in scale?

In the same vague, wandering frame of mind, Heller reconsiders the tiny pinprick at the base of the skull. Nothing notable or detectable found in the bloodstream in the Lazo-Wasum autopsy, and, yes, the Lazo-Wasum autopsy was botched, and, no, they weren't equipped to do a full one on Trish, but there is nothing at all learned from either one—certainly nothing definitive about this pinprick.

His mind vague, wandering, he begins to wonder: maybe that pinprick, that barely detectable pinprick, is there to tell a different tale.

The recurring theme of Antarctica's mix of the sophisticated and the primeval, of the ancient and the new comes back to him of how, in the absence of autopsy evidence, he has gone back to the old methods—interviews, instinct. Is that what's going on with the crime itself? Old methods?

What if the poison didn't enter the bloodstream via that pinprick?

How else would it enter?

Via the most traditional path for poison, especially a whole class of hard-to-detect poisons.

The way arsenic, roots, and other poisons have done their sinister work since the time of the Hebrews and the Greeks.

Via food.

Via the food supply.

Not the general food supply, of course (there's been no general event), but by a specific placement in a victim's own food—nicely disguised by the fact that everyone, the whole base, was eating the same foods, and no one else got sick.

And, of course, he thinks immediately of the supervisor in charge of food service.

The same man who quite unobtrusively but quite suddenly emerged to take the lead in Trish Wong's funeral, with his religious knowledge.

Robert Manafort.

Overseeing the food system closely.

Always, because it's so central, so important every day to the function of the base. It's one source, after all: one cafeteria, one mess hall, no choices.

And now, even more important, because the food supply is suddenly limited, potentially critical. It's now an enormous responsibility.

Robert Manafort. Heller opens his binder, breezes through the records toward him, stops at his page, rereads it.

A veteran of wintering-over. An old hand. A bulwark of the secondary staff. Relied on. Not much thought about. A ready smile.

Manafort. A religious zealot in hiding, here in a scientific community? Heller has thought of that, of course, listening to Manafort's service. His easy, unthinking command of Bible verses. Is the zealot about to be unleashed, amid approaching, unpredictable end-of-the-world scenarios? Would zealotry in turn unleash followers? Heller has no idea.

But he does know one thing:

It's time to take a kitchen tour.

49.

"Welcome, come on in. I'm surprised you haven't taken the tour of our humble kitchen before," says Manafort, acting expansive, but the gesture of welcome feels very careful—quite calculated—to Heller; all of Manafort's movements seem a little robotic and orchestrated.

He sits in Manafort's tiny closet of an office, receivables receipts piled high around him in perfectly neat stacks. Corners squared up. There's only one chair at Manafort's small, makeshift desk. He's shoved a second chair in temporarily for Heller to take, but, obviously, no one besides Manafort is ever in here.

Heller would label the office obsessively neat. Somewhere beyond the expected and welcome order of a food services chief. One part of him is glad to see that level of obsessiveness at the top of polar food services. Another part of him wonders about it—that care, that thoroughness.

Manafort smiles. "First of all, you should know, despite all the impressive advanced degrees and impressive, cutting-edge experiments and genius IQs around here, I feel like I'm the most important person at McMurdo," he says. "What can I tell you? Everyone's got to eat, and polar life all stops if we don't." It's the words—the sentiment—of a rotund, jelly-jowled chef, but Manafort is rail lean, has big hands, looks more like a ranch hand.

Heller nods. "Look, Robert."

He doesn't say *Call me Bob.*

"I want you to take me through the whole process of food prep. Receiving, storage, menu selection, nutritional decisions, preprep, preparation, postprep, leftovers, refrigeration, the whole deal."

"Why?"

"I want to understand."

That's for starters.

"And as we go, I want you to tell me who does what. Introduce me to everybody else involved."

Manafort cocks his head, looks at him. Is preparing to walk him through it. He walks him over to the receiving palettes.

Looks up. And says suddenly, unexpectedly, "Look, Mr. Heller, I feel we should talk."

Heller looks back at him.

It's no longer just a food-prep and food-processing discussion. It's no longer just show-and-tell.

"I know why you're here."

Heller waits.

"Because these are the last palettes. You know that and I know that. There are no more palettes coming. And we have to make a plan for that."

That's not why Heller is here, of course, but he waits. Maybe the visit is becoming more important. Maybe the visit is going to reveal something about poison, or about even more than that, or different from that, heading down another path.

Manafort gestures to the palettes. "These are basically half-full. I know you don't know what a full palette looks like. I know how much food we have here. I know how much I can stretch it. I alone know, down to each meal. I've been doing this a long time. I know what I can do, how far I can get with what I have. And I know what the end of the line is." He looks with challenge at Heller. "I can give you a countdown to the day," he says. "If everyone here stays alive and maintains a certain calorie count, I can give you a countdown to the day. Do you want to know exactly what day it is?"

Heller shakes his head no.

"You don't? Don't you think you should? Our peace officer? Or the closest thing to it? I think it's a little irresponsible of you not to know what we're dealing with. I could just say it right now, blurt it out, and then you'd know."

"Don't," says Heller. "Please."

"You don't want to be in a countdown mode, do you? You don't want to know too much. You want to still get some sleep." Manafort smiles creepily.

Enjoying himself, Heller notices. Actually enjoying himself.

"I could blurt it out." A little game from Manafort. A little threat. Making a little game and threat out of basic humanity. Of living and dying. Of end-times. Making a little game for Heller.

It all echoes with what a serial killer would do. A sweet spot, a joy for a serial killer.

"How secure is the food supply?" Heller asks. As if ignoring everything he's heard. Everything he's intuiting already. "How secure from tampering?"

Manafort blinks. "Tampering? What do you mean?"

"You know what I mean."

"I take it you don't mean food poisoning. That's unintentional. Has to do with shipping and refrigeration. I'm pretty careful about all that. We can't afford any contamination. Especially now."

"No, I mean tampering. Intentional tampering."

Manafort shrugs, sighs. "Well, not secure at all."

An unguarded, undefensive answer, Heller notes. Not defensively crying "Impossible!" or even trying to hide the possibility. Appearing honest—intentionally? . . . calculatingly?—knowing, of course, that this opens as possible suspects virtually everyone at the station and hardly corners him.

"I mean, so many people have access at so many points along the way . . ."

"But it's likeliest during food prep, no? And during food prep, there's only a few of you, the same few of you, and you'd obviously notice anyone else, anyone unusual in the kitchen."

Food tampering.

Food tampering for a single victim only. Fatal meal service for one. A single victim at a time.

But it could be a specific victim.

Or it could be a random victim.

Serial killers come in both varieties. Specific victims. Random victims.

If it was a specific victim and poisoning, it points more to Manafort or someone near him—someone near the end of the food-prep funnel.

If it was random, it's a wider circle of possibility. Someone dropping something into a random serving—even possibly after the dish was served.

Something occurs to Heller suddenly. "Does anyone have a special diet?" Because that plate, a special-diet plate, is tailored specifically, after all, and can be specifically doctored.

Maybe Trish Wong. Maybe Sandy Lazo-Wasum.

"Yes, some people do have a special diet," says Manafort. "A handful."

Heller's sensors pick up a little.

"Including me," says Manafort. A shrug. A quick little smile.

So he's the only one *not* at risk of being a random victim, if it is random victims, thinks Heller. The only one with his own eyes on his own food at all times.

"Gluten-free. Dairy-free. Low sodium. Do you want me to list for you who gets what?"

Trying to be cooperative—or pretending to be cooperative, thinks Heller.

"No, thanks, that won't be necessary," Heller says.

• • •

As Heller turns and leaves, Manafort says something behind him that he can't quite make out. A whisper, an offhand comment.

Heller whirls on him, brow furrowed. "What did you say?"

Manafort shrugs, smiles a little. "Nothing."

"Nothing? You muttered something."

Manafort looks at him, confused. As if he hasn't said anything. As if Heller is hearing things. Is confused. Manafort's look is part sympathetic, part pity, part puzzlement, part concern.

"Just going back to food prep, is all."

Heller doesn't press it. He experiences it as a passing thought. Somewhere between a thought and an utterance. Maybe he *is* having a little T3. Maybe this is a warning to him of how it will affect him as the winter wears on.

But Heller swears he heard it. A whisper, at the back of his brain.

A little warning. A little statement. A truth that either Manafort uttered, insinuated under his breath, or that Heller's own thinking has brought forward from somewhere in his unconscious, dreamlike in the form of an utterance in Manafort's voice.

But an indisputable and alarming little fact, T3 or not.

A whisper, in Manafort's voice:

I've got the food.

50.

Fissures. Cracks.

Not in the ice. The ice stays solid, frozen, unchanging.

Not in the ice but in the little community assembled on top of it. In the interactions. In the eroding faith. Individual, collective.

In certain ways they are all together. They all sense now, implicitly, the race that they are in, the stakes. They don't speak of it, but they all feel it, and whether they accept it personally or not—whether they have personal doubts or beliefs that supersede or intervene—no longer matters because it is the race, the struggle that everyone around them has accepted. It is unstated, but obvious. Too big to state. Too big to discuss. No longer philosophical, because it feels so real. So pressing, so everyday, undeniable.

The issue is now survival.

But more than that: what form survival takes.

For how many of them.

It's a project of survival. The ultimate science project.

All these science-fair winners. All these brainiacs.

This is their final science fair. They need an A.

• • •

There are some odd effects, right off.

The fact that, suddenly, everyone is important. Everyone is suddenly aware of his or her own importance.

It too is unspoken. But Heller can feel it. And he knows he is not unique. Suddenly you matter. Your health, your strength, your reproductive potential. People begin to observe themselves. To care about cuts or infections. The cooks. The service people. They notice, feel, experience their value. *My little life suddenly matters.* Has exaggerated, outsize importance for our species. *I am one of the chosen, the few. Simply by default? Or maybe by design? Why me? But why not me?* And with this sudden individual importance that they sense, that they absorb—with either humility or grandiosity or awe—they naturally, incessantly question it. Are nervous about it. *When resources get short, am I going to be cut out somehow? Is my secondary status going to make me expendable? Where do I stand in the pecking order? In the McMurdo lifeboat?* They feel nervous, anxious.

Their heads are down. Noses to the grindstone. Ready to contribute, to do their part, to go the distance, for the social good.

But their minds are all over. Wandering frantically.

Fissures. Cracks. Not in the ice, which remains solid, opaque, unforgiving. But in the souls wandering on top of it—cut loose, in a new world, in an endgame that has no start and no finish. That is held still in time.

It is both ending and beginning.

It is both creation and destruction.

They are nothing.

They are everything.

It is a strange position to be in. As unprecedented as it is unpredictable.

No wonder there are fissures, cracks. Widening around them, beneath them, despite the solid ice.

51.

Polar T3 syndrome is a condition found in polar explorers, caused by a reduction in levels of the thyroid hormone T3. Its effects include forgetfulness, cognitive impairment and mood disturbances. It can exhibit itself in a fugue state known as the *Antarctic stare.*

Triiodothyronine, also known as **T3** . . . affects almost every physiological process in the body, including . . . metabolism, body temperature, and heart rate.

Heller reads the Wikipedia entries again. He had printed a copy when he was first told about the syndrome, intending to do more research, but without the Internet, he's had to live with what he has. Before they lost the Internet, he had managed to look further into the cognitive impairment described—which identified hallucinations, dream states, and other mental disturbances in documented cases of T3 syndrome.

And as far as the body's physical changes caused by the endless night's havoc with the hormone triiodothyronine? Well, it could be as tough to handle as it was tough to pronounce. The body's systems could compensate for a while—that's why it was a rare problem in Scandinavian countries and the subarctic. But you apparently get to a point in the endless night when the body cries uncle. It crashes in on itself, floods itself with problems. The body holds out and defends itself for as long as it can, then collapses in the ceaseless darkness.

And like all hormones, it's different for different people. There's no predicting who will be affected, who won't be, and to what degree. Nothing to do with gender, body type, weight, overall fitness—no markers at all. And people tend to hide their own symptoms. Nobody likes to admit that they're going crazy. Especially scientists. Especially those who pride themselves on their hardiness, their readiness for the Antarctic challenge.

The printed page now in front of him is one more indication of his own antiquity, he knows. His research: printed, handwritten, and tucked into manila folders in a three-ring binder. It's how he began thirty years ago, and his methods haven't changed.

It's perfectly possible the killer suffers from the severest effects of T3. Are the effects severe enough to turn someone into a killer? To unleash a latent murderer? A chemically coaxed Mr. Hyde? It would make sense, in that there were no killings during the summer, during the light. This of course forgives nothing but could explain a lot. He imagines it isn't quite like the loosening of impulses caused by alcohol or drugs that accompany so much crime, but more akin to a dream state that also suspends the controls of the conscious mind. And yet there's such precision in the killer's methodology, such care and meticulousness, could this go side by side with the temporary hallucination, the extended fugue of T3? But he returns to the fact that everyone's thyroid is different, and that the syndrome is profound—and profoundly unexplored. Damn that NASA defunding.

The thyroid. Mysterious organ. Mysterious functioning. Even to doctors, apparently. Who are good at issuing hormones and pills to rebalance its functioning, to getting the numbers back into normal range, but still do not really understand the thyroid's structure.

And the relation of the thyroid to that other mysterious organ, the brain? The relationship is ill understood. Nil understanding, as he has read between the lines.

And if he can find the killer, identify him or her, and prove the effects of T3 in the killer's state of mind, would and should that be part of the decision about punishment and sentencing? In the old world of conventional justice, of prosecution and defense and attorneys and expert witnesses and a jury of peers, that would be a significant issue. But in this new world, is that all suspended? In this new world, he doesn't know what they will do for justice. He doesn't know if there is even a justice system intact. *Who* will determine punishment? *How* will they determine punishment? He originally told himself that isn't his job. His job is finding the murderer. Other entities will take it from there. But he now knows that isn't necessarily the case. He's involved in the making of this new world. This temporary, stand-in world—until they know more. Or this inconceivably permanent new world—if they aren't ever going to know any more. Both, at this moment, equally possible.

52.

He is summoned to Hobbes's office.

Hobbes shuts the door behind him.

He doesn't look at Heller as he says it:

"We need to talk about guns."

In truth, Heller is not surprised. He hasn't been aware of any; they are not part of daily life in a scientific community, a research facility. They are explicitly outlawed by the rules of the National Science Foundation, but Heller has had the vague sense that there might be firearms of some sort stowed here on the base somewhere. They're clearly not part of any of the murders, not part of the killer's MO with their forensic traceability, their ballistic signatures, their serial numbers. Any firearm at McMurdo—a sidearm for Hobbes as station manager, say— would have a recorded serial number and would be kept safely.

"There are four AR-15s and six semiautomatic Glocks."

Heller can't help smiling a little. "What the hell for?"

Hobbes looks at him uncharacteristically hard. "For exactly a situation like this."

"Where are they?"

"Different unmarked lockers at different places around McMurdo."

"A first line of defense in a Russian attack?" Heller teases.

"Yeah, something like that. One locker is actually behind you . . ." Hobbes points to the closet behind Heller. Heller turns and looks, a little startled—like someone snuck up on him from behind.

"Who's got the key?"

"I do. As station manager. Simmons also has a key."

"Any others?"

"A closet off the cafeteria."

"Who's got the keys to that one?"

Please. Don't say Manafort.

"I've got those keys too. But look, these gun closets, if things got frantic, took a bad turn here, people with enough desperation and force could get into any of them."

"Where's the ammunition?"

Hobbs looks morose. "It's in the lockers with the guns."

Ready for an attack, thinks Heller cynically. Ready to defend themselves against . . . competing scientists?

"A lot of ammunition," Hobbes admits, shifting uncomfortably. "And even though the lockers are unmarked, I can't say for sure no one knows about them."

"Well, the thing to do is remove the ammo," says Heller. "Store it somewhere safe. Somewhere no one can get at it."

"But then we don't have the guns ready if we need them . . ."

"Need them for what?"

"You know for what. Don't pretend you're naive. I know you're not."

"You mean they're not ready if *you* need them," says Heller.

"Yes. Yes, that's what I mean," says Hobbes.

"Well, then you've got a little dilemma, don't you?" says Heller. "If you want to leave the ammunition there for you, then you need to leave it there for someone else." *You can't have it both ways, Manny.*

Hobbes takes his point. "So when, and how, do we separate the ammo so no one sees, so no one gets wind of what's in there? It would have to be done in secret . . . and I don't feel comfortable about that . . ."

"Practically or morally?" says Heller, pointedly.

"Come on, Joe, you know me by now. You know I'm just trying to stay one step ahead of events here."

One step ahead of events—to control them or prevent them?

One step ahead of events—meaning, ahead of a catastrophic breakdown? That could come in a moment or in slow motion, step by stealthy step, barely recognizable?

A breakdown where it is the have-guns versus the have-not. The have-food versus the have-not. The have-shelter versus the have-not.

"Preparing for the worst," observes Heller. "I'm not sure that's the spirit of leadership that would rally me behind you, Manny."

"I'm the station manager. I'm leading in title only," says Hobbes. "Let's be honest. It's something we've all noticed." Hobbes shifts heavily in his chair, the weight of the last days, the last weeks, falling on him. "We're sliding into the system of hierarchy, of authority. Everyone seems to be accepting it temporarily. But if . . . if these conditions are permanent, we're going to have to go with some other arrangement. Something everyone else buys into."

"Which isn't necessarily democracy, Manny. You realize that, right?"

"Well, that's the system people know."

"But it's not the only system. And it's not the simplest system."

"What are you saying? That some kind of totalitarian system, some authoritarian or autocratic system will make more sense?"

"I'm saying that might be what happens. Seems quite possible to happen. Given the tensions, given the conditions. Scarcity, anxiety, worries about survival—those are the breeding conditions for totalitarianism, not democracy."

Manny Hobbes is silent. Brooding. "All the more reason to have the guns and ammo standing by, I guess," he says.

"You mean, standing by for you."

"Yes, standing by for me." Hobbes tilts his head at Heller. "Look, maybe I *am* the right leader. Maybe I'm their best chance. Or as good a chance as anyone."

"You see what I mean?" says Heller, with a wry smile. "Maybe a totalitarian system is the right way to go here. With a benign dictator, a benign presence, like Manny Hobbes."

Heresy and reason, intersecting, dancing with each other, Heller notices. It is a new world.

• • •

Heller is heading for the door when Hobbes continues, more quietly, half to himself. "You know, Joe," says Hobbes, "when I imagined Antarctica's long-term fate, as a scientist, it was a tale of global warming. Our destruction of the planet through melting poles and sea rise and the associated natural catastrophes that got triggered, and in a hundred years, the balmy, temperate green paradise of Antarctica being all that's left of mankind. Our last, best hope. A place for a new start. You and I wouldn't be around to see it, of course, but our descendants would. And they'd inhabit a new Eden. A chastened Eden, where we'd have to be a lot more careful this time with the tree of knowledge, but where we'd learned our lessons, learned them the hard way, mankind paying a heavy price, but we would now do much better. The consequences of global warming. That made sense. But my typical scientist's vision has been challenged, and it may never have its green, temperate moment as paradise. We've managed to turn my long-term dream of an Antarctic paradise into a short-term nightmare. Global warming is too slow a way for us to kill ourselves. Too extended and inefficient. We've come up with something quicker, infinitely more lethal. Leave it to man, huh? Leave it to man."

53.

He had agreed to Trish Wong's funeral. Thinking it might draw out the killer somehow. And recognizing how it symbolized taking on the responsibilities for their own world.

Passing the cafeteria the next morning, between meals, he happens to see it.

A prayer meeting—fifteen people gathered around. Arms and shoulders linked, in spiritual support, in spiritual solidarity. Praying vocally.

A prayer meeting—and, at its center, leading it—Manafort.

The funeral has inadvertently created a star. Stepping from the shadows of food services—volunteering to handle the prayer. A simple charitable, good-willed act? Or a calculated way to step onto center stage?

He notices the linked arms and shoulders. It's not a conventional Christian ritual. It's a stance, a formation, conceived here. And practiced enough, for long enough that they are doing it comfortably, naturally, expectedly with one another.

How long has this been going on?

A little bit of a football huddle, he notices—as if excluding, shutting out the world outside. As if planning their next play. Their next drive down the field.

He's surprised to see it in a scientific community. Where science, research, observable phenomena are the ethic. The standard. He is surprised, but he certainly understands the turn to faith, defaulting to faith under the current extraordinary stresses and circumstances. And these are kitchen workers, lab assistants, administrative assistants.

For now.

• • •

He understands the impulse, of course. Has always understood it, even sitting at the back of the Shaftsbury Congregational Church as an eleven-year-old. People's perfectly understandable need to believe that life, or the soul, or *something*, goes on after physical mortality. That we—or if not we, somebody, something of us, something human—continues in some form.

But he also understands how this belief is suddenly more acute. Suddenly more present on and in the surface of things. Suddenly more pressing. Because they are facing nothing. An immense, overwhelming, and actual nothing. They are surrounded, to begin with, by the natural nothing of Antarctica, stretching out around them visibly, nearly infinitely. And they used to have their digital web of connection to friends and family, to knowledge itself, to all of humankind, which let them tolerate, defy, or smile comfortably and even affectionately at the white infinity around them. But with no connection, knowledge cut off, the rest of humankind suddenly, apparently, inexplicably extinguished, through some still-unimaginable event (and the "unimaginable" aspect of it is part of its power, the incomprehensibility of it lets the "event" work its dark magic even better), with only each person next to them as an unsubtle, constant human reminder of the end of humanity, he understands the resurrected need to seize upon something more, something beyond. The end looms up close. The end is all around them.

Endless darkness, endless ice, endless night—hell, literally. *Ah, so this is what they meant.* It's like a dark prophecy come true.

But Heller also recognizes the prayer meeting immediately for what else it is—another power base.

I've got the food.

A shiver goes through him.

• • •

He purposely passes through the cafeteria the next morning, at about the same time. He carefully counts, to compare.

It's twenty-five people now.

54.

"Any more from Pritchard and Dolan?" Hobbes asks.

"Their last contact was the Australian farmer, and that mountain ranger before that. Nothing since then," says Simmons.

"But they're still trying?"

"Every minute, every day."

"Check on them, Joe. See how they're doing."

• • •

Heller goes to see Pritchard and Dolan again in the Comm Cave, the makeshift-looking roomful of equipment where, even before their current round-the-clock duties, Dolan and Pritchard could pretty much always be found together. They've been occupying the Cave intensely, of course, with little break, for the past several days. But right now only Dolan is there, at his seat, looking at dials, adjusting knobs, surveying the controls from above almost haughtily, like a commander inspecting his troops.

"Where's Pritchard?"

Dolan looks at Heller. Is silent, downcast. As if trying to solicit sympathy from Heller even before he speaks. Trying to prepare Heller for a little-known fact, as it turns out. "He has a tough time with T3."

"He does?"

Dolan shrugs. "Nothing new. Every year. We've both come to expect it."

They share a double, Pritchard and Dolan. They have for years. It's an extension of the Comm Cave—geographically, functionally, spiritually—and you'd be hard-pressed to say where the office ends and the sleeping quarters begin. Classic wooden radios, eccentric old equipment, a tangle of boxes and wires and electronics that they've somehow gotten clearance for by their seniority and smiles and the goodwill they've built up over the years. There are several snickering nicknames for their lair. But there's general agreement that they are the best of friends. Pritch and Doley. As Pritchard says—boasts, in fact—Dolan has taught him everything he knows. To which Dolan shrugs, smiles—wanting you to know that "everything he knows" is a slight exaggeration.

Perfect communications guys, some have mused, because they seem to communicate practically telepathically, finish each other's sentences—a level of communication that is especially handy on equipment-inspection tours out in whipping wind and dark, where you can't see or hear each other.

Heller goes into the bedroom to see Pritchard. Pritchard is sleeping with a pillow over his head. He is moaning slightly. There are multiple pill bottles by his bunkside. Heller takes a moment to look around a little further. Each man has a picture prominently by his bunk. Pritch is standing with a woman and child somewhere in the American West, the Rockies behind them. Wait—a wife and son? Dolan is sitting with a woman in the bend of a palm tree trunk in what looks like Hawaii—a classic honeymoon pose. But both men confessed to casual summer girlfriends here, when he'd interviewed them again. Okay, so both are cads? Still, something doesn't feel right—feels staged—about the photos. The two have bunked together forever. Heller has of course considered the possibility of a long-standing sexual relationship between them (Pritchard always wakes Dolan, they had laughed, that's their routine), then had dismissed the idea, but it's now crossing his mind, vaguely, again. Bisexual? And the photos are here to tell others—or themselves—that they're not? *You have to understand the culture here,* both Sorenson and Hobbes had said. A science place. A place to experiment. And what does a relationship between them have to do with anything, anyway?

"Pritchard," whispers Heller, gently.

"Leave me alone." Slurred. Shifting the pillow against Heller's voice. Annoyed to be bothered. A side of Pritchard that Heller has never seen. Usually upbeat, eager beaver, talkative, wanting to please.

"How you feeling?"

"Like shit. Total shit." But he turns a little, lifts the pillow off his ear. He wants Heller to hear, to know. "Migraine. Pounding. Pulsing. A sledgehammer swinging gleefully on my brain."

"Anything else?"

"Everything else."

"Meaning?"

"You name it. Confusion. Depression. Things are all a little unclear. I'm in fog. I'm fogged in."

"Suicidal?"

"Keep the knives and sharp objects away from me," mumbles Pritchard. A pretty good sign he's not actually suicidal, thinks Heller.

"Dolan says it's an annual thing for you," says Heller. So why do you do it? Why do you suffer it? Heller wonders.

"Not this bad," says Pritchard. "I guess the end of the world tends to bring it on," he says.

Pritchard struggles to sit up. He wants to talk. At some level he welcomes this.

"We don't know it's the end of the world," says Heller.

"Yeah, we do," says Pritchard. "We've been trying to raise someone—anyone—and we haven't. Dolan's a genius at this stuff. If there's a voice loose in the universe, he can find it. So let me tell you, there's no voice loose in the universe. And I think it's pretty reasonable to be depressed about that."

But despite what he's saying, Heller senses that Pritchard is valuing the human connection. He's always been the talker, the upbeat, communicative one. They've been described more than once as an odd couple, but always affectionately. Always that they'd do anything for each other—and for anyone else, for that matter. The kind of teamwork, of trust in one another, that is a model for Antarctica.

"Dolan needs you."

Pritchard smiles. "Not really." He smiles more. "That's a common misconception."

"Okay, then *we* need you. We need you helping him."

"You mean you need to know I'm out there trying. Trying and not getting anywhere." Pritchard looks like he's trying not to tear up. "Let's be honest, Mr. Heller. We're doomed."

"We don't know that."

"Yeah, we do."

"We need you. You're our chance. You're our chance to know more, and knowing more, maybe escape doom."

Pritchard is silent. But he hears him.

"The tower inspection you guys do," says Heller. "I'd like to come on the next trip."

Pritchard sits up a little more now, straightening. He frowns. "It's pretty dangerous going out there this time of year, you know. That's why we use the cameras. It's not a good idea. And *really* not a good idea to have anyone extra go. No need to take on additional risk."

"In theory, yes. But maybe you guys are missing something."

Pritchard gets quickly, sharply offended. "Hey, we're not fucking missing anything!" Then muttering: "Asshole . . ."

Sharp, sudden mood swings. A manifestation of T3. Heller tries to defuse it. "Hey, I'm sure you're not. It's just another set of eyes in the cold and dark, that's all."

"And another heart and set of lungs to worry about out there."

"We don't have much choice here, either of us. Hobbes and Simmons and Bramlett have asked me to go."

A little white lie. Heller isn't quite sure why he's even said it.

"Jesus. They don't trust us? Why don't they trust us? What do they think?"

Paranoia—more classic T3.

"They think it's on this end somehow, don't they?" says Pritchard. "That's the only way they can explain it. Well, it's not. They can't believe there's nothing out there at the other end of Comm, so they figure it's gotta be this end. Typically reductive scientific thinking."

The hostility. More indication of T3. On the other hand, the anger seems to be lifting, clearing, his T3, defogging and energizing him.

Heller decides to shift the conversation elsewhere. He opens the bunk door, calls Dolan in.

"Listen—Hobbes and company want me to go with you to inspect the towers." Repeating the little lie to Dolan . . . doubling down, as if to make it true, make it real . . .

Dolan doesn't look at Heller. He looks at Pritchard. Searchingly. "Boy is that a useless idea," says Dolan. "You won't even know what you're looking at out there."

Heller shrugs.

"Do you? Do you have any idea?"

Heller shakes his head. No, not really. "But you could tell me. Tell me so I'll be of some use to you."

"But we don't have a choice, do we?" Dolan is a quick study.

"No. Not really."

"Okay then," says Pritchard.

And stands up.

In a definite attitude of *It's your funeral.*

Which, Heller realizes, it actually could be.

221

55.

The history and purpose of the two comm towers are straightforward enough: The second is there for backup, in case the electronics fail in the first one. Or if a supply plane clips it on a windy approach.

A backup tower. Cautious, responsible redundancy.

A lot of good that did.

The two tower sites (one just a few hundred yards from McMurdo, the other almost a mile away) were originally chosen in the 1960s for their adequate distance from interference. Equipment was updated in the '70s and '80s, but nobody saw any reason to shift the towers closer. At one point, it seemed they would both be artifacts. Wi-Fi and modems base-wide would switch to the Iridium phone satellites in geosynchronous orbit, touted to be a big improvement over their jury-rigged, spotty, and untrustworthy terrestrial system, but the Iridium solution quickly proved not only too expensive but no more reliable, just as spotty. So the Wi-Fi and modems were still served by the original two comm towers, and the fickle phone service was Internet based.

And now, nothing. No signal from anywhere.

Everyone reasonably assumed that any problem, any failure, would be at this end. Here on the harsh, frozen, unforgiving continent.

No one ever imagined the failure would be from the other side. From the north.

Ever since their arrival, Pritchard and Dolan have been charged with maintaining the towers, which they have always been glad to do, old radio hands, tinkerers. Like modern-day mechanics asked to keep that old car on the corner running. Just in case. No problem, sir. Kinda fun, sir.

Until now. Until all possible communication, until any further sign of life, hinges on these antiquated structures.

"We go at zero six hundred hours," says Dolan. "It's typically a few degrees warmer at that hour. You might say fifty below, fifty-five below, what difference does it make? But at these temperatures, with all our test equipment, *that* five degrees might be the difference between the equipment functioning or not," he explains. "Including"—he gestures to his heart and his brain, and wiggles his fingers—"all this equipment." He continues. "We take two ATVs. For the headlights, first of all. And in a situation—an engine failure, not unheard of at these temperatures—the three of us can fit onto one. Internal combustion engines were never designed for fifty below. But it's all we got."

Pritchard piles on. "That five degrees might be the difference between getting it done in ten minutes or in twelve minutes, which might be the difference between getting back into the Quonset hut or ending up a hundred yards from it—permanently."

• • •

Zero six hundred hours.

Bleary, half-awake, Heller watches as they check all their equipment. He watches Pritchard search a shelf, shaking his head—"Come on, where the fuck?"—shifting things around on the crowded shelf and pulling things down until he finds a roll of sealing tape at the back. As they fit their packs, tape their gloves, check their flashlights, he listens to them banter about the two ATVs. "Let's have the One-Four go first. That's got a better headlight." "Nah, I think the Cat's better. It spreads wider." "No, let's have the One-Four." And then—he is thankful—both check him over carefully too. Check all his clothing seals. Both of them inspecting together, expressions furrowed like concerned spinster aunts. Pritchard slaps Heller on the shoulder—an indication that preparation check is done, he is ready to go.

• • •

The single headlight of the front ATV carves a hard, narrow tunnel of light ahead of them, focused and intent, a path of light surrounded by a universe of night. The wind whips snow across the single beam, making the wind visible, like visual proof of its insistent and relentless anger, although the whistle and hum, both high and low in frequency, a sheer scream and low rumble rolled into one, make its anger clear as well. It's fifty below, and the cold seems to hang in the air visibly too—crystals of shifting air that would sting like an attack of hornets if they were hitting bare skin.

Heller is on the back of the second ATV, driven by Dolan. The roar of the ATV engine is completely swallowed up in the wind. Strange how the normally insistent, arrogantly loud ATVs are rendered mute, as if meek and docile, subsumed in sound and fury much more substantial, much more primal and elemental.

They reach the first tower in under a minute, Heller guesses. They leave the ATVs running—would never risk turning them off and having one or both not start—and they head toward the permanent tower scaffolding. Dolan gestures to Heller: "Follow me."

The wind whips through the scaffolding so forcefully as they climb the stairs that Heller feels himself lifted a little. It's a giddy feeling. He holds the handrails with both gloves, as previously instructed. They stay close. Dolan and Pritchard each carry a tool case. The electronics pod they need to reach is about four stories up. They take each scaffold step carefully. The three of them are packed together like a single animal on the move, rising up off the icy terrain, climbing higher into the night. In this wind and cold, there can be no talking. It is, for each of them, about preservation of energy, about paying close attention to the steadiness and solidity of each step, and then making the next. They are conscious of their companions. But their job out here is attention to themselves.

When they reach the electronics pod at the top of the first comm tower, Dolan takes out a couple of tools—a long-handled needle-nose pliers, an odd stubby screwdriver, and, last, a sealed plastic envelope, which he opens carefully in the wind to remove a single, oversize key. Now he takes from an inside pocket of his parka a folded-up, heavy-grade piece of clear plastic that he has obviously prefitted to the job at hand. By shifting the clear plastic only slightly in his hand, it opens automatically and forcefully in the wind. He slides the plastic over the pod, as a protective measure against the elements, a temporary barrier against wind and wet. Now, with the stubby screwdriver, sliding it beneath the plastic, he chips the ice off the pod—the whole pod is only a foot and a half square—and then, using both the pliers and the oversize key that Heller can see is fitted to just this pod case, for security and protection, he pries the pod open in the wind. Both Dolan and Pritchard train their helmets' miner lamps on its interior—shining them through the protective plastic into the inner workings of the pod. Heller can see an array of wires, transponders, chips, and electronics. He has no idea what he's looking at, of course. A sea of electronic connection. Or of disconnection. Dolan reaches both gloves in. Shifts one wall of electronic connections aside to reveal a second set behind it.

He and Pritchard shift their heads to move their helmet beams around. Covering between them the full interior of the pod. After a minute or so, Dolan carefully reverses the process. Brings the little wall of electronics back into its original position, checking once more, before closing the pod, clipping and sealing it, and locking it with the specially fitted key and, as a last step, rolling up the protective plastic barrier.

There is no acknowledgment or satisfaction that passes between Pritchard and Dolan. Heller has the sense that only if there was a problem would they signal to each other. Proper function doesn't earn any high fives or acknowledgments out here where every movement must be thought out, measured, conserved. He's impressed with their professionalism.

They all descend the scaffolding carefully, climb carefully back onto the still-running ATVs, head to the second tower. The one farther off.

It takes two minutes or so to reach this one. Two long minutes. Heller wouldn't have imagined it could be noticeably colder as they reached the second tower, but it is. And this further comm tower is taller, Heller notices. Maybe an extra story or so. A different scaffolding. A little sparser arrangement of steps and rails to the top, Heller sees.

Same plan. Same toolboxes. Same careful climb. Same tenting and taping of the electronics pod, before Pritchard, this time, deices the pod, opens it, begins his careful helmet-beam inspection.

Heller can't help but notice again how comfortably they operate together. No words can be spoken, out in the wind; no words should be spoken against the pressures of the cold; all attention is on the efficient but thorough use of time and energy. But still, Heller has the sense that even inspecting a comm tower on a balmy tropical isle, they would do it with wordless satisfaction.

All goes the same in this next inspection, just as smoothly.

Until they start to descend from the scaffolding.

Which is when Joe Heller apparently faints dead away.

Trips and tumbles down a full flight of the scaffolding.

One moment feeling fine, and the next moment collapsing, falling . . .

He remembers cracking his head on something.

Hitting the scaffolding with his head.

His body bouncing down the scaffolding.

The steps, the steel, all blurring around him, scrambling together in his brain.

And then nothing.

Blacking out.

As if the Antarctic cold and night, long held at bay around him, like a wolf impatiently prowling the perimeter, suddenly sees its chance, gets the better of him, finally invades, rushing insistently into his body and his mind.

• • •

He comes to in considerable pain hours later.

Lying in a position he has never expected to.

Staring up from the examining table, in the small, all-too-familiar infirmary.

The examining table where Sandy Lazo-Wasum and Trish Wong preceded him.

Pritchard and Dr. Calloway are sitting next to him, looking down at him. The doctor is searching his eyes with a penlight, as Pritchard catches him up on the last few hours.

"You blacked out in the cold. You went tumbling down the scaffold. You would have kept going all the way down the next three flights, but Dolan grabbed your parka collar to stop you. We managed to drag you down the scaffold. Dolan got you slung over the ATV, steered it from the back with you passed out in front. We figured you had just minutes."

Dolan enters the room, stands behind Pritchard and the doctor.

"He saved you," says Pritchard. "Dolan saved you. You were a goner."

Heller shifts his eyes up to look at Dolan.

Dolan looks back at him expressionlessly.

56.

He recovers quickly. He has to. He doesn't want to be seen as taking up any extra medical resources. Or seen as weak in any way.

Dr. Calloway checks his vitals for the next few days. Heller gathers that while it was technically a sudden life-and-death, touch-and-go situation, most of the station takes it largely in stride. Close calls—close encounters with the extreme cold—are not uncommon, par for the course. They're seasonally recurring cautionary tales, like repeated car crashes at a notoriously bad intersection.

"You know, even mild hypothermia causes mental confusion, and muscle mis-coordination, and loss of judgment, and with any repeated incidents of hypothermia, those tendencies become more pronounced," Calloway tells him. "Plus some people are just more susceptible to extreme cold than others, and your susceptibility increases as you get older. I'd recommend against any more of these little excursions . . ."

Heller doesn't know whether he tripped first, then hit his head, or hit his head first, then tripped. The sequence matters greatly—because if he hit his head first, then he's confused by how and why he could have hit something on the way down that was not in his path on the way up. Both Dolan and Pritchard were just above him as they descended the scaffold. So when he tripped and fell, Dolan had acted pretty quickly to grab him by the collar. Quicker than Pritchard, Heller notices.

He doesn't know whether it was some strange symptom of T3 he experienced—a sudden disorientation, a momentary mysterious symptom with particularly bad timing. Something unstudied so far. The extreme cold triggers all kinds of physical strains and reactions. That's why NASA was here. That's why it all still needs study. Especially when combined with mild or moderate hypothermia, according to Calloway.

But the blow to the head has certainly not been enough to dislodge an observation already planted there. That's already taken root and is slowly, slowly growing.

"Let me ask you something," Heller says to Dr. Calloway, as he is about to be released. "Those red needle marks at the back of Sandy's and Trish's necks. Reasonable to assume the poison entered that way, right?"

"Yes. Some fast-acting poison. Something very sophisticated."

"And what about that choice of entry point?"

"Just about perfect," says Calloway. "No more efficient path into the nervous system and the bloodstream."

"But it's been hard for me to figure out when a killer would have done it. If it's someone sneaking up on them in their sleep, let's say, and it's a fast-acting poison, as you say, why aren't they dying in their bunk? How and why are they dying dressed, out in the snow? But if they're awake and aware and dressed, like god knows you are in the snow, how is a killer, or killers, able to place it so perfectly, so accurately? And twice? Why isn't there evidence of them defending themselves? In that situation, it's a very risky, impractical way for poison to enter the body."

"Okay, granted," says Calloway.

"And certainly it's not the typical way for a poison to enter a body."

"No."

"Other methods . . . food, gases . . . are much more typical."

"Certainly."

"Dr. Calloway, could those needle marks . . . could they be nothing?"

Calloway looks confused. "What do you mean 'nothing'?"

"Just . . ." Heller shrugs. "Just that. A needle mark? Just . . . misdirection?"

Calloway smiles. "Well, with ideas like that, I think I have to keep you here longer for observation. The T3 seems to be talking."

"I know it's a little elaborate. Borderline crazy. But unexpected—you'd have to give it that, right? And if someone knew your autopsy was going to be limited, it's a smart piece of misdirection, isn't it?"

"Bizarrely smart. As an actual act . . . *and* as far as your even thinking of it . . . I'd say, yes, borderline crazy."

Heller shrugs. "Just a thought."

"A very weird one," says Calloway.

Okay. A very weird one.

But it's Antarctica.

You gotta adjust your thinking.

57.

Heller stands just outside the doorway, listening to the prayer meeting.

He feels like an intruder. But he also feels like he has to know what's going on. That he has to know if it goes beyond simple prayer. From thought to action.

"O Lord, we ask you to watch over us. Because, Lord, this kingdom of ice has never known a more fiery time. It is a fire—an unknown fire—that burns a thousand miles beyond us, but it is an equal fire that burns within us. The fire for survival with your truth. For survival in your trust. In your capable hands. We put our hearts in your hands, O Lord.

"For you have just proven your might to us. If we ever doubted it—and certainly we did, for we are scientists, secularists, many of us, so doubt is our job. It is our professional nature to doubt. And as if to answer our doubt, O Lord, you have unleashed a poison on the globe, to prove again your might, and as before, you have kept a chosen people, a chosen few, as witnesses—and what better witnesses than a scientific community, O Lord. How well chosen—proof of your own superior and almost scientific intelligence—to have chosen this community as your witnesses, as your way forward, but this time, forward in *your* name, forward in *your* shadow. This time, we walk with you.

"These are the end-times. The end-times that we have always heard about and assumed were far off—an issue for our progeny many generations from now—but you have reminded us of our responsibilities to you. Of our *current* responsibilities. You have reminded us of your presence, in a way we doubters cannot doubt. You through your word in the Bible you have given us, have always warned of end-times, and now in your mercy, you give us the chance to heed your warnings."

And clearly it is answering a vast hunger in them. A hunger that has gone unanswered. A hunger that is spreading, for today there are almost forty of them. A hunger that, like the food he serves, Manafort seems to know just how to season, how to make it taste, how to serve it up hot and flavorful and palatable.

Does Manafort believe it? It seems like he does. But it hardly matters, since *they* believe it. Since they have clearly been waiting to believe it.

And if Manafort does incite them, what is Heller supposed to do? What if that's what the majority wants? What if they want Manafort's leadership? What if they buy into his point of view? Won't Heller's responsibility then be to defend them? To make sure the will of the majority gets done?

He has been looking for a poison. An exotic, custom poison.

But he realizes there are many poisons.

Seeping, leaking and leaching, insinuating themselves.

The unknown poison that has so speedily and efficiently, it seems, afflicted and infected the planet above them. And whether its doom turns out to be nuclear or biological or chemical, natural or man-made, accidental or purposeful, whether they discover what it is or not, it is a poison in every sense. Spreading lethally, uncontrollably. A powerful poison that appears to have changed the world.

But there is this other poison too. The poison he is hearing spoken now. A poison seeping, leaching, leaking into consciousness, into susceptible minds. The poison of belief. The poison of magical thinking. The poison of T3, come to think of it.

He thought he was dealing with only a specific poison.

But he is now investigating other poisons. Far subtler. Far more lethal.

And these poisons, can he discover their ingredients?

Can he check their spread?

Can he contain it?

58.

Manafort is in Hobbes's office.

The two men are across the desk from each other. Both standing.

Manafort has asked for the meeting. He has brought a couple of people with him. Holson. Pike. Heller recognizes them from the prayer meetings.

Hobbes has asked Heller to be here for this meeting. Hobbes must have asked Simmons too, who is at his side.

There is obvious tension in the room.

"Okay, Bobby," says Hobbes, trying at the outset to disarm it, informalize it. "What's this about?"

"We are praying for your able leadership," says Manafort, formal, almost scripted, as if from the pulpit. "But our membership—our membership growing daily," he adds, with a little smile, "is having some questions, some concerns, which are getting in the way of their faith in your leadership."

"And you're here to ask those questions, voice those concerns, in the hope of bringing back some answers to your group, yes?"

Manafort gives a little nod—he has no choice but to say yes.

"Well, as I'm sure you know, Bobby, I'm doing my best under some trying circumstances," Hobbes says. "And I think you have to cut me some slack on that. I think we all have to work together, do you agree?"

How can he not? But Manafort says nothing. An aggressive, insolent silence.

"So how can I help, Bobby?"

"The food supply," says Manafort. "We're concerned that you're not being honest about the food supply. There's a feeling that you're putting aside some food for the self-appointed leadership, stashing emergency supplies."

This is of course a surprising question for Hobbes. Because there is one other person who knows exactly what the food situation is, and that is Manafort. In fact, he presumably knows it even better than Hobbes. So he is not really talking about the food supply. He is talking about something else.

"Well, you've seen how we've ramped up the hydroponics program. We're lucky that was in place, and it's expanding." He sounds a little like a salesman, a huckster. "It's no longer supplemental and experimental. Now we have to count on it . . . and the thing is, we can."

"And then there's the matter of the guns," says Manafort.

"What do you mean 'the guns'?" says Hobbes blankly, evenly.

"Rumor has it they're here and locked up, and you have the keys," says Manafort.

Hobbes pauses for a moment, before answering. "Rumor has it right."

"Well, there's a problem with that. Why do *you* get to decide about stashing and locking guns, at this point?"

"Because I think that's the safest option, under the stress of our current situation. That's the way to reduce the risk of anyone getting hurt or killed with them. Obviously."

"And *you* presumably are the only one with access. You and your lieutenants."

"Well . . . yes."

"And given everything that's happening, Emmanuel Hobbes is now simply in charge? No discussion? No decision?"

"Bobby, this is still a research facility. A science center. The National Science Foundation and the US Marshal's office have put me in charge. You know that."

"But things have changed. Dramatically. You'd certainly agree with that, yes?"

"Yes, but maybe only temporarily. Let's not jump to conclusions. It still might be a communications issue only."

"You're deluding yourself."

This from the leader of the daily prayers, thinks Heller. Hobbes stays silent.

"Maybe we need to elect someone," says Manafort. "Someone we all agree on to be in charge here."

His implication is clear. That Hobbes's leadership is provisional, previously appointed under different circumstances, and actual leadership has only now been called upon in this extraordinary current situation. That Hobbes is not the leader they need.

"We need access to those guns," says Manafort.

"What, to shoot each other?"

"To defend ourselves against each other."

"Listen to yourself, Bobby. Defend ourselves against each other. Does that sound like the society we should be heading toward?"

"Don't be naive, Manny. We both know what the food supply is."

"Ah, so you admit it. You know we're not hiding any."

"We both know what kind of world we could be heading toward. What kind of competition."

"But it's up to us to stop that kind of world. To be smarter than that. To head it off before it happens."

"More people should have access to those guns. People who everyone agrees on. That's only fair. That's only democratic."

That's the problem with democracy, thinks Heller. Everyone gets to claim it as their own. No one's in charge. Not the best system when survival is at stake.

That's only fair. That's only democratic. Heller understands for the first time that Manafort is being authentic. That Manafort not only is a believer but truly believes he is doing right. A righteous man. A particularly dangerous thing.

Hobbes looks evenly at Robert Manafort.

"So you're saying that if more people have access to those guns, that's going to make us all safer? Is that really what you're saying?"

"I'm saying that it's wrong that the only person who has access is you. You and your lieutenants. You're playing God, and only God gets to be God."

"But you're putting your faith in God, yes?"

"God is the only fair one. The only unbiased one."

"And what sort of God, Bobby? A kind and benevolent one? Or a cruel and harsh and vindictive one?"

Manafort's only response is a smug, superior smile. Smug enough, superior enough that Heller feels he can read the thought behind it. *Whatever kind of God it is, he's on our side.*

"We need access to those guns," says Manafort. "We can't have a society of haves and have-nots, because the have-nots in this case risk having nothing. Nothing but death."

There is silence in the conference room. Theatrical, threatening, extended, operatic. Hobbes stares balefully at Manafort and his sudden lieutenants, Holson and Pike, who stare back. A stare-off. A standoff.

"How many guns are there?" Holson asks.

"Too many," Hobbes answers.

"And where's the ammunition?"

"Not with the guns," Hobbes lies. Fluently, easily, Heller notices. A stalling tactic, Heller figures. "Keeping them separate creates one more chance for safety. One more hurdle against chaos."

"No ammunition? What if we do have to defend ourselves? What if we have to use them?"

"If you have to use them," says Hobbes, "then it's already too late."

"People want to defend themselves," says Manafort.

"Against who?"

"Against harm. Against bedlam." And then he narrows his eyes and says what he knows will be inflammatory. "Against the godless and the faithless."

"Now wait," says Hobbes. Now uncomfortable. Now somewhat alarmed. "So are you starting to conceive a society of believers versus nonbelievers? Of the godly versus the godless? Is that what's going on in your prayer meetings?"

Knowing that is exactly what's going on.

"Us and them? Is that what's happening in your prayer meetings, Bobby?"

But if he is hoping to shame him, thinks Heller, he may only be helping Manafort experience his own power. His own specialness. His own separateness.

He sees a flash of anger in Hobbes's eyes. Something he has never seen before in the gentle, modest, methodical scientist he has come to know. He sees Hobbes straighten, thrust his chest out. He sees the eight-year-old schoolboy on the playground, the primitive instincts of aggression and defense and survival, suddenly surface, in that stance, in that flash of eyes.

He sees the schoolboy standoff matched by the bully. The bully so ineffectively disguised as a man of God.

"If you don't distribute that firepower real soon," says Manafort, "lots of people are going to get real angry, real fast. They're scared. They're anxious. They need a way to feel less scared and anxious. A way to defend themselves against fear and anxiety."

It goes unsaid, but Heller feels it. *You give us some of those guns, or we're gonna take them.*

Heller feels it getting real ugly, real fast.

Hobbes has the guns. Manafort has God. Neither source of power has ever been tested or called upon in Antarctica before.

Heller is somehow certain that both sources of power will come into play.

Heller isn't sure what's going to have more power here. A few guns or God?

"I need to protect our food supply," says Manafort. "That's our lifeline here, and you know it. I have to protect that food, for all our sakes. You get me those guns."

And Heller hears it again, at the back of his brain. The little whisper again. *I've got the food.*

And if he has the food and the guns, then he has everything.

Real ugly. Real fast.

59.

Manafort quickly proves himself unnervingly adept at the politics of perception.

He locks up the kitchen supplies. Puts padlocks on all the cabinets and industrial pantries.

"This is for us," he tells his acolytes at the prayer meetings. "This is for us, for each of us—so that no man or woman has greater rights than any other. We are all God's creatures. We all have equal value in God's eyes. But this is to protect us from man—any man—usurping that view. Deciding selfishly otherwise."

This, Heller realizes, does a few things:

It is a parry directed at Hobbes and the still-locked guns. *If you can lock up the guns, I can lock up the food.*

It appears to his flock, his growing group of followers, that he is protecting them. Keeping their food safe. Vouchsafing their survival.

It puts Manafort more in charge. Makes him look benevolent, paternalistic, righteous—just what the God-fearing would expect and accept in their leader.

And most of all, it sends a message about a power shift, about a fundamental change at McMurdo Station. In Antarctica. On the planet, possibly.

The power is shifting to the kitchen.

From the laboratories, from science, from exploration to meal prep. From the consideration of the cosmos to the number of cans, the pallets of potatoes, the number of calories. From advanced degrees to basic muscle and brawn. From light years away to the primitive safety of the three square feet around you. Heller sees the shift. He knows that Manafort sees it already too. Maybe Hobbes sees it already, or doesn't, but they will all eventually see it. And Heller is blessed and cursed to see it first.

60.

On his own—unaccompanied, unescorted, but moving carefully, atten-
tively, across the dimly lit paths of McMurdo, dressed correctly for
even this short trip through the winter cold—he makes his way to the
observatory.

He's drawn, yes, by the prospect of another look, another peek at
the vividness of the cosmos. There's no need to interview Green again.
No follow-up questions. Just the need to be there.

Something to lift him out of the sure knowledge of the coming
conflict, some moment of peace and elevation before whatever ugliness
is to come.

He finds Green sitting at the telescope. Crouched in the driver's
seat, bent and positioned to thrust into deep space. Heller realizes it
is akin to the thrill of speed, of racing into the colors and joy of the
unknown, and yet it is that deep thrill coupled with stillness. A thrill
of stillness.

He knows what he is doing here. He realizes it somewhere in his
preparations to visit Green:

He doesn't know if he'll have the chance to look through the telescope again. He doesn't know if anyone will.

Yes, Green is sitting there, in the driver's seat, the jump seat to the
universe, but he is not looking through it. He is not working at all,

Heller notices. No paperwork. Just staring down. Staring out. He barely registers Heller's entrance, it seems. But he proves that he is aware of it.

"Everything's changed since your last visit, hasn't it?" says Green. Listless. Unmoored. A new vacantness in his manner, in his eyes. "It's no longer the stars, the heavens. It's now survival. It's going to be our basest instincts, isn't it, Mr. Heller? The kinds of things you've seen your whole career. The kinds of things I've never had to think about. That now I'll be forced to think about. That we're all now forced to think about."

"We don't know that yet. It's still too soon to be so demoralized. We don't know what happened yet."

"Something bad. Something very bad."

Heller doesn't want to violate the natural, unspoken trust that has built up between them. A thin but strong little string of connection that he wants to remain intact, so there's no use prevaricating or being falsely cheerful. "Yes, probably something bad," Heller admits.

"We're idiots," says Green, shaking his head. "We can explore the cosmos, we're within inches of understanding our arrival on Earth, our presence here, our interaction with matter, and yet left to our own devices, left to our other, accompanying impulses, we're idiots. We achieve the worst. We prove our idiocy, over and over. It rises to the top, quashes everything else about us."

Heller is silent. There's no use arguing with that—it tracks pretty well with Heller's own darkest thoughts.

Green gestures to the gleaming telescope. "It was my object of desire. My lifelong passion. Now it's as useless, as valueless as a pile of junk." He looks at it disdainfully, turns away from it. "Hundreds of millions of dollars to build, Mr. Heller. A can of beans is now worth more."

Green hangs his head. "What was the point of my sitting here in this chair, all my late nights focused on the sky, my absenting myself, devoting myself to something bigger, grander. What was the point? It's all going to die with us. All this knowledge. All this effort. I've been wandering around this observatory in aimless circles, asking all these unanswerable questions. Thinking about my life. How a life dedicated—a life focused—became so suddenly a life wasted. How a life of intelligence became in an instant a life so foolish."

The telescope. It's magnifying man's foolishness right now, isn't it, thinks Heller. Amplifying it, clarifying it, bringing it close, painfully close, in all its vivid colors and hues, too bright to look at, too bright to put your eye to the eyepiece. So Green does not.

"I'd like to look," says Heller.

"One last time?" asks Green dolefully. "Is that what you really mean? Look one last time?"

Heller nods. It is what he means. There's no denying it.

He is looking for Trish. Looking for Amy. Looking for himself. Looking while he *is* himself, before the inevitable chaos and ending descent.

Green flips off the eyepiece cover. Spins several dials. Squints as he adjusts the view. He can't help himself. He is still the ambassador of the universe. Ambassador to our best impulses, our better natures.

He gives a nod and a sad smile. "Take a look, Mr. Heller. Our universe, there for the taking. And now, it will slip past us. Slip past mankind, return to stasis without us. It was all ours. And now we'll melt back into it in a different form of matter, I suppose, and the universe will hardly know and certainly won't care."

Green checks the eyepiece one last time, slides out of the seat, and gestures to Heller to slide into it.

"Remember, you asked about the feeling of insignificance?" Green says. "Well, now I feel it. But it's not the multitude of stars that brings on the feeling for me. It's mankind's own failing, our own stupidity and avidity and greed that make me feel insignificant. Make me feel small and useless, like the lowest and most untrainable of creatures."

He makes a final adjustment as Heller ducks to put his eye to the cosmos.

To drink it in. To drown in it. To forget. To remember. To absent himself. To be himself fully.

As Heller is first looking through the eyepiece, a bright object passes surprisingly close across the lens's field. Close enough, sudden enough to startle him, and he is about to ask Green about it, when he realizes— a satellite. Still in orbit. Unobserved, unmanned, circling uselessly, for hundreds more years. A symbol of their technological achievement. And of their ability to help themselves, to save themselves, remaining forever out of reach.

● ● ●

He doesn't mention it to Green. Green has undoubtedly seen the satellites pass too.

He focuses instead on the sky beyond it.

Which takes his breath away once more.

Green knows it. Green can see it.

"We never got to the stars, Mr. Heller," he says.

And then is silent, letting the thought hang there, simple and unadorned.

And after a moment: "It's just us, now. So it dies with us, Mr. Heller. It dies with us."

61.

Word spreads quickly about the locks on the food cabinets. It amplifies the undercurrent of anxiety. There's enough food at the moment, plenty of food, but the fact that the food is now locked up indicates to many at McMurdo that there *isn't* enough.

Manafort knows there's enough food, thinks Heller. He knows it better than anyone. So locking the cabinets is only a way of accelerating the panic, accelerating the confrontation. Manafort is pretty clever. Making stews, cooking for hundreds year after year, brooding and plotting the whole time. Stirring up trouble, literally.

There are soon efforts to get into the locked cabinets. Silent night raids. People trying to jimmy the locks. Sawing and cracking the wood around the hinges. News of this only panics people further.

Food is found hidden in rooms. It indicates preferential treatment. It causes fights.

"Locking those cabinets has caused a host of problems," says Simmons bitterly.

Just as Manafort knew it would, thinks Heller. But he keeps quiet.

"This is insane. We have plenty of food. We have to meet with everyone in the cafeteria to reassure them. To talk them through it," says Hobbes.

It won't do any good, thinks Heller. They won't believe you. It will only make it worse.

"Meeting with everyone means Manafort will be there," Heller points out. "Locking the cabinets was his doing. He'll have something to say. It could come across as a standoff."

"We've got no choice. We've got to get everyone together about the food. We've got to try to talk sense."

Good luck with that, thinks Heller.

62.

The meeting is at 9:00 a.m. The cafeteria is full. Shoulder to shoulder. All 156 of them.

Hobbes faces the room. Manafort stands by a chair in the first row. Already standing, as if ready to speak, ready to defend, ready to lead.

They are surrounded by a nervous, anxious, agitated population.

No longer really a scientific community. Now, this morning, a community of survivalists. A town meeting against the approaching storm, thinks Heller. The approaching hurricane. Will we work together or duck and cover separately?

"There's been an undue amount of worry about the food supply . . . ," Hobbes begins.

"Well, what do you expect? Suddenly all the food is locked up!" someone shouts.

"It was locked up because a sizable contingent here felt it was safer, more prudent to lock it," Hobbes says, diplomatically.

"Maybe we should have a vote," someone else shouts from the back.

"Maybe we shouldn't," says Robert Manafort suddenly—confident, forceful—turning to the room. "Who says a democratic system is the best for us? That's just the kind of system that may have finished everyone off north of us. Democracies, all over the planet. And when there was trouble, there were too many opinions on what to do. Too many voices. And it was too late, too fast. Let's not make the same mistake twice. Mankind can't afford that."

"Bobby, we don't know that's what happened. You're jumping to conclusions."

"We better jump to some conclusions, Manny. We better start to. Or we could be finished. Finished forever."

Hobbes and Manafort stand and stare silently at each other.

Heller can feel the room divide. Divide in two.

Divide evenly? He can't say.

The old way—*steady, stable, trust me, hang in there, everything will be okay*—personified in Hobbes.

The new way—*change, extraordinary times, heaven's trumpets, humanity's last stand, everything is NOT okay, don't be fooled, this is serious, everything is different now*—manifested in Manafort.

And why shouldn't the cook lead them now? Why not their cook, instead of some scientist? Why not the person who feeds them—for they have never had such a need of sustenance as now.

Heller realizes: Hobbes is the old system. The old system that by all indications finished them off. That didn't work. Manafort is the outsider. Something new. At least a chance.

And Manafort of course has something else that Hobbes doesn't. Manafort has God. And God would never have been such an ally, but the prospective end of the world has suddenly brought him back. Suddenly resurrected him. The prospect of nothingness—of an ending, of finality, of a void—has suddenly reignited the power of the concept of God. Brought about his renewed presence. Whether Manafort believes in God or not—still an open question—he is putting God on his side. He has invoked him. And God, apparently, has been waiting for this. Waiting as if patiently, or impatiently, for this.

Particularly clever because people need to believe in something beyond themselves. Heller realizes Manafort will win. Election or no election, process or no process, Manafort will win.

"The Lord is with us, Hobbes. I know you're not a believer, but the Lord is with us, and he will see us through, as long as we acknowledge him, as long as we see him and feel him. I'm sorry it took this—this catastrophe—to bring him back to us, to bring him alive in each of us, to awaken us to his presence always in us, but it did, and for us, it is not too late. For whatever reason, unfathomable to us, we are chosen . . ."

"We are not chosen," says Hobbes, red faced, irate, frothy, fulminating. "We happen to be here. It's a random fate determined by the science of weather or wind pattern or the extremes of surface temperature or ocean current, some climatological effects either common or peculiar that science can eventually help us work out and comprehend. It's the whim of the pathogen, the whim of the poison, that's all. Let's not let a different kind of poison get us, Bobby. Don't let a different kind of poison, poison us. Let's pull together. Let's stay together."

"I'm all for pulling together, staying together. But I have a different leader in mind. A more experienced, more trustworthy leader than you or me, that's all. I think this takes someone and something bigger than us, Manny, don't you? Don't you think so?"

Heller senses again that Manafort truly believes. It's not cynical on his part. He believes. He's doing what he thinks is right.

Manafort and Hobbes stare at each other again. Silently. Balefully.

But it's not a standoff anymore, thinks Heller. Manafort will win. And they will all lose.

And that is what he is thinking when Calloway leans up behind him and says, very quietly, "Can you come to the infirmary?"

Heller nods.

"Ten minutes." Adding: "Make sure no one sees you."

63.

Heller knocks. The infirmary door opens. Calloway is standing behind it, waves him in. Shuts the door quickly behind him.

He motions Heller to sit down. He looks at him. He allows the silence to descend on them. Heller detects a liveliness, a sense of irony, a sense of wistfulness and eagerness and wisdom in Calloway's eyes. *I've got something. Something to tell you, Heller,* those eyes say plainly.

"I know this will not be pleasant for you, but it's important."

He opens a manila folder, fans the pictures out. Photographs of Trish Wong's corpse. Calloway took them, as part of his effort to perform at least a partial autopsy there in the infirmary, with Sorenson's help, when it was decided that Trish would be cremated. As they thawed the stored body, they had to at least try to learn what they could. In his preoccupation, in his grief, Heller hadn't even considered the existence of such photos. There is, of course, no avoiding them now.

In the top photos, she looks very much like herself—herself distressingly transformed. Whiter, paler, immovable, eyes open, facing up, empty. An empty vessel. Although he tries, Heller finds he is not able to absent himself. He feels an instant nausea, visceral, his stomach muscles involuntarily reacting. He takes a breath to control it. Grips the edge of the desk.

Calloway shuffles to a close-up of the base of Trish's neck. The little red mark left by the hypodermic. The needle never found, but the evidence of its pinprick right there. "That little red needle mark. The barely detectable way that a poison would have been injected. At the base of the skull. You said you couldn't figure out how someone got it into Sandy Lazo-Wasum and then into Trish without their fighting it or reacting in some way, right? Could a poison be *that* fast acting? Mere seconds? So instantly paralyzing, let's say, that you couldn't even move to defend yourself? Obviously, they were somehow surprised from behind or were sleeping or otherwise preoccupied. And the base of the skull, a brutally efficient way of injecting poison, whatever it is, directly into the bloodstream, right at the neural cluster of the upper spinal column, maximally effective point of entry, right?"

Heller nods. "Right."

Calloway looks at Heller. "Take a breath, Joe. Sorry to have to show you this, but as I say, it's important. With what's going on at McMurdo right now, maybe real important."

He fans out some new photos of Trish.

Further into the autopsy effort. Photos where the skin at the base of her neck is peeled back, her ligaments and muscles and spinal cord exposed. Photos civilians aren't subjected to, not even in court.

Heller's whole chest heaves. He feels like retching. He swallows. Holds it down.

"The pinprick that so obviously indicates the injection of poison, right? And the obvious conclusion about that injection site—poison injected highly efficiently. But when I looked at these photos again, looked really closely, I saw that the path of the needle doesn't penetrate to the bloodstream. It goes only as far as the surface tissue and ligaments. There's no damage to the muscle and the nerves at the point of release. In normally warm, ambient temperatures, there'd be no path indicated, the needle would be withdrawn, and the tissue would close around it. But luckily for us in this climate, the tissue is slow to close over, slow to respond to that kind of intrusion, even one as slender as a needle, and all the tissue kind of freezes in place for a little." He looks up from the photos at Heller. "There was never any poison in that hypodermic. That hypodermic was injected only to leave the mark on the skin's surface. Only to have us *think* it was poison. We thought the killer was trying to hide it, hoping we wouldn't find it. But the killer was hoping we *would* find it. And assume it was an injection of poison. And head any investigation in that direction."

Calloway taps one of the photos of the red mark. "I think that pinprick mark was left *after* Lazo-Wasum and Trish were dead. And *that's* how someone got to the base of their skulls, and that's how they never responded. You were right, Joe Heller. Your crazy instinct was right." He begins to put the autopsy photos back in the manila envelope. "This is a killer who is incredibly careful and calculating."

"But, if it wasn't poison . . ."

"Oh, it was still poison," says Calloway. "But the killer is trying to point us to an *injectable* poison. A certain kind and class of poison. And point us away from something else." He looks at Heller and allows himself a tiny smile.

"You have something you want to tell me."

"There is a species of snake we have here at the base, in one of the research labs. Its venom has enormous potential medical and pharmaceutical value, and interacts with the cold interestingly, so a couple of the scientists—Tallent and Blevins, I'm sure you met them—have been doing research with that venom here for several years. Their research is sponsored by two big pharma companies. It's proprietary and potentially hugely lucrative, so they don't share their findings, even between themselves. Anyway, the species' venom is among the deadliest toxins in nature and very fast acting. Of course Tallent and Blevins are modifying the venom—distilling and reconstituting and reprocessing—but the pure poison can directly penetrate the pores of your epidermis, and go undetected until it's too late. Which is only a minute later, at most. Asphyxiation due to respiratory paralysis. For generations, that's how certain Amazonian tribesmen have used the venom for their spear tips, to incapacitate local prey, which is how these powerful toxins were originally discovered."

Heller is silent. Motionless. McMurdo, the world to the north, all of it has momentarily fallen away.

"Tallent and Blevins' supply of snakes is shipped each season from the Amazon, and after the venom is extracted, the specimens are euthanized. Because of their toxicity, and because this is a scientific community, the original specimens are all accounted for when they come into the labs and destroyed immediately after they've made their contribution to science, but . . . someone could have gotten ahold of a couple, and been breeding them. It wouldn't take much to steal a specimen or two, feed them, mate them—not all that hard, and not that hard to keep anyone from knowing. Someone who's very careful, obsessive, like this killer seems to be. I could see a certain kind of person, a certain kind of scientific mind getting very excited about these snakes. Excited about the prospect of killing in this way. And fooling and misdirecting the investigation—the so-called experts—with a pinprick."

He tilts his head, slightly bemused. "Simple contact with the skin. But we never looked merely at the skin. Why would we? We cut in. We go inside. We look below the surface. We're scientists. We're doctors. We look deep." He holds out a last photo—Trish's torso, pale, bloodless—before putting it back in the manila envelope. "Plus, in this climate, the super cold skin quickly disguises any epidermal evidence. The cold body temperature hides the visual evidence, sends the whole body pale. A rash we'd easily see on a recently deceased person in the Amazon, let's say, or even in a temperate climate, disappears here in the body's uniform paleness."

He lifts the manila folder. Taps it on his desk. "People have their odd private hobbies during the winter-over. A reading plan. A weird science project. In this close community, we try to give people their privacy. I can definitely see someone pulling this off. Their own little hobby."

Calloway leans back. "I don't know who, Joe. But I know how."

• • •

Venomous snakes? So unpredictably primitive, so bizarrely tropical in this environment. And just a theory, at this point. An old-fashioned poison, in contrast to but in synergy, somehow, with the unknown pathogen that may have doomed the planet to the north of them.

Heller feels the rage surge in him. Angry, hot, his fists clenching, looking for a place, any place, to land. Stunned rage. Rage at being duped. At feeling like a fool, as he had felt with Paul. Left in the dark.

"Venomous snakes here at McMurdo?! And no one says anything until now?!"

Calloway looks at him. "Like I said, Tallent and Blevins are actually competing with each other. Funded by competing pharma companies. So they don't like to reveal anything they don't have to, least of all to each other. I promise you, those guys are immersed in their chemicals and their compounds. Trying to treat diseases, preoccupied with the glory of new patents. And like I said, the specimens are destroyed almost immediately. I'm telling you they've half forgotten that there are even snakes involved in the process at all."

He had interviewed Tallent and Blevins, of course. Perfectly pleasant. Seemingly forthright. But he did not ask them about their research, which they implied was fairly technical, and they might or might not have volunteered much in any case. As Calloway says, they might not even think of it in terms of poison anymore.

The locked-room mystery. A primitive poison. The tropical united with the polar, as if to bring Earth's extremes together, as harbingers of its end. And the snake, Heller can't help but notice, that slithering slippery symbol of evil in the Garden, working its destruction in their cold private Garden too. He pushes away the biblical. But sees how easily he can be sucked into Manafort's view of the universe. How anyone can be.

64.

"We need the guns to guard the food supply."

The guns again. Not letting it go. Focused. Determined. Part of a plan, Heller can't help but feel.

Manafort makes the demand—wrapping it in concern, reasonableness, prudence—then stares at Hobbes, defying Hobbes to challenge him.

"Now there's hard evidence that the supply is under threat," Manafort continues, citing the cabinet break-ins, the hoarding, problems he himself created. "There's distrust, there's about to be insurgency, we have to make everyone feel the food is protected for all of us, that it's fair."

He is there in Hobbes's office with Holson and Pike again, both arrayed behind him, and others behind them, an instinct toward phalanx that Heller has observed a few times now.

Hobbes stares back. Silent for a moment. Then says, cautiously, "Who appoints the guards? Who decides who protects the supplies?"

Legitimizing Manafort, Heller notices. Preparing to meet Manafort halfway. Demonstrating his own fairness, his willingness to listen. A mistake. Heller is alarmed.

"We appoint two guards for each locked food area. So they'll also watch each other. You choose one, and I choose one."

Making it sound fair to the assembled. But Heller notices how Manafort is quick, adept in playing a role in his own legitimization. He isn't letting it look like Hobbes is merely granting him the power. He is granting *himself* the power.

Making himself into a de facto leader, by his appointing half the guards.

Taking a half step, on his way to getting all the way there. Half control, as the first big step toward full control.

Leaving Hobbes little choice.

Because if Hobbes says no now, it's a rallying cry for Manafort. It's enough justification—potentially enough motivation—for Manafort and his soldiers of God to seize everything, in the perception that Hobbes is trying to control them.

Or does Hobbes say yes to this seemingly "fair" system of two-guard teams, one guard appointed by each of them?

Which reinforces the sense of "sides."

Which legitimizes the view of "us" versus "them."

All steps in the wrong direction. Steps down a slippery, wintery slope.

But saying yes—acquiescing—also staves off ugly confrontation. Staves off a holy war. Provides peace for another day. Another few days. While Hobbes tries to figure out something else.

"Look, Bobby, why don't you select your people, I'll select my people, and we'll have them guard the pantry and stockpile points, as you suggest, but without guns, okay? They keep an eye on each other, but without guns."

A clever way to cede Manafort a little control. A first step, but too much of one.

Manafort shakes his head. "The food supply is more important than that. It could be compromised by anyone. Our guards need guns." As if Hobbes and Manafort are now a team. The leadership team. A further clever way to legitimize himself. Manafort is a clear danger, thinks Heller. Ingenious. Treacherous. A slithering, sibilant, hissing, poisonous snake.

"Guards need guns," says Manafort. "You pick your people, I pick my people, and we get them the guns. Not just to keep an eye on each other but on the whole base. On all of us."

Hobbes pauses a moment, before answering. "Let me think about it," he says.

Heller can tell by Hobbes's tone that it's no longer just a stalling tactic. That he *is* thinking about it. That he may give in. *Don't do it.*

"Think fast," says Manafort. "We don't want anything bad happening in the meantime."

Heller can't tell if that's a threat. He notices how Manafort says "*We* don't want." Making it a shared goal. Including himself in leadership. Manafort is so naturally skillful at this.

A sudden police force, thinks Heller. For just 156 of them.

Manafort will have the food, *and* he'll have guns, thinks Heller.

Food. Guns. It's gone primitive and elemental already. Science is far away, far out of the picture already.

65.

"What is it?

"It's Dr. Calloway."

"What about Dr. Calloway?" demands Heller. Already angry. Already upset.

Because Heller already knows. Bramlett's stricken look, her eyes even wider than usual behind her black glasses, her pale skin flushed, as she stands at Heller's door—it is already telling Heller. Already causing his fury and frustration to rise at the messenger.

Heller looks at her, pulls on his boots, and follows Bramlett wordlessly.

• • •

Sorenson does the autopsy. Such as it is. No one at McMurdo has the skills or knowledge for a full one. Calloway didn't, and couldn't even bone up online, but called upon his medical school cadaver training, which came back to him at least in part. The cool, beautiful nurse does her best, but her hands are shaking. She merely assisted at Trish Wong's, and at Sandy Lazo-Wasum's botched procedure. And this is her boss on the table. Who taught her. She did not expect to be practicing on him. She's barely able to. She is an RN. Dispenses prescriptions, dresses wounds, treats coughs, colds. She can barely bring herself to make the incisions, much less probe what's beneath them.

Heller stands with her. He knows she needs him there. Needs someone.

It is above and beyond Sorenson's training, but it's not really going to take much.

An RN will be more than adequate for this medical investigation.

The back of Calloway's skull has been cracked wide open. Right here in the medical exam suite. Found slumped next to the exam table. So the amateurish, abbreviated autopsy and crime scene investigation are one and the same. Body doesn't even have to be moved. How convenient. How wretchedly convenient. Heller wonders vaguely if this is a first. A murder precisely where the autopsy will occur.

"Blunt-force trauma," says Sorenson. "Obviously. Death had to be instantaneous, or pretty close to it. By the way, this is the exact perfect spot to strike. Like, to the inch. Right between occipital lobe and parietal lobe, with a little upstroke to hit both at the get-go. So this isn't necessarily spur of the moment or just sudden fury. Could be very calculated. But more than that, calculated by someone who knew what he or she was doing." She pauses. "Although, obviously, there's plenty of rage involved."

"Can you say how many blows?"

Because Hobbes, Simmons, and Heller can't tell at all, the skull damage is so extensive.

"Four blows. Quick succession. I can tell that by the blood-drying pattern. Four blows. Just to be sure, I guess."

"What kind of object?"

She shrugs. "Large and heavy. Could be a lot of things. One of our metal braces we use for twisted ankles. Edge of a jack, edge of a construction hammer. And where that object is now, that's your department, Mr. Heller." She looks at him. "But I've already looked around here, and on first glance, nothing seems to be missing."

"Well, as you say, if it was premeditated, they probably would have brought the perfect weapon with them. One that wouldn't be missed. One that could probably be disposed of without being missed."

They are speaking formally. Trying to keep it clinical. Trying not to vomit.

"Can you examine the wound further? See if there's any metallic residual of the weapon. Anything to give us a clue?"

She nods. "Sure. I can do that. I know how to do that."

Blunt-force trauma to the back of the skull. As common a method as snake poison was not.

She has a medical light on. Shines it on the back of Calloway's neck, leans close.

"Well, no red needle mark this time," she says.

No time for it, thinks Heller.

No need for it, thinks Heller.

The world has changed. In your favor, thinks Heller, addressing the killer directly in his head. *Now you don't think it matters. You don't need to be so secretive, so cautious.*

Blunt-force trauma to the back of the skull. A murder that sends one of two messages.

This is someone else. Not me, the serial killer is saying back to him. *You've got a compounding problem here, Heller. It's someone who has some independent beef with you, some other issue, a newly expanding problem for you, Heller, but it's not me.*

Or:

It's me. It's still me. And as you can see, I don't really care anymore.

• • •

What did Calloway find that earned his death? Something beyond what he already speculated to Heller? Something he hadn't yet shared with Heller? Because it was just a hunch? Because he wanted to be a hero and bring Heller a solution? *I don't know who, Joe, but I know how.* Because he didn't recognize the danger of investigating it himself? Snooping around himself?

Or was it just the discovery of the snake venom? Had someone somehow realized that Calloway cracked the methodology?

Is there something in Calloway's desk drawers or in his notes that could be a clue to what he thought he discovered?

But if there is, isn't it highly likely that the killer has already looked and taken it?

Heller senses already that the crime scene will yield him nothing. This is a careful killer.

Who is figuring that he doesn't need to be as careful anymore.

Or who got rattled or pissed that Calloway was getting close.

So maybe there's a chance. In the abandonment of his previous stealth, maybe there's a chance.

That is, if they all survive long enough for Heller to find out.

66.

The hydroponic experiment is compromised.

Someone was in pilfering vegetables and potatoes and left the door ajar on the way out—rushing, ashamed—and the whole crop has been destroyed by the cold. Theo Cohen, the botanist in charge, discovers it the next morning. He's in tears. Word spreads quickly.

It was going so well, the potential yield was so substantial that they had shared the food calculations with the whole base. Cohen had known, for a shining moment, the feeling of a scientist who might actually save humanity.

It also occurs to Heller: this is the one food source that Manafort doesn't control. This is an option that science has provided. Cohen's—and Hobbes's—pride and joy, and a symbol too of ingenuity making survival possible. Tying ingenuity to survival. A formula for hope.

Could it have been a Manafort acolyte behind the break-in? Behind the foolish mistake of leaving the door ajar? Maybe no mistake at all.

In light of the pilfering causing an accident that now *has* truly jeopardized McMurdo's food security—Hobbes feels little choice. He unlocks the guns.

Heller sees the guns on the hips of the guards appointed to watch the pantries and the food lockers. In each pair, one assigned by Hobbes, the other from Manafort's camp of believers. A loaded Glock for each. Their mute black barrels, their weight and presence a new tenor to

Antarctica. Heller knows it will not be long until the guns make their presence fully known. Fully felt. Literally. He hopes he's wrong. He knows he's not.

• • •

He hears secondhand, but very quickly, about the conversation that precipitated the incident.

You believe in God?

Hey, I can't afford to believe in God.

But that's what we need right now, don't you see? To believe in something beyond ourselves.

See, I think now more than ever we need to believe in ourselves.

You really think mankind is smart enough to make the judgments we need to make right now? Look what just happened to our planet . . .

We have to try. Do our best. And falling back on some medieval belief in God is not how we'll survive.

Medieval? God has been part of who we are since Creation, and you dismiss him as medieval?

The two pantry guards had talked, argued, discussed into the night. And the talk—the argument—had apparently escalated.

Escalating tensions. Between nations. Between pantry guards.

And one of them is dead.

• • •

Who knows exactly how it elevated into insult or fury or belittlement— but however those interacted and combined, all were heightened by the terrors of survival.

In the morning, they have only one version of events. The survivor's version. The Manafort version.

Pike is the surviving guard. One of Manafort's lieutenants.

And Cohen—Theo Cohen, the botanist—has been killed.

Theo Cohen—who volunteered to serve as a guard after his experiment was ruined. To still be useful somehow? Or out of anger, rage, and self-destruction, wanting to get his hands on a Glock?

Theo Cohen—Lazo-Wasum's lab friend—who felt depressed, felt ruined himself? Angry? Antagonistic? Who didn't care what he said anymore, didn't care what happened to him anymore? Would he lash out at anyone?

No one will ever know exactly what occurred. What was said.

No autopsy necessary.

No mystery.

No investigation necessary.

And no punishment? No justice? No criminal proceeding? Pike is instructed to stay in his room. Meals are brought to him. Normally his detention would be a nonissue, his actions would be dealt with on the mainland, but right now there is no mainland. And everyone is too distracted and preoccupied with survival to worry about justice.

Cohen the botanist is dead.

And now there are—more and more defined—two camps. Believers and nonbelievers? Theosophists and scientists? However you define the two camps, Manafort's and Hobbes's.

And each camp must realize, thinks Heller, that its chances of survival double if it has half the mouths to feed. If the other camp is not here to feed. To consume resources.

Heller tries to stay outside any camp. Tries to stay neutral. Keep to himself.

Tries to figure out what Calloway may have learned. What Calloway knew. Or was about to know.

A blow to the back of Calloway's head.

Heller thinks inevitably of his own misadventure in the cold.

That was a blow to the back of the head too, wasn't it? Accidental. Self-inflicted.

But he's asked himself repeatedly. *Did* he slip? Slip on nothing and whack his head on the metal of the scaffolding just above him, as they said, a part of the scaffolding that he didn't remember on his way up the metal stairs? He doesn't remember seeing it. He'd like to go out there again and see it. But he can't in this weather.

Or was he pushed? With low visibility, compromised mobility, fogged goggles, bundled up out there in the cold?

Both Pritchard and Dolan standing above and behind him, as they descended the metal stairs in the dark.

He'd pretty much dismissed the idea. Too crazy. Too attributable to his confusion in the moment. But here is a murder with a new MO—blows to the back of the head. Did he escape, fall away from such blows, when Calloway couldn't? When you consider breeding exotic snakes to create a deadly toxin, or needle marks as a diversionary tactic, or research scientists listening to a cook and backwoods minister—is that idea so crazy?

You gotta adjust your thinking.

He doesn't know—he'll never know—if it is Calloway's manner of death returning him to speculation about his own fall, or else his slow but steady recovery from his fall and blackout, or his mind shifting away momentarily from relentless thoughts about Ann and Amy that causes a few memories of that inspection tour with Pritchard and Dolan to finally surface, arrange themselves in his mind in a way they never have before.

Seemingly small things.

Seemingly unrelated, but now, for whatever reason, aligning.

How, as they prepared that morning, Pritchard went searching for a roll of sealing tape, impatient and annoyed—until finally a roll turned up, buried at the back of his shelves.

How Dolan took the key out of a sealed plastic envelope when he removed it from his toolbox at the first tower.

And a certain snippet of conversation. *"Let's have the One-Four go first. That's got a better headlight." "No, I think the Cat's better. It spreads wider." "No, let's have the One-Four."*

Wouldn't they have had that conversation before?

Wouldn't Dolan have taken the key out of that sealed envelope before? When and how would he have put it back in the envelope and *resealed* it?

Wouldn't Pritchard know where the sealing tape was if they were regularly using it during inspections?

The conclusion is inevitable.

They haven't been out on previous periodic inspections, as they've always assured the leadership they have.

They said they have, but they haven't. They had to go on this one because Heller wanted to go with them.

So they've lied about going out previously.

Lied, or at least misled, or prevaricated. Lied and hedged when regular equipment inspections are a standing order from Hobbes and Simmons and the leadership. (Heller himself has heard Pritchard and Dolan referencing previous inspections. Talking confidently, affirmatively to him about their schedule, their diligence in making them.)

Lied or misled, Heller notices, together. Both of them. In sync. Watching each other's backs?

Lied, and the question is, why?

Laziness? Inexcusable, but understandable.

Fear of the weather? Of the hazards? Inexcusable, but understandable also.

Or because they know everything works? They just know, confidently, arrogantly, that the comm towers are fine, even though they're hearing no one, getting no signal, but they know it isn't them. It's the rest of Earth—evaporated, zapped into incommunicative nonexistence.

Or:

And this boggles him. This is where his headache instantly returns.

Because they know everything *doesn't* work.

Because they know—confidently, arrogantly—that the comm towers are *not* working.

• • •

The knock in the head—has it knocked this crazy idea into him? Or knocked some sense into him?

He saved you. Dolan saved you.

Does Pritchard believe that? Does Dolan? Did Dolan really save him, catch him by his collar as they said?

Save him for what?

Did Dolan save him impulsively? Heroically? Or save him purposefully? For some less obvious reason than heroism, or competence, or quick instinct? To prove Heller's own vulnerability to him? To send him a message? Or just to prove what a good guy Dolan is? Putting some good feeling in the bank. Confusing him. Letting him chalk it up to T3.

He saved you. Dolan saved you.

Maybe. But he can't know. He can't be sure of what happened out there.

Or what's happening in here.

67.

He is standing in Pritchard and Dolan's suite.

He has surprised them. They won't know what he's doing here. He's come to confront them about his fall out at the second tower—but he's not sure exactly how to approach it. It's just an intuition, after all, which still feels a little primitive—foolish—on this continent of science.

Pritchard is stretched out on his bed. Dolan isn't around. It occurs to Heller, just then, that it's the first time he hasn't seen them together. Even on Heller's previous visit, when Pritchard was curled up in pain, which Dolan attributed to T3, Dolan was right there in the Comm Cave next door.

Heller is suddenly aware of something crossing the floor and disappearing—he could swear—beneath Pritchard's bed.

Mere shadow. Mere movement. He doesn't know what it is, or even *if* it is. It could merely be an effect of the low light in here. A tracer in his eye. No more than a shadow across his senses. Not even there. A mild hallucinogenic effect of T3.

But then he hears a tiny rustle beneath the bed. Faint. Barely audible. A slight thump.

And he sees Pritchard's eyes look down—just for a moment—so that he knows he isn't the only one hearing it. And maybe wasn't the only one seeing it a moment before.

"What's that?" Heller asks.

"What's what?"

Pritchard stares at him purposefully, unyielding. Stiffening a little, Heller can see. He seems, Heller notices, suddenly a little vulnerable without Dolan here. A little nervous. When he has always seemed like the more relaxed, open one when they're together.

"Whatever you looked down at," says Heller.

"Oh, that's nothing," says Pritchard, with a nervous shrug.

Heller looks at him. He doesn't think Pritchard even realizes his mistake. *Oh, that's nothing.* It's like a version of that scurrying shadow, that slight sense of something running along a back wall of Heller's brain, a tiny firing synapse of illumination: there's something a little off about Pritchard that he's never noticed before.

"Well, if you tell me it's nothing, that tells me it's something," says Heller. As if reasoning with a child for a moment.

While Pritchard is still lying there, Heller suddenly bends down to look beneath the bed.

Radio equipment, electronic components, in cardboard bins, all jammed together in there. Transistor boards, tubes, hobbyist junk.

Creating a little wall, Heller notices.

He shoves aside two of the cartons.

Even in the low light, he can see: There's a terrarium behind it. Heated—a wire running from it to a plug.

He pulls the terrarium toward him.

"Be careful," says Pritchard, leaning off the bed toward Heller. "Don't pull the plug out. They need the heat."

Heller has been acutely aware of Pritchard lying on his bed, *not* trying to stop him from bending down by distracting him, *not* trying to physically restrain him, not moving, not reacting until this moment, when he's worried about the plug.

Now Pritchard swings his legs off the bed and bends down alongside Heller. Pulls the terrarium carefully toward them, out from under his bed. *Sharing it.*

Heller recoils as it gets closer. Snakes. Dozens, writhing in there.

"Snakes," says Pritchard, with a certain, unhidden amount of pride. "Snakes—in Antarctica! Pretty impressive, huh?" His eyes gleam, drink in the squirming, bustling terrarium. "I know there's some weird winter-over hobbies, Mr. Heller. Well, so okay, I've got mine."

"Are they poisonous?"

Pritchard looks at him. "Poisonous! Of course not. These are *Enhydris anteriori*. They're happy to be together like this."

"So this is what I saw slithering by in the shadows?"

Pritchard looks uncomfortable. "Sometimes I let one out in the room. They're well behaved. Look, please don't tell anyone. You're not supposed to have pets of any kind. That's why they're under the bed. Please . . . please don't. They're not hurting anyone."

But I'm exactly the person you wouldn't tell, thinks Heller. *Why are you telling me?*

"Dolan knows?"

"Oh yeah—but he doesn't know I let them out." He looks down. "But he's not here right now."

Confiding in him. Asking him not to tell Dolan.

"Oh, that's nothing." Heller had no idea that Pritchard has compromised social function. Mildly childlike. It has always been hidden behind his radio expertise. Or is it T3 effects? He knows that Pritchard suffers it acutely. Is this just Pritchard right now? Temporarily less functional? A different Pritchard?

He watches the snakes with Pritchard silently. He hopes Dolan doesn't suddenly appear. He is disgusted. Watching them slither, climb each other. But he manages to act fascinated. To gain Pritchard's trust. This is obviously a new experience for Pritchard. The chance to share them. The chance to show them.

"No one can breed snakes in Antarctica," says Pritchard. "I promise you this is unique. Well," he frowns, "except those snakes they have in the lab."

"Snakes in the lab?"

"Yeah—and those, we hear, *are* poisonous. One that's super poisonous. So they don't let anyone see those. They won't even let me in when they get them, and I love snakes."

Heller squints into the terrarium. He's sure that Pritchard never moves his terrarium to the front of the bed. Leaves it hidden behind the radio components. He's betting it's at Dolan's insistence.

"Hey, what's that bright snake at the back? A little smaller. Is that a baby?"

Pritchard squints. "No, it's not a baby. Over there—*that's* a baby *Enhydris.*"

"But that other one looks different, though. What is it?"

Pritchard looks silently.

Then admits, with a shrug, but more than a note of fascination: "I don't know."

68.

That blow to the head, out there with Pritchard and Dolan.

His memories of that little excursion got overwhelmed by the blunt fact—the blunt single impact—of that blow, he senses now.

But the smaller memories have kept circling back to him, a little clearer, a little more insistent each time.

And suddenly seeing Pritchard in a different light—childlike, a covert herpetologist, separate from Dolan for the first time, kneeling on the ground with Heller, looking into a writhing terrarium, like two pubescent junior high teenagers after school—certainly it colors his chain of understanding . . .

Pritchard not being able to find the sealing tape . . .

Dolan unsealing a tool that would have been unsealed before . . .

The two of them arguing about which ATV light is better, when they would have decided that long ago . . .

Thinking back to their preparations for the inspection of the comm towers, Heller hears Dolan's question again in his head: *You won't even know what you're looking at out there. Do you? Do you have any idea?*

He'd thought it was just disgust, judgment, an insensitive passing comment aimed at Heller the outsider.

He realizes now: It was making sure. Making sure he *didn't* know what he was looking at. Making sure the comm towers would not be understood. That it would just be a bunch of incomprehensible wires and diodes and dials to Heller. So they could *keep* them not working.

Why?

To cut everyone off obviously, to cut off McMurdo, but why?

To create an alternate world. Their own world. And why?

Why would you attempt something so radical, so wholly unimaginable, so strange and unthinkable?

Even as he forms the question, he knows.

To protect—to *perpetuate*—something equally radical, equally unimaginable and unthinkable.

To insulate the unthinkable.

To extend the unimaginable.

A radical cover-up that might only occur to Pritchard and Dolan, via the radical act or acts that preceded it.

He is instantly fascinated.

He is instantly nauseous, dizzy, sick.

He is thrilled, salivating with the solution, with finality.

He is aware of a feeling of sudden light.

He is aware of a feeling of sudden darkness.

Jesus. They are the only experts. The only radio people.

And what else has he heard, but misheard?

Understood one way, when there is another.

• • •

Heller and Pritchard both hear Dolan coming down the hallway.

Pritchard pushes the terrarium back. Pulls the cartons in front of it.

"He wouldn't want me showing you," he says to Heller.

"I won't say anything," Heller assures him.

• • •

Dolan is a little disconcerted to see Heller there. It is just a moment—a twitch, like a snake's shadow—that Heller detects, before Dolan goes opaque again. "You feeling better?" Dolan asks.

"Yeah, I am, thanks," says Heller. "Much better. The fogginess is finally lifting," he says, gesturing to his head.

Yes, the fogginess is finally lifting.

"Hey, Hobbes asked me to come down, see how you guys are doing with the radio."

"Same, unfortunately," says Dolan. "I mean, you went out with us to inspect. We don't know what else to do."

"Can you walk me through it, give me an update? I need to report back, reassure him. As you know, it's getting a little desperate around here."

Dolan shrugs. "Follow me."

●　●　●

Pritchard reaches for his key, to open up the corridor door to the Comm Cave, before realizing that Dolan just came from there, so it's still open.

Heller has noticed before that the Comm Cave is kept locked from the corridor side, and never thought about it much. It seemed somehow prudent to lock it. But now he wonders whether their keeping it locked has nothing to do with the safety or value of the equipment.

Pritchard throws some switches.

He dials through a few frequencies.

Static. Nothing.

"The last thing was that Australian farmer, wasn't it?" says Heller.

Pritchard and Dolan nod, glumly.

"Hey can you play that again? I remember you recorded it. That was smart."

Dolan pauses for a moment, Heller sees.

(A snake, a shadow, slithering across the edge of the periphery. The edge of Dolan's eyes.)

Pritchard nods cheerfully. "Sure." And flips some other switches, to load the track.

• • •

It's as scratchy and muffled as before, just as you'd expect from a jury-rigged ham radio system.

"Hey, blokes, this is Aussie 2094, broadcasting from the Brindabella Range. Anyone out there? Anyone know what's happened? The grid is down. We've been operating on generator plus batteries and flashlights here since Monday . . ."

Son of a bitch, thinks Heller to himself. He stares at the radio equipment—to avoid looking at Dolan or Pritchard.

"One more time," says Heller.

"Hey, blokes, this is Aussie 2094, broadcasting from the Brindabella Range. Anyone out there? Anyone know what's happened? The grid is down. We've been operating on generator plus batteries and flashlights here since Monday . . ."

Son of a fuckin' bitch, Heller thinks again.

He is thrown back to his first months without Paul. When he wanted to be left alone, but there was that ridiculous Global Police Technique exchange program, and they made him partner for a month with an Australian kid named Bailey, and they had a stakeout together, when Heller asked Bailey to hand him the flashlight, and Bailey looked at him puzzled for a moment, and Heller pointed and asked again, and Bailey laughed and said, "Flashlight? What in fuck's name is a flashlight? I'm handin' you a torch, mate. 'Cause that light ain't flashin'." Whereupon Heller, smiling, turned it on and off a few times. "See it flashing? Flashlight," said Heller. "Torch," said Bailey. Both smiling, as they headed out into the dark on stakeout. Heller remembers it vividly.

The accent is perfect. A perfect Australian accent.

The voice is at a pitch and timbre that no one would recognize.

But an Australian doesn't say *flashlight*. An Australian says *torch*.

Only an American would say *flashlight*.

An American, with the help of filters and static and radio effects, pretending to be Australian.

Heller knows. It's Dolan's voice—altered perfectly, ingeniously, convincingly, all the static of the recording, all the interference and the primitive radio transmission, helping to convince and persuade, helping them all accept it, covering any sins nicely—except for the wrong word at the end of the sentence. A word an Australian farmer would never use.

It was their last communication with the world.

A world that the Australian farmer—like the conveniently primitive, also-faked Morse code communications with Ranger Winslow before it—had confirmed was undergoing some disaster, some global catastrophe.

A fast-moving, lethal, unprecedented pathogen, they had guessed.

But all the poison, it turns out, is right here.

"Keep trying. We know it's grim work. But we need you to keep trying," Heller manages to say evenly. And he thanks them for trying. And backs out of the room, without looking directly at either one of them.

Son of a bitch.

Torch. Not flashlight.

Literally a moment of illumination.

Of seeing into the Antarctic dark.

• • •

Does he tell Hobbes? Hobbes who is in the middle of a slow-motion revolution? In the middle of the breakdown of the social order? Or is the slow-motion revolution and breakdown of the social order just the setting Heller needs for justice?

277

69.

He's thinking as fast as he can.

Trying to piece together still unimaginable strands and fragments.

Realizing that this is a kind of master criminal who has managed to manipulate his whole environment. Bringing a radical level of control to it that is almost inconceivable. Cutting off communication entirely, leaving everyone literally and figuratively in the dark. A dark where he can choose them, pick them off, one by one.

He thinks about what he's dealing with. What to do next. It's not so straightforward. It's not so simple.

If he tells Hobbes or anyone that their communication has been cleverly and purposefully cut off by Dolan and Pritchard, Dolan and Pritchard will simply deny it. It's his word against theirs. His crazy theory versus their diligent-looking efforts, their jury-rigged Morse code machine and primitive ham radio and their scratchy recordings, their heroic round-the-clock exertions.

If they don't restore the communication, they will have until the weather warms enough to let the first plane and ship in—like every year.

Another eight weeks or so. Another eight weeks in the dark, incommunicado.

Obviously, the rest of the world has been trying to get in touch with them and knows McMurdo is having communications problems, presumes that they're working on them, knows they have more than enough food and fuel for the season, that everyone will be back in touch as soon as the weather permits and the first plane and the first ship arrive. For years there was no winter communication with McMurdo. It's a temporary return to the old days, that's all . . .

And suddenly he realizes:

It's much more than that.

If Dolan and Pritchard can switch *off* communications, then they can switch it *on* at will.

Switch it on as necessary, to tell the world: *Comm problems here at McMurdo. No reason to worry, everything fine. Supplies excellent, as you know. We will continue to work on problems. Can solve!* And either they made clear that they can only send and are assuming that their communications are being received or, it occurs to Heller, Dolan and Pritchard have been receiving confirmation communications back and simply not saying anything about them. Burying them.

It isn't much different from any other winter-over. The rest of the world is fine, McMurdo is fine, and as always, McMurdo, we'll see you in the spring.

For almost all of McMurdo, the world has ended.

For Pritchard and Dolan, the "world" will end with the first plane or ship.

Maybe sooner. Because the first visit, before a plane or ship, might be from the Russian or Argentine station.

Hey, McMurdo let us know they're having some communications equipment problems. Can you go see what's going on over there? Make sure they're okay? We're pretty sure it's just a communications issue that they haven't been able to fix, but we haven't heard anything from them lately. Can you send over some new equipment and some communications experts to give them a hand? Thanks so much.

Will the residents of McMurdo inadvertently destroy themselves in the silence of the next eight weeks? The war of Hobbes and Manafort? Armed camps. Will they survive eight more weeks?

Heller is still staggering. Still trying to process it. The flip of a little switch out there on the comm towers. Flipping a tiny switch or two and cutting off the world. Flipping a tiny switch or two and altering everyone's perception of the world, of the future, of themselves. How did they think they could get away with it?

Because they *had* gotten away with it. Had gotten away with murder, and it had only emboldened and empowered them—and then they saw, with Heller's arrival, that they were going to be cornered, trapped, and their choices came down to something radical, unthinkable, unimaginable . . .

And—Heller knows—because there are two of them. Because they look like a team. Teams are trusted. Partnerships are trusted. Longstanding partnerships, especially. Always teams of two in the silos, to set off nuclear devices, needing to turn the keys in unison. Maybe one person goes a little crazy, but not two together. (And yet, Manafort is showing that a whole continent can go crazy together, step by step, little by little.) He thinks of Paul again. Of their partnership. Partnerships are hollower than you might think.

He pictures Pritchard and Dolan again, shuffling nervously in to the leadership in the wake of the communications blackout, both of them visibly uncomfortable and distraught. But their anxiety wasn't really about the prospective "causes" of the communications outage. Their shuffling, their anxiety, were due to the immense lie they were about to perpetrate.

So far, Heller only has the proof—the slim and circumstantial proof—of a misused Australian word. And Dolan may have "inadvertently" erased the recording already anyway. May have picked up on the mistake after Heller's request to hear it again, and destroyed it. One misused noun. On only Heller's say-so. Hardly proof of anything.

And Pritchard may have already told Dolan about Heller's visit. About looking at the snakes and the weird snake in the back. So Dolan may have already gotten rid of the brighter, smaller snake at the back of the terrarium.

Heller knows what that extra snake at the back of the terrarium is doing there. He doesn't know the details, but he knows the broad outline. It's been liberated from the lab by Dolan. Maybe bred in the lab to increase its poisonousness. Its venom harvested. As Calloway said, it only takes being spread on the skin. Undetectable in this environment. Quick acting. Neurotoxic to an astonishing degree. After all, tiny doses of anthrax or botulinum or other customized chemical agents have the calculated capacity to kill a billion people in just hours. The kind of catastrophe McMurdo scientists have been so vividly imagining. It's just as easy—easier—for Heller to imagine one person, a patch of skin, a valid neurotoxic experiment in the unique environment of low-temperature reaction, with its promise for pharmacology and anesthesiology, an experiment gone awry. Not controlled closely enough.

And it occurs to him: McMurdo's isolation, its thousand-mile perimeter of relative safety . . . wouldn't it make sense that there are experiments going on here that can't be done safely anywhere else? The private pharmaceutical companies, it was explained to him, contribute significantly to funding the station, and their competing projects are allowed to be "proprietary," secret from one another. Hobbes never mentioned toxins or venom, maybe because it never even occurred to him, maybe because he didn't even know, but maybe because "proprietary"—meaning secret—is part of the pharmaceutical companies' operating agreements with McMurdo, so Hobbes is contractually prevented from discussing those experiments, and maybe there are several of these somewhat dangerous projects going on.

The competitive, secretive nature of such experiments. He could see how competing groups would stay mum if a specimen or two went missing.

Finding new treatments, new cures, but creating questionable byproducts along the way.

The good with the bad.

Beauty and possibility, with danger and darkness.

Antarctica in a nutshell, once again.

This is what Calloway must have figured out. And this is what Dolan must have realized that Calloway had figured out.

But just as big a mystery. And maybe, Heller thinks, a possible path, a possible solution lurking there . . .

The relationship between Pritchard and Dolan.

He's taught me everything he knows, said Pritchard. *He's a genius.* A Svengali? *He saved your life.* So it had seemed. But did he? Or was Dolan shaping that moment, as he has apparently shaped so many.

He's taught me everything he knows. Has he taught you incorrectly, Pritchard? On purpose? Provided you with knowledge that is actually ignorance, year after year? Used you as his tool, his toy? *He's a genius.* Oh yes, definitely. But not merely the technical, radio-and-electronics genius you think. A different kind of genius. A deeper, more malign kind of genius.

He saved your life. You think so, Pritchard? Like he has saved yours?

Susceptibility to T3 is as variable as any other disease or propensity to disease. As variable as one thyroid to the next. Some people remain normal. Some have trouble. Some have extreme trouble. Pritchard's headaches and absences. Does Pritchard suffer extremely? And isn't that something that Dolan has come to know pretty well, after years of rooming with him? A T3 susceptibility that created an opportunity for Dolan? An opportunity every year of wintering-over. And perhaps an opportunity that he resisted, and quelled within himself, burying it in his work, in his electronics expertise, until he couldn't anymore. Until the murder of Lazo-Wasum.

Or an opportunity that he was preparing, for years. Cultivating, carefully planning, enjoying all the preparation in some way. Until it was time to try it. Until the snake experiments had progressed far enough.

An opportunity built for years. Until Pritchard is an instant, fool-proof, complete alibi for everything. Because he doesn't know any better. Because he's been trained.

And maybe there is an opportunity here. A little window. Because Pritchard has asked Heller not to say anything to Dolan about finding the snakes. A little window of communion with Pritchard?

Heller wonders if he's brought this on himself. If it is his presence alone, or the threat of his presence, by which Dolan (and Pritchard, cooperating with him, a dutiful, obedient, highly suggestible follower) hatched this unimaginable scheme.

He can't ask Dolan for the recordings. If he does, Dolan will know for certain there's something telltale in them. Not knowing what exactly, he'll know they reveal something, and destroy them.

The closest proof of anything is the poisonous snake under Pritchard's bunk. But even there, Pritchard, the self-admitted secret herpetologist, is the one who will be blamed. Dolan can shrug, say he knows nothing about snakes or venom.

Both could easily be gone already, in the wake of Heller's visit to the Comm Cave—the recording erased, the off-color snake gone from the terrarium. Even if he half believes Heller's crazy-sounding tale of a faked recording and a poisonous snake, Hobbes would never take action on such flimsy evidence. Hobbes is a scientist; Hobbes abides by the rules; Hobbes will require more substantial proof. And if Hobbes *were* to act summarily, without further evidence, Manafort would act summarily against him.

And most of all—Hobbes is no longer in control. Hobbes's system—the system he represents—is no longer trusted, dominant, reliable. Do evidence, due process, proof even matter in this environment where all bets are off? Where everything is up for grabs? Dolan, trying to protect himself by temporarily shutting down outside communication, has created another world that even he could not have foreseen. But one that works to his direct advantage. A psychopath's wet dream.

And if Heller simply confronts Dolan, couldn't that make it worse? Couldn't the murder rate go up exponentially, for a sick pathology like Dolan's to know that Heller is onto him, that his time is running out?

Heller is running out of options.

He finds himself weighing a very strange one that would never have occurred to him, but—in their increasingly unmoored present, their current situation—it seems surprisingly viable.

Tell Dolan the truth.

A convincing, motivating version of it, anyway.

You've done such a good job, Dolan, you'll never be convicted. No one will ever believe me.

There's no adequate justice system in place here, even if your crimes could be proven, which they can't. The autopsies show nothing, and the radio and herpetology evidence is circumstantial at best, if you haven't destroyed it already, and it could all be Pritchard anyway. You're safe, Dolan. Maybe that's something you already know, but as a law officer, I can confirm it for you. You're safe, you bastard. You're safe.

And you're going to be a lot safer, if you restore the comm towers. Because if you don't, I'll kill you myself, right now—knife, strangulation, suffocation, make it look like an accident. Nothing to it for a cop like me, believe me, and in our cutoff isolation, it'll be easier than ever to pull off, so don't choose that, Dolan. You're way safer, safe from me at least, by restoring the comm towers.

Make him fix the comm towers.

Heller has the sense they will repair easily. A few switches flipped. No one would know what the problem had originally even been. Dolan can even look like a hero. More heroism for the guy who saved Heller out there.

Of course, repairing the towers, without telling Hobbes or anyone else, involves going back into the cold.

Going back into the cold with Dolan, again. A psychopath. A murderer. A maniac.

The comm towers where Heller still doesn't know for sure what occurred the first time.

Maybe Pritchard—T3-suffering Pritchard—comes with them. Heller has to think about that. Where do Pritchard's loyalties lie? How much has he been programmed? How much free will and moral judgment does he have left? Has he in fact been a silent, helpful partner in the murders, at Dolan's beck and call? Heller doesn't know.

But Heller does know he saw a clue—the infantile, trembling, childish Pritchard. *He taught me everything I know,* says Pritchard. And Heller now has a sense of how deeply true that might be.

It's still confusing, still a dilemma.

The faster he can get communication restored, the faster the escalating Manafort-Hobbes conflict can neutralize, melt away.

But the faster he can get communication restored, the more quickly it might force Dolan to act again. His opportunity running out. Forcing him, encouraging him to go out with a blaze of glory? Cornered, trapped, with no other choice? Backed into a corner at the bottom of the world?

It's another "Catch," isn't it? Another "Catch" in a situation that's piling them on.

70.

McMurdo, a scientific community, has no jail or holding cell.

The closest thing is a sturdy locking room off the infirmary. (For those whose T3 symptoms are severe enough to risk harm to themselves or others.)

Hobbes, Stanford, and Bramlett have demanded that William Pike, Cohen's murderer, be kept there until they figure out what to do with him.

Which Pike is willing to do. Remorseful, confused, shocked by his own impulses, his own actions, Heller can see. Keeping a constant eye on him is partly a suicide watch.

But Manafort does not agree.

He bursts in on a conference-room meeting, energized, surrounded by a sense of his own growing power.

"Why should Pike be held like that?"

"Because he killed a scientist in cold blood."

"But we don't know what happened," says Manafort.

"He *told* us what happened," says Hobbes. "An argument escalated."

"He was being taunted," says Manafort. "His beliefs were being ridiculed. He had to do something."

In another setting, another context, Manafort's statement would be simply outrageous. Crazy. You can't kill someone over words. Over beliefs. But Heller senses that Manafort might have burst in, might be saying this to demonstrate something to Hobbes. To all of them. To show them how it is no longer crazy. To show them that this is the new world they are living in. The new logic, at Manafort's command. To show how instantly, how thoroughly the world is changing before their eyes. Not the world-in-question to the north of them. The world of McMurdo.

"You don't *kill* someone over beliefs!" says Hobbes. And Heller hears, senses, the answer even before Manafort says it.

"Yes, you do. All the time. That's what we've always done. That's what every war on our planet has been about."

"But . . . we have laws."

"Who says what laws we have? Maybe the laws are changing. Changing because *we* are changing." Chin, chest, thrust forward, defiantly.

And the unspoken issue rises between them again. That there are no laws. That there is no precedent. That the mainland was going to deal with all these issues, once Heller found the killer or killers and solved the case. But now they are on their own—or so Hobbes and Manafort think, at this charged moment.

And if Heller suddenly tries to interject—if he suddenly says, *No, the comm towers have been disabled, and can be reenabled,* who's going to believe him? Dolan and Prichard, the communications experts, will laugh. They'll chalk it up to Heller's inexperience with his own T3. Taking the common-enough form of paranoia and mild mania. His inability to control it. His understandable inability to handle the changed circumstance. The enormous unprecedented stress of it, for all of them. The horrifying fate of Heller's special friend, Trish Wong. Affecting his mind. Affecting his judgment. Not to mention the dizziness and the serious fall Heller experienced in the cold a week ago. Further evidence of his struggle in this environment. After his fall, apparently still not thinking straight. The world to our north collapsing is the result of a trick from our radio experts? The world disappearing can be rectified—brought back to life—with the flip of a switch? Welcome to T3, Mr. Heller. Welcome to T3.

"We might as well have Pike contributing," says Manafort—as if reasonably. But in fact, challenging. "Helping out. Until we agree with each other on what to do. How to handle this. I mean, he's not going anywhere."

But really, turning Pike into a hero for Manafort's growing contingent, thinks Heller. To be celebrated. No consequences. A first example of no consequences. A precedent, he realizes. A symbolic victory for Manafort. And a kind of carte blanche for Dolan. Holy Christ.

• • •

The rules and presumptions are changing. For Pike, for Dolan, for Manafort, for all of them.

But they are changing for the lone law officer too.

Because a whole other solution occurs to Heller. An option unprecedented in the annals of Heller's career, in the annals of his thinking and his outlook.

The option:

To not say anything.

Leave the communications down. Leave them disconnected.

Giving him the chance to exercise his own brand of vigilante justice. Or just threaten Dolan with it.

Frontier justice. When you have to create the justice yourself, because there's no other way to do it. Make the judgments yourself. Prosecutor, judge, and jury. Efficient, shorthanded, shorthand law.

A scenario that becomes more real when he is summoned to Hobbes's office.

• • •

"The system is breaking down," says Hobbes, glumly. "I pretend it's not, I say it's not publicly, I project confidence, but I know . . . I'm not blind . . . the system is breaking down. I feel at fault on that."

Heller looks at him silently. Sympathetically.

"I'm a scientist, an administrator. Not a politician."

Jesus. Don't give in so easily to Manafort's demagoguery. Don't fold so easily. Fight, Heller thinks. *Hang in there.*

Hobbes unlocks the bottom drawer of his desk, lifts a thick stack of documents out of it, and then, to Heller's clear surprise, removes a false bottom of the drawer and gingerly lifts out a Glock automatic and a box of ammunition beneath it.

Heller can tell it's never been out of that desk drawer. Maybe, in earlier, happier times, even forgotten about. Seeing Hobbes bring it out now, Heller thinks, is a clear indication of the state of things.

Hobbes sets it on the desk, frowns at it.

Shoves the Glock and the box of ammunition across the desk toward Heller.

"No one knows I have it. Take it. I trust you more with it than me. At this point, I'd do something . . . stupid."

"But even just for personal protection?" Acknowledging the degenerating state of things. "Don't you want . . ."

Hobbes holds up his hand to stop him. "You're the professional." He looks more closely at Heller. "I've gotten to know you these last weeks. Who you really are. What you're really about. You take it. I hope you don't have to use it. But if you do, you'll be wiser with it than me."

Not just a Glock. A Glock no one knows the existence of, and that no one will know Heller has. Heller doesn't hesitate. He sees all the advantages. Hobbes is right. He grabs the gun, puts it into his belt strap, zips his parka over it, scoops up the ammo box, and pushes it deep into a parka pocket. He only looks back up at Hobbes once the gun is hidden, off the desk, once it has its new owner.

"Hope I don't have to use it. But I won't hesitate if I need to. I guess you know that about me too," says Heller.

Hobbes nods.

"Manny, you're doing the right thing. You've done the right thing all the way."

"Hasn't done much good."

"Sometimes it doesn't. But we still have to do it."

Wordlessly after that, Heller gets up.

Exits Hobbes's office.

Armed.

Frontier justice now in his belt.

Civilization is falling apart.

But the Glock in his belt may be just what Heller needs to restore it.

• • •

He doesn't try to tell Hobbes about Dolan and Pritchard and the broken comm tower.

He's tempted. He wants to. He feels guilty withholding the information. But not just yet.

First, he has a deal to offer.

Fix the communications, Dolan. Fix the communications in exchange for my silence. There isn't enough evidence, it's inconclusive, contaminated, the prosecution process and jurisdiction are unclear, all of which you know. I can't get you, Dolan.

That's the case he's going to make to Dolan. Which unfortunately may have the power—the persuasiveness—of being true.

He has to act—get communications restored—before civilization on McMurdo degenerates further.

Civilization to their north, it turns out, goes on unimpeded.

It's civilization at McMurdo that's now at risk.

He has to get communications back up.

With threat. With force. Right now.

71.

Heller opens the door to the Comm Cave.

They are both at their consoles.

Both exactly where everyone at McMurdo has pictured them.

Diligently, dutifully trying to reach the world.

Looking that way. As if trying to fool Heller once more, one last time.

Dolan avoids looking at him.

Heller senses Pritchard has told him something.

He doesn't know, of course, exactly what. Exactly how much. Whether he told him they were on the floor together, looking at snakes. Whether he told him he saw the other species at the back.

He sits down behind them. "Don't let me interrupt. You keep working," he says, sarcastically. A sarcasm he assumes Dolan can hear, loud and clear, with no static.

"It was you on that recording, wasn't it, Dolan? That Australian farmer. That was you. Accented, filtered, scratchy, pitched down a little, but you."

Dolan continues facing the console, expressionless.

"That was Dolan. Wasn't it, Pritchard?"

Pritchard shifts. Like he wants to answer. He looks over at Dolan, who keeps his eyes on the console. Pritchard stays quiet.

"See, no Australian farmer has ever said the word *flashlight*," says Heller.

Dolan and Pritchard are both silent.

"I'd love you to play that recording again for me, but I know what you're going to tell me. You're going to tell me it got erased, aren't you, Dolan? Because you got nervous when I asked you to play it for me last time. Because you thought you might have screwed up. Because you're very careful, aren't you, Dolan?

"Turn around from that console and face me. Slowly. I know you're not doing anything there. I know your sitting there is bullshit."

They both turn slowly.

To see Joe Heller pointing a Glock at them.

"I know everything," he tells them. "I know you've cut off all communication, managed to fool the whole station into thinking it's the end of civilization thanks to a few deft radio tricks, all to cover up a murder, and then another murder, and then a third, trying to cover your tracks, to keep me from getting anywhere. So, you know as well as I do I've got no evidence. The bodies are gone and the autopsies missed the real causes of death, and even in the case of Calloway, you've probably been smart enough to get rid of the murder weapon. I can sit here pointing this gun at you and hope you confess, but we all know that's not going to happen. So my only chance for justice here is to just shoot you . . ."

He calmly cocks the Glock, aims it at Dolan.

"And if we were really alone here, if I really *was* the last cop on the planet, that is exactly what I'd do." He uncocks it. "But as only the three of us know right now, as soon as the spring thaw comes, new communications equipment will be sent, communications will be restored, flights and supplies will arrive, and I would be on trial for shooting two radio experts in cold blood, on an unproven hunch. Maybe I'd get lighter time for suffering from T3," Heller says. "The point is, I can't just shoot you"—he cocks it again—"unless it's in self-defense. Unless I'm attacked, two on one." He uncocks it. Cocks it again. Uncocks it. To show them he's thinking it, feeling it, weighing it both ways, undecided.

"Now even if we do nothing, all three of us know that your charade ends as soon as spring comes. Or as soon as there's communication. And all three of us know you'll get more and more desperate as we approach that time." More desperate and more dangerous. "I can't have you growing more desperate. Look what you've done already.

"So, here's what's going to happen. You're going to restore communication right now. Obviously, you'd never even had that key out of its envelope when we did that first inspection, when you couldn't decide which ATV should go first. You'd never even been out there to inspect, so I'm sure you can restore communication from right here. Flip the switches. Now."

And he lifts the Glock, cocks it, and, as if with no greater thought, as if with the casualness of shifting in his chair or rearranging reports on his desk, puts the gun against Dolan's forehead.

Against it, so Dolan can feel the barrel's metal. A cold, Antarctic, anarchic cold.

Cocked, ready to fire, because that is how the gesture will have the most meaning.

It's so sudden, so unpredictable.

The room goes frozen. Motionless. Breathing stops.

Frozen.

A different kind of frozen from the vast black wasteland around them but directly related to it.

A tableau that holds for five, six, seven seconds. Until Heller uncocks the gun and withdraws it.

The silence holds for five, six, seven seconds more.

Dolan speaks first. Low. Somber. "To restore communication, we have to change some settings here but also go out to the comm tower."

"That makes no sense. You're bullshitting me. I saw that you'd never been out to the comm towers when you did this. There was nothing wrong with those comm towers."

"That was true before," says Dolan, quietly. "But when you came out with us, we were nervous that you were getting close to the truth, so we changed the settings out there too, in case you figured it out here at the console. Now to get it up and running, we have to restore things here *and* out there." He gives a little shrug.

On the one hand, Dolan admits it. Admits the bizarre premeditated interruption of all communication. Will he admit to the murders too?

On the other hand, Heller will have to go back out there with them. Go back out there into the cold and dark, where he still doesn't know what happened to him, exactly. Go back out into the cold and dark with them one more time.

"Then we're going to make another little inspection trip of the comm towers. The three of us. And you're going to flip the switches back, restore communication, and prove it to me—really prove to me it's working—while we're still out there. A little victory call to Hobbes, or Simmons or Stanford or whoever you want, to confirm it. Hey, Hobbes, we finally fixed it. We're heroes. Check for yourself. We're back online.

"Because if you two don't prove it to my satisfaction, we're not coming back in. None of us. You took Trish from me, you bastards. And I'm happy to pay the ultimate personal price for making sure you don't take anyone else. You know how much I cared about her. The mistake you made is unleashing another killer. One who really doesn't care what happens to him at this point."

Of course, that's no longer true.

No longer true at all.

Because Amy and Ann are suddenly alive, of course.

And now that they are suddenly alive, he wants to live to see them.

These two odd, crazy radio techs have wiped out the world, and now, suddenly, they can save it.

Maybe they believe him about Trish Wong. Maybe they don't.

It's Pritchard who speaks next. "You really want to go back out there? When you had such a hard time before? You almost died out there! Dolan saved you."

Pritchard's intellectual deficiency becomes clearer with every sentence, every moment, thinks Heller. Dolan stays silent. Dolan seems to know it. Heller stares hard at Dolan. Dolan looks away.

A kid who loves radios and snakes, thinks Heller. Perfect for someone like Dolan.

"No," admits Heller, "I don't want to go back out there. But I have to make sure you do it."

He watches their reactions closely throughout. Watches Pritchard's blinking acknowledgment. Dolan's pathological blankness. Just as he would have expected. "The venom and its undetected application to the skin. The little red hypodermic pinprick. Just as cleverly misleading as the Morse code transcriptions and ham radio broadcasts. I know everything."

"Everything?" says Pritchard. A little wide-eyed, naive looking. But it is, nevertheless, in his way, a pointed question, Heller notices. An unnerving question.

As Pritchard watches, Dolan unscrews a panel, pulls it out, switches some wires and inputs out of the tangle behind it (it looks for a moment like the writhing snakes, thinks Heller), changes a couple more wires, reattaches the panel, then looks up at Pritchard and nods, before turning back to Heller. "Step two is out at the comm towers."

Dolan suddenly tilts his head a little, quizzically. "I don't know if a handgun will fire in fifty below," he says with a shrug. "Do you know?" Ever the technician, thinks Heller. Unfeeling. Psychopathic. Interested in the ballistics. Human disconnection.

"It will," Heller assures him. "It definitely will. Maybe I'll have the chance to show you."

72.

Hypothermia—Signs and symptoms

Symptoms of . . . hypothermia . . . [include] shivering, high blood pressure, fast heart rate, fast respiratory rate . . .

Low body temperature results in shivering becoming more violent. Muscle mis-coordination becomes apparent. Movements are slow and labored, accompanied by a stumbling pace and mild confusion . . . As the temperature decreases, further physiological systems falter . . . Difficulty speaking, sluggish thinking, and amnesia start to appear; inability to use hands and stumbling are also usually present . . . Below 30° C (86° F) . . . muscle coordination [becomes] very poor, and walking almost impossible, and the person exhibits incoherent/irrational behavior, including terminal burrowing, even stupor . . . Major organs fail. Clinical death occurs.

—*Wikipedia*

He has not told Hobbes, Bramlett, or anyone that the world still exists. He wants to, of course. He wants to be the bearer of the best news in the world. But he is afraid that if that word gets out to Manafort and his acolytes, they might panic, act quickly, do something forceful and irreversible, since their rise, their "chance," would so clearly be coming to an end. They might want to control their ending. They have the guns now.

• • •

They make the same preparations. Will take the same two ATVs. There's no risk taking two ATVs that Heller can see. Nobody can escape on one of them. There's nowhere to go. You'd be heading off to your own demise.

"We have to go to the far tower first," Dolan says.

"Why's that?"

"Because the other tower doesn't really do anything. We told you before. It's backup. The far tower can operate everything."

The far tower. Almost a mile away. The tower where he fell. But Heller remembers from previous discussions and explanations that what Dolan says is true. That the two towers are primarily about redundancy. Can Pritchard and Dolan just switch on the lower, closer tower? Will that reestablish communication? Is the far tower really the essential one? It appears to be. Somewhat taller, somewhat newer. But he doesn't really know.

• • •

The wind is howling. The cold is excruciating. Even though Heller has gradually acclimated to Antarctic winter, these are conditions everyone would normally avoid.

Sixty below, on the outside thermometers. "That's right on the edge of the equipment being functional," Pritchard observed earlier. "Just so you know."

"You guys are gonna tell me that every day, aren't you? Let's go," says Heller. "We're going."

Showing them he doesn't care. Showing them he's willing to die. And take them with him.

Do they believe it? Are they as willing to die too? Do they believe him that he has no case, that they will go unprosecuted?

Pritchard and Dolan have brought the same toolboxes. Heller has inspected them to make sure all the tools in them are appropriate. That there are no extra tools made by Glock or Colt or Smith & Wesson in there.

There's no discussion, no talk. It was wordless last time too, but this wordlessness has a different feel. They are alert to the wind, to the elements, but they are alert to one another too. They are fighting the wind. Squinting in the dark. Heller is keeping his eyes on both of them.

It is, as always, man against the elements, but there are extra elements this time—elements of unpredictability, of opaque motivation, of watching your back.

On their previous trip out to the tower, all Dolan's, Pritchard's, and Heller's attention had been on the task at hand. For Heller, observing the inspection. For Dolan and Pritchard, fooling him into believing it was one.

This time, Heller is thinking about . . . everything else: his unleashed wrath at what he's just discovered, his focus on the perpetrators, his continuing speculation on their strange relationship, his sense of Pritchard's mental deficiency, of being shaped by Dolan, his frustration at no proof (all circumstantial, he doesn't have the bodies to re-autopsy their skin, exotic poison undetectable—he's sure that Dolan has researched that, made sure of that). He is still shocked, stunned at their audacity and arrogance, still wrapping his mind around it, and he is thinking too, inevitably, of Amy and Ann alive and well, countervailing this literal and figurative darkness. All of it circling inside him, blowing around in his brain. All of it distraction. You're not supposed to be distracted when you come out into the cold in Antarctic winter. You need all your concentration. All your faculties. That's Antarctica 101. And he's violating that rule in a big way. Add to which, there are two of them. And it's still not clear to him how these two—these two parkas leaning into the cold and wind—relate to each other.

He keeps the Glock at the ready, his gloved hand gripping it, gun and gloved hand zipped inside his parka's chest pocket. It's awkward for him, but he knows he has to keep the gun somewhat warm. Because he doesn't actually know if it will fire at these temperatures. He knows the cutoff for firing is somewhere around this temperature.

• • •

In a few minutes, out of the night, in the narrow beam of light from the lead ATV, he sees the far comm tower ahead of them. The struts of its scaffolding are the first thing visible, the metal cross braces completely coated with ice, glistening in the ATV beam's reflection, a fantasy seeming to float in the light and the sparkling snow dust of the crosswind—fifty miles per hour or so, making it feel even colder, deliriously colder. The floating ice-coated struts of scaffolding are like pieces of a dream. And as the ATVs move closer, Heller notices it doesn't make the dream element fall away and reality take over—it only makes the sense of a dream stronger, more vibrant and complete.

The dreamlike quality is enhanced too because it's a dream he has had before. The same ATVs, the same two radio technicians in the same parkas, the same route, a powerful sense of physical déjà vu, and yet everything is different—all the feelings, the stew of anger and astonishment at their stunt and how to prosecute them for the murders, all the knowledge. A dream that he has relived, trying to understand and process exactly what happened to him out here last time. Calloway's warnings about the hypothermic susceptibility of some people—of how it may even interact with T3, there are no studies yet—are reverberating in his head too.

They leave the ATVs running. They start up the scaffold stairs. He observes the scaffold overhangs this time as they climb up, paying extra attention to see if there is one where he knocked his head, as they told him, but he sees nothing precarious, nothing in his direct path, and that confuses him.

He has to climb the stairs with them because they are not going to leave until they have made contact with Hobbes or Bramlett or Simmons or Stanford, surprising them with the good news, testing the connection with them, until he's been assured by the base that the comm connection is back.

Same procedure. Dolan taking the odd wrenchlike tool out of the box.

It's Dolan who opens the panel on the electronics pod. Heller and Pritchard standing over him.

Dolan, the silent, brooding one.

Dolan, the mad genius.

Opening the panel and then turning to Heller and Pritchard.

"I can't do it," he shouts at them, into the wind. Barely audible but loud enough to be unmistakable.

"What do you mean?" Heller shouts back, his hand squeezing the gun inside his parka's chest pocket.

"I can't do it. I want to, but I can't."

I want to, but I can't. Heller is trying to process this. It's confusing. Incomprehensible. Is he feeling T3; is it hypothermia?

It is only later that Heller will understand the meaning.

A meaning that would have been perfectly clear if Heller had only been a little smarter a little sooner.

I want to, but I can't.

Because he won't let me.

Once again, the scaffolding, as impulsively and unpredictably as before, comes alive from behind him to smash Heller on the back of the skull, and he crumples.

Antarctic night, endlessly black, goes even blacker.

As black, as blank, as vast and measureless as death must be.

73.

McMurdo in summer is a bustling, industrious place, every corner of it occupied. McMurdo in winter is hunkered down, quiet, but, of course, has the same physical geography, the same real estate as summer McMurdo. Which means there are hundreds of places, in winter, where no one goes. Places that are shut up tight. Or everyone assumes are shut up tight, anyway.

He is in one of those places. Hog-tied. Plastic ties tight around his wrists and ankles. Dark. He has no idea where he is. He'd guess that most of McMurdo has no idea where either.

There's no slap and sting of wind in here. But there's also no heat.

About the size of a closet. Some kind of storage. Not to be opened up until spring.

A locked-room mystery. The phrase comes back to him. With its new, twisted, personalized meaning. Those mysteries that Robert Trebor loved to read over the winter, and gave up as too irrelevant, too unrealistic, too beside the point. Irrelevant? Unrealistic? Heller is in—he will end up—a locked-room mystery. Unknown. Unsolved. Unread. Until spring.

The last thing he saw was Dolan. Dolan and then blackness. Dolan in front of him, uncomfortable, upset. *I want to, but I can't.* Meaning it was Pritchard behind him. Pritchard who delivered the blow. Heller never took a step. So he didn't trip or miss a metal stair. He was standing still.

With Pritchard behind him.

The back of his head pulses. But he notices that he is sore all over. He closes his eyes. He opens them.

There is suddenly a penlight in his face.

Pritchard's voice behind it.

"You moved your head," the voice says flatly, evenly. "You moved your head and fell away from me, so I could only hit you on the back of the head once. One time ain't enough—as I guess we've both discovered," he says.

Heller can't see Pritchard's expression behind the penlight, but he imagines the little smile. Wry and toothy with meaning.

One time ain't enough.

One blow to the back of the head.

One murder. Sandy Lazo-Wasum's.

One time ain't enough.

Heller can't move his feet or hands but nevertheless can tell that the Glock is no longer in his parka pocket. As he lies there on the floor in the dark, he can feel the emptiness—the hollowness—of that pocket.

"This time, you fell down a flight of stairs, and your fall has saved you. For now. Until I figure out what to do with you," says the voice. Pritchard's voice behind the penlight.

In a moment, Heller knows exactly where the Glock is.

It is against his forehead. Barrel icy cold.

Pritchard holds it there for a long beat—in clear, mocking imitation, mocking repetition of Heller holding it against Dolan's forehead.

Pritchard suddenly draws it away, pockets it. "I'm going to kill you," says Pritchard flatly. "I just have to figure out how." Like a little puzzle. Like the kind of puzzle he enjoys. His little hobby, his way to pass the time, during the winter-over in Antarctica.

• • •

Once again, Heller has misunderstood, misinterpreted a partnership.

It is Paul all over again. Paul who continually deceived him. Paul who made him look stupid.

But this time, his stupidity will cost him his life.

● ● ●

"You were watching Dolan, weren't you? Dolan, the radio genius, odd, quiet. Dolan, the brooding mastermind. I saw you watching him," says Pritchard, leaning close in the penlight, unable to resist the satisfaction of a smile. "Not looking so closely at Pritchard, the talker, always so forthcoming, slightly childlike, why I'd even excitedly shared my secret snake hobby with you. Pritchard who always credits everything he knows to Dolan. Innocent-sounding, innocent-seeming Pritchard," says Pritchard.

So he's not childlike at all. Just cleverly childlike when he needs it. When he has to be.

"Those are all my snakes. They're all venomous. The smaller brighter one at the back is just a different subgenus. Dolan doesn't like them, but he tolerates them. And Dolan thinks I suffer T3. That I suffer it terribly. Like I fooled you into thinking I suffer it," says Pritchard. "Dolan feels bad for me. Very sympathetic. Very forgiving. He attributes a lot of my behavior to that. He wishes I'd get professional help." Pritchard checks the ties on Heller's wrists. "Truth is, it's Dolan who suffers T3. Makes his judgment very cloudy. All his thinking goes soft. But the most interesting thing is it makes him completely forgetful. I discovered that years ago with him."

Heller has read the relationship exactly right—one dominant and one subservient, one forceful and one malleable, one demanding and one beholden, one in charge and one in trancelike obedience and trust—but he has read who is who, which is which, exactly, entirely wrong.

Pritchard's hearty sociability. Dolan's furtive diffidence. Heller has completely misinterpreted.

Unfortunately, he knows exactly why Pritchard is telling him all this.

Because Pritchard is planning to kill him. And he wants Heller to know how he will get away with it. How he will continue to get away with it.

Heller knows by now that cruelty is part of Pritchard's MO. In thinking about the two murders, in searching for a common thread, Heller had eventually noticed a cruel connection—in both cases, the victim's lover had to observe the victim's autopsy. Sorenson had to suffer seeing Lazo-Wasum's naked body on the examining table. Heller had to endure seeing Trish Wong's. Both of them not only had to bear the autopsies but in the moment had to stay silent about their relationship to the victim. Watching the examination. Watching others poke and prod the bodies that had been warmly next to their own just hours before. All this was somehow part of the thrill for the killer. Heller theorized that it might even be what determined the choice of victim—and might be the whole motivation for each murder.

But Heller realizes only now that Pritchard has always had the opportunity to be nearby for each of those autopsies. To be near enough to see, gauge, enjoy the reaction of Sorenson, then of Heller. To see, gauge, enjoy both their shock and their shamed silence. That's somehow the thrill.

He likes the cruelty. He needs the cruelty. Heller hopes that extra need for cruelty will somehow be Heller's chance to survive.

Survival. Always the subtext of life in Antarctica. And now for Heller, an extra hurdle to Antarctic survival.

He searches Pritchard's words again. *This time, you fell down a flight of stairs.* This time. Meaning last time, it was different. Meaning last time, you were pushed. That's all it could mean.

Meaning last time you were pushed, but we said you hit your head and fell, to make it look like an accident. Which it wasn't.

This time, your fall down the flight of stairs *was* an accident. Not in the plan. *Your fall has saved you.*

Meaning the plan had been more blows to the head. Sufficient blows to the head.

Then why didn't they finish him off out there, once he stopped falling?

More of Pritchard's words come back to him: *Dolan saved you!* He had assumed Pritchard said it mainly to make Dolan look good. To make the story be Dolan, take attention away from Pritchard. But Heller has always heard something odd, some other meaning, in Pritchard's repetition of the fact, in the overly upbeat tone of Pritchard's voice. Now, he hears the mockery, the cleverly disguised, cleverly expressed annoyance. Frustration with his partner. *Dolan saved you!* What if Dolan *has* saved him? Emerging temporarily, just enough, from the fog of his forgetfulness, the haze of his T3 symptoms, from his fluid mental "softness," to convince Pritchard not to kill him. To convince him that Heller is not in the way, or doesn't deserve it, or isn't really a problem. *Dolan saved you.* Does it mean that Dolan has saved him again? Because after all, Heller is still alive.

• • •

Hobbes, Simmons—all of McMurdo—will be missing them soon.

So Pritchard will have to do something quickly.

Beat him up some more, bruise him badly—lethally maybe—to show he died falling down the metal stairs.

Sorenson will never know the difference. Sorenson's a nurse. A good one, but a nurse.

Heller goes through the possible scenarios in his head.

But he seriously underestimates Pritchard. He miscalculates Pritchard's cruel genius once again.

74.

Paradoxical undressing

Twenty to fifty percent of hypothermia deaths are associated with paradoxical undressing. This typically occurs during moderate to severe hypothermia, as the person becomes disoriented, confused, and combative. They may begin discarding their clothing, which, in turn, increases the rate of heat loss.

—*Wikipedia*

Heller lies in the dark.

He has no idea where he is at McMurdo.

Somewhere closed up in the winter, he is sure. Somewhere no one can hear him yell for help or scream in tortured pain.

A locked-room mystery.

He notices he's getting steadily colder. He's starting to shiver.

He knows it's only a few minutes until he's shivering uncontrollably.

• • •

Pritchard comes in again, this time with Dolan.

Dolan barely looks at him. Heller registers it now as autistic. High-functioning autistic.

"Ever heard of paradoxical undressing?" Pritchard asks Heller.

Heller shakes his head.

"A symptom of hypothermia. Happens in almost half of all hypothermia cases. Your metabolic function changes so dramatically you feel like you're burning up, and you take off all your clothes, which, of course, just accelerates the problem. Accelerates it until death."

Heller is silent. Pritchard continues.

"The victim becomes very combative. Won't let anyone near them to help them. It's often followed by a further effect called terminal burrowing. The victim looks for a place to bury himself, hide from harm. Obviously, it's some kind of holdover from our primitive animal brains. Shows you what level the brain is working at, how hard it's working, when hypothermia sets in. But don't worry. Terminal burrowing is never going to happen to you. There's no good place to burrow out there. It's all hard-pack ice."

Terminal burrowing, no.

But paradoxical stripping, yes.

"It's almost time to strip, Joe Heller," says Pritchard. "Almost time to strip and get back out there to the comm tower."

Where Heller's hypothermia set in so violently (Heller can already imagine Pritchard's version to Hobbes and company), *where he defended himself so vigorously from our help, there was nothing we could do. That Joe Heller is a strong guy—and this time, it worked against him. He wouldn't let us near him. He was so crazy. And what could we do anyway? The guy had a Glock!*

We should have read the signs from his earlier episode, when he got disoriented and fell. We should have taken his proclivity for hypothermia much more seriously.

But he was as excited as we were about a breakthrough in our communication effort. We thought we had one. That's why we were all out there together, risking the cold and dark.

Unfortunately, we were wrong, Hobbes, sir. We were wrong, Stanford, sir. It didn't fix anything. We've still had no further communication. There still may be no one out there.

Heller looks at Dolan.

Dolan saved you.

Dolan is not even looking at him.

75.

The frozen Antarctic continent.

In winter, as dark as it is vast.

As vast as it is cold.

A frozen, empty continent.

A man naked on it.

Naked, in the shadow of a communications tower.

Naked, running in circles.

Two men in parkas, watching.

Shining their helmet lights on him.

Watching, waiting . . .

Pushing the naked man away from them, when he comes at them desperately, grabbing at them, at their clothes . . .

When they first push him away, it requires some strength, some agility from them.

But very soon, the naked man is stumbling around, can't walk straight, can't even take steps; he is delirious, speaking nonsense.

They watch, they wait . . . it is fascinating to see . . .

His clothes are scattered randomly—convincingly—around the base of the satellite dish tower, as if he has ripped them all off.

Someone will eventually come and retrieve them.

• • •

Heller can imagine the scene so vividly.

His cognition shutting down.

His frantic shivering, his racing in the snow.

In the end, a painless death. All the literature says so. The nervous system shuts down self-protectively. Does it shut down before or after brain function? Of course, no one can know for sure. No one has lived to report back about it.

• • •

They will have to rush his naked body into the infirmary, to make it look good, of course.

They will have to risk Sorenson being able to revive him.

But they will undoubtedly try to wait long enough so they know he's dead.

Which, in sixty below, won't be that long.

It is a little science experiment for them, Heller realizes. A matter of timing it just right. Making sure he is "dead enough" for Sorenson to not revive him, but to look like they acted to save him as soon as they could. As soon as he would let them near him, as soon as he would let them help him. And Sorenson is a nurse—she might not even be able to tell the difference anyway, might not be able to judge how long they were out there. They could say they brought him in as soon as they could. She'd have no way to know if they did; it would never even occur to her that they didn't.

The poison is a science experiment too.

Pritchard enjoys these science experiments.

That may be the most enjoyable part of the process for him.

Maybe Pritchard came originally to Antarctica to cut himself off from people.

To cut himself off from all the temptation—and it worked for a while, but it didn't work forever. And maybe when he learned of the experiments by the pharmaceutical companies, it stirred his imagination, and there was no going back. But it's a little late to be psychoanalyzing Pritchard. A little late to be speculating. Pretty useless now.

. . .

Advanced hypothermia. It's a brilliant idea, Heller thinks. Criminally brilliant.

Simple. Elegant.

Going out of the world as naked as he came in.

Going out of the world with the most primitive impulses and autonomic responses and needs—just as he came into it. Cold. Warmth. Fear. Wonder. Breathing.

Disappearing into the black void—the endless black void of Antarctic night and the black void of unconsciousness—as he emerged from a measureless black void into the world almost fifty years ago. Full circle.

It is easy to imagine. Terrifying to imagine. As vivid a scenario as a pandemic occurring on the rest of the planet.

But an idea that requires no extra oomph, no extra persuasiveness, with fake radio recordings.

An idea that is different in one major respect:

It is about to go from vivid imagination to reality.

. . .

A brilliant idea.

With a practical problem that dulls its brilliance considerably:

If Heller is to strip, they have to take the wrist and ankle ties off him.

If they take the ties off him, he can move, he can attack them.

They can't defend themselves with the Glock, can't defend themselves by shooting him, or their brilliant little tale of hypothermia won't work.

They can't even threaten him with the gun. He knows they won't shoot him, because they want—they need—the hypothermia story.

He realizes that, oddly, Hobbes is helping him here. Hobbes and Simmons, Stanford and Bramlett, and all of McMurdo. Because Pritchard still has to make it look good. Still has to satisfy the powers that be, knowing that the world north of them *does* still exist. If McMurdo was really on its own—all that was left—then Pritchard and Dolan could shoot him now. But they still have to make a convincing case for what happens out here; they still have to convince Hobbes, Stanford, and the others. So they can't just shoot him. Civilization or, at least, its vestiges and veneer are still working for Heller. As if making one last stand. Pritchard knows he can't actually use the gun. *Heller must have been suffering from T3. Or from hypothermia. He suddenly tried to attack us. We had to shoot him.* Really, Pritchard? Shooting Heller in the head or heart? With Heller's own gun? How'd you get his gun, Pritchard? No, Heller and Pritchard both know that version will never fly.

So their only chance is to wait for Heller to get cold. Too cold to defend himself vigorously. Too cold for him to attack them.

He realizes that's exactly what they're doing.

"Almost time to strip, Joe Heller."

Waiting for him to become weak enough, docile enough so they can remove his ties without any risk. So he'll strip and do what they say. They'll walk him out there naked or ride him out there naked on the ATV. He'll stumble around out there. He'll be fairly hypothermic already, halfway to delirium, mentally incapacitated.

It won't take them but a few minutes.

He feels the cold surrounding him.

What would Paul do?

Invoking his old partner. Master of deceit. What would Paul do? How would he work around this? Paul ruined his career, but he was his partner, and when he wasn't a criminal, he was a great cop. *What would Paul do?* Can Paul save him?

Heller feels his descent beginning. Feels the drop of temperature, feels the cold surround him, invade him, and feels himself starting to not feel it anymore.

Welcome to the end of the earth, Hobbes greeted him on his arrival.

And then it *was* the end of the earth.

And then, it turned out, it wasn't—though he'll never get to share the good news with Hobbes.

And now it's the end of the earth again.

But this time, just for him.

• • •

A short while later, Pritchard and Dolan return to the shack—a small storage shack at the edge of McMurdo.

When they enter the dark shack, they see Heller's limbs shivering and shaking.

"Shit, are we too late?"

"Jesus, it's happening fast."

Pritchard shines the penlight in Heller's eyes.

He sees Heller's pupils dancing wildly around the dark room.

Pritchard and Dolan both notice that his breathing is rapid, shallow.

"Cut the ties," says Pritchard. "You'll have to help him get his clothes off. He's already lost motor control."

Dolan takes out a pocketknife.

Pritchard watches, the Glock in his hand.

Dolan has to hold down Heller's shivering legs and feet to cut the plastic ties around his ankles.

Freed up, his legs and feet shiver and shake rapidly, uncontrollably, even more.

It makes it harder for Dolan to cut the ties around Heller's shivering wrists and shaking hands and fingers. It's frightening, gruesome looking. Heller's contorted fingers. Wrists bent back extremely. They have to work fast.

As soon as the ties are off Heller's wrists, the terrible shaking suddenly stops.

Stops completely.

Enters a new stage, apparently.

Dolan finds himself pulled suddenly, forcefully against Heller's body. Spun around suddenly, his back now against Heller's torso.

The pocketknife he has been holding is suddenly in Heller's hand, against Dolan's neck.

Both of them are facing Pritchard. A stunned, confused Pritchard holding the Glock.

The shack is tight. Dark. The beam from Dolan's helmet is now pointed at Pritchard, of course. Suddenly in Pritchard's eyes. Pritchard blinks.

● ● ●

What would Paul do? He'd fool you. Completely fake it.

Make you believe he was suffering from hypothermia when he wasn't. Not yet, anyway.

The shack is tight enough, dark enough that one hard shove from behind Dolan lands Dolan hard and sudden against Pritchard.

Hard and sudden enough to knock Pritchard down backward.

Surprised, confused, the thin beams of light swinging wildly, Pritchard inadvertently fires the dangerously cocked Glock into Dolan's chest.

The sound of the discharge in the tiny shack is enormous, disorienting; the flash is blindingly bright. Certainly disorienting for someone who has never seen a firearm discharged. Not quite so disorienting for someone with thirty years' police experience. Experience in tight, dark spaces, waiting for a drug deal to go down, for a suspect to show. Shoving Dolan so hard against Pritchard, Heller was half expecting the shot.

And when they collapse together, Dolan onto Pritchard in the tight, dark shack, it's Heller's chance to grab the Glock.

• • •

Pritchard starts struggling to get out from under Dolan . . .

He's forced back down by the extra weight of Heller's boot on Dolan's back, pinning him there beneath Dolan.

In the narrow beam of his own helmet light, Pritchard can see the Glock pointing down at him.

He smiles up at it.

"We both know you won't shoot me," says Pritchard. Trying to shift, but immobilized, beneath Dolan. "Only in self-defense, and I have no weapon," says Pritchard, still smiling, and Heller can, once again, see Pritchard's version so clearly:

Dolan is dead.

Heller's prints are on the Glock.

First, he shoots Dolan, then tries to shoot me.

We should have all paid attention, Hobbes, sir, when Heller fell on the stairs that first time. Classic effects of T3. Obviously a serious sufferer. Add in the fuzzy thinking of hypothermia. He's not used to these extreme conditions . . .

He should never have had a Glock, Hobbes, sir. He forced us out there. He was convinced we were keeping the comm tower from working. Classic T3 paranoia and delusional thinking, Manny, you know that . . .

316

There in the tight darkness, Dolan's body starts to lift toward Heller.

For a disorienting moment, Heller thinks Dolan is levitating, reanimating.

The cold and dark are having their effect.

His mind is suddenly feeling cloudy, somehow tightening up at its edges, constricting. His thoughts are going fuzzy on him, softening, leaking, starting to float around him. *T3? Hypothermia?* It would make sense in this frozen shack that it's now setting in . . .

Heller watches motionless, while Pritchard pushes Dolan up off him . . .

Maybe to race for the door and the ATV, leaving Heller stranded here in the cold, unoccupied fringes of McMurdo . . .

Or maybe, with no other choice, to reach for, tussle for the Glock . . .

The Glock Heller won't use.

I want to, but I can't.

Dolan's mysterious words coming back to him. Words of pained powerlessness.

I want to, but I can't.

Because he's too much a cop. Locked in the tight black box of the rules. The rules that forced him to turn in his own partner. Sacrifice department friendships, and then his marriage. Come alone, to the end of the earth.

Frontier justice.

Antarctic justice.

The problem for him being that word: *justice.*

I want to, oh, I want to, but I can't.

• • •

And then, in the next second, it's suddenly the Glock he *will* use.

In a lesson, an insight that cuts sharply through the softness of his thoughts.

A lesson, an insight that does not come from Paul but from Pritchard.

Pritchard, pushing up off the floor.

Something Heller has learned from him.

The hard way.

Twice.

Pritchard, who now has Dolan off him . . .

Is standing up, gathering his legs under him . . .

His helmet light dancing wildly against the walls . . .

In a descending haze of hypothermic, polar T3 dizziness and confusion, Heller hears voices.

A voice of resignation: *I hope you don't have to use it. But if you do, you'll be wiser with it than me . . .*

A voice of darkness: *One time ain't enough . . .*

Blinking purposefully, pushing the dizziness back, Heller leans in . . .

Slams Pritchard across the back of the head with the butt of the Glock.

One blow.

One time is *enough.*

Pritchard crumples back to the floor.

Head and limbs go slack.

Suddenly silent.

Suddenly motionless.

There in the tight, cold dark.

• • •

The bewildering butt end of the earth—

Calling out to him, instructing him somehow to use the butt end of the gun.

Contrary to all his training. All his years of crouching at targets, patrolman's stance, firing thousands of practice rounds.

Contrary to everything drilled into him as a cop.

The Glock's other end.

Using it like a thug, not a cop.

But that's the end where justice could begin.

You gotta adjust your thinking.

• • •

Heller drags Pritchard out of the shack to the ATV. Still running.

The violence and effort have shaken Heller into alertness. Got his metabolism running. His juices returning.

He slings Pritchard across the front seat, gets on in back—just as Pritchard described Dolan doing for Heller, saving him after his first "fall"—and heads toward the light and warmth of McMurdo.

BOOK THREE: DAY

76.

The first C-130 of the season swoops down out of the northern sky, steadies its mild wing roll, and lands without incident—and with much fanfare—on the McMurdo runway.

A ceremonial cheer goes up from the assembled 153 surviving residents of McMurdo winter. It's a half-century tradition to bundle up and gather outside in the finally rising sun of early September, to herald the first arrival of supplies—palettes of fresh milk, butter, eggs, fresh fruit—and, most of all, to greet the first of the busy season's fresh personnel.

Hobbes and Heller stand together, watching silently.

• • •

As soon as the reassuringly constant flow of messages from Pritchard and Dolan had stopped for several days—"having communications issues, but we're okay"—the Russians had traveled over from Vostok station, over a hundred miles away, to see if everything *was* okay. A parade of winter tractors, checking on their Antarctic neighbors, not knowing exactly what had happened. They had received concerned calls from United States Antarctic Program (USAP) headquarters in Centennial, Colorado, conveyed to Moscow via both diplomatic and scientific community channels. Not knowing exactly what was occurring or had occurred, alarmed at the sudden cessation of communication, and wondering then about the veracity of the previous communication, the Russians had come armed.

Of course, if they had ventured over several days earlier, their American colleagues might not have allowed them in, fearing contagion from a catastrophic global pandemic. The Americans would probably have been armed themselves. Who knows exactly what would have occurred, although one likes to think that scientific heads would have prevailed.

As it was, the Russians were welcomed in. They had brought their team of comm experts, given the reported communications equipment issues, who restored all satellite and Internet connections in less than an hour. The flip of a few switches, the restoration of a small component that had already been found in the suite of Daniel Pritchard and Patrick Dolan. Hidden at the back of a terrarium, actually, beneath one of the bunks, a terrarium teeming with snakes, slithering thickly over it, which had to be destroyed to get to the component safely.

(Privately, later, some of the Russians laughed at the whole thing. Most shook their heads, amazed. The way the entire McMurdo winter-over community had been hoodwinked by a couple of radio techs. A couple of very disturbed radio techs. That would never have happened at Vostok, they said. They maintained more tech support than the Americans. They felt a little flush of superiority over the Americans, a flush of pride at their more rigorous and rigid system. Although deep down, they knew it could have happened to them too. It could have happened to anyone.)

The initial amusement and amazement were soon subsumed in the sobering discovery and spreading understanding of what had occurred at McMurdo during the winter-over. A second poisoning. The base doctor bludgeoned. A botanist, Cohen, killed in an argument. Dolan, one of the radio techs, inadvertently shot by the other. Four dead. Five, counting the first poisoning of a scientist the previous winter. A hefty death toll, when for all the previous winters at McMurdo, there had been none. The riskiest conditions, it turned out with ringing irony, were within the warmth and presumed "safety" of McMurdo's walls. The greatest risk wasn't the harsh landscape. It was other humans.

The murders of that winter-over captured their moment of media attention, as does any murder story. This one had, for the media, the extra appeal of potential victims being stuck there, trapped, for long months of continuous night. Fish in a barrel. A dark, cold barrel. It captured imaginations, lived on a little longer than the next murder story, because of the setting—the inherent mystery and drama of Antarctica, for most people. Many of the "survivors" were interviewed subsequently. What did it feel like? Were you terrified? Could you sleep?

(It was noted, of course, how it was in such contrast to the experience at Amundsen-Scott, the smaller base a thousand miles to the south, relying on the same communications system. The forty winter residents of Amundsen-Scott had remained comfortable, snug, secure, well fed, as in any other winter. Quietly doing their projects. Unfazed, unchanged. The communications disruption was actually cheered by a number of them, it turned out. A welcome quiet. A happy hibernation. Curled in for the long night. The "good" sibling station. The well-behaved sibling station.)

The radio communication from McMurdo, though intermittent and fractured, had been so specific—detailing the specific components the radio techs were repairing, detailing the health conditions of specific patients, sending medical reports, updating supply reports, even communicating some birthday wishes. It had been so detailed, so comprehensive, so reassuring, that there had been no reason to worry. It was, after all, still better than the Antarctica of only a few years before, when there were no winter-over communications, and they were not as well equipped, so there was much more reason to worry.

And anyway, Centennial command always dutifully checked the transmission images when the satellite passed over McMurdo. The satellite images always showed everything normal. All buildings lit. The smoke of cooking from the cafeteria. The exhaust plumes from the fuel and gas of heating. All the normal, plentiful projections of heat and light. The normal limited movement of orange parkas around the base in winter. All looking good from up here.

The same satellite that Heller saw circling—silent, drifting, useless, he had thought.

As it turned out, he was right. All that diligent satellite observation of them was pretty useless.

• • •

The off-loading of supplies is efficient, as the first C-130 always is. Because all eyes are on it. Because everyone has extra energy, extra spring in their step. Glad to have made it through another Antarctic winter. Particularly glad, in this case.

And once the off-loading is done, the loading of the C-130 begins immediately. The first round of the collected trash, to maintain a zero-tolerance waste policy. The first few personnel to leave the station and head back north to the world, a privilege won by lottery—again, a raucous tradition, always accompanied by good-natured teasing and ironic cheering.

And then, what Heller and Hobbes are specifically standing out here to supervise, to confirm:

Pritchard is brought out manacled. Led by Simmons, carefully flanked by three of Simmons's staff. No sunglasses on Pritchard, Heller notices, so keeping his eyes closed against the rising sun's brightness. No gloves. His head is exposed, his head wound still bandaged and wrapped. As is Heller's. Pritchard faces forward, eyes to the ground, doesn't look around him at all, as he is led to the plane.

He will be heavily, carefully manacled aboard the plane. There is a seat already designated.

The international bureaucracy has found a way, given the heinousness of the crimes. The fact that Lazo-Wasum was an Austrian national—normally a hurdle requiring cumbersome judicial proceedings—has worked unexpectedly in their favor. His murder was so clearly perpetrated in precisely the manner of Trish Wong's, the Austrian judicial system waived its separate rights and drafted a document allowing Lazo-Wasum's murder to be tried as part of a wrongful death suit alongside the two murdered Americans, Wong and Calloway. And the complex agreement from the Austrians allowed the American judicial team to insert certain prosecutorial powers they wouldn't be entitled to otherwise. The cross-border, transnational Antarctic experiment usually impedes the administration of justice. But this new working document—unbound by previous rules or conventions—makes justice uncharacteristically swift. The rules of evidence, adequate legal representation, the right to a defense. All that has been streamlined in this new American-Austrian accord—thanks to the brutal nature of the crime. Murder as a rallying point, a place of common ground—not something Heller would have ever predicted of the scientific community of McMurdo, and Antarctica.

• • •

When Pritchard has been settled into his seat, manacles and locks attached and tested, Simmons signals at the airplane hatch door.

Joe Heller comes aboard to inspect the arrangements. To make sure Pritchard is fully secured in his seat. That no objects are near him.

"He'll be received by US Marshals when you land in Hawaii. Do not unshackle him. They'll come aboard and do it.

"No conversation with him of any sort, for any reason, for the duration of the flight. No getting out of his seat for any reason." And then, turning to Pritchard, to say the one thing he'll say directly to him, to deliver the last communication between them:

"You'll have to piss in your pants."

Heller heads to the hatch door. "You're all set," he says to the crew, to the pilots, as he ducks out and descends onto the ice again.

Antarctica's first, and only, acting peace officer.

• • •

Manafort has gone back to cooking. The prayer meetings continued for a while but now have dwindled. The faithful, usually five or six of them, still meet in the cafeteria in the mornings. Heller walks through occasionally, exchanges a head nod with Manafort. *I'm keeping an eye on you.* Manafort is leaving Antarctica at the end of the busy season. Going back to Idaho. *I'm keeping an eye on you until you go.*

• • •

He would never forget the nature, the sequence of his thinking on the two-minute ATV ride back to McMurdo, Pritchard the genius, the serial killer, slung unconscious in front of him.

The fuzziness, the fogginess, dropping away suddenly, a crisp clarity with the bracing cold. As if his mind, his brain—in that instant of survival, of victory, of being alive—had suddenly, finally, acclimated to Antarctica. And offered him a sudden clarity about himself:

How he had always assumed the truth. Had been raised to value it, cherish it, advance it at every opportunity. Truth for him was reflexive. His only real act of faith. Paul had teased him, called him a regular Boy Scout, when he was first on the job. And Paul had shown him how foolish he was, how blind and naive, how the truth, the facts, could be much more malleable, more fluid and shifting, than he would ever have thought.

And here in Antarctica—land of harsh and irreducible truths, you'd think—Pritchard and Dolan have shown him a malleability within the

truth, a massive flexibility in the facts that he never would have suspected. He had learned so slowly from his partner, Paul, and learned
so extremely from Pritchard, that truth is not the unbending, supreme,
reigning value that he has spent his life believing. So he appropriated it
as he saw them do, bent it briefly to his own purposes, pretending he
had hypothermia to save his own life. The hypothermia effects that he
happened to read about—fascinated, terrified—along with paradoxical undressing and polar T3 syndrome, on that initial flight down to
Antarctica.

He had also packed the paperback of *Catch-22*, figuring that on the
long flight he'd finally get to read it.

He realizes that if he had read it, if he had gotten absorbed in it
instead of immersing himself in the terrors of Antarctica, learning from
Wikipedia about all the signs and stages of hypothermia, he wouldn't
have been able to fool Pritchard and Dolan by imitating its symptoms
so convincingly there in the shack. Not reading *Catch-22* had saved
him. Now there was a "Catch" for you.

Thank you, Paul. Thank you, Dolan and Pritchard. Your lessons in
lying saved me. Finally penetrated my thick skull.

Sometimes the lesson has to hit you over the head.

Sometimes being hit over the head *is* the lesson.

• • •

As for the why? The why that barely matters to the wheels of justice,
that doesn't hold a candle to the who, what, where, and when. The why
that always fascinates but never satisfies. Pritchard had refused to say
much of anything at all. The cleverly, constitutionally, and ingeniously
talkative Pritchard went essentially mute.

Heller knew it was true, knew he was right; the parallels were too
perfect: there was some deep, cruel impulse in Pritchard that arranged
for the suffering of Sorenson seeing Lazo-Wasum on the table, naked and

cold in front of her, as he had been naked and warm with her just hours before. Then Pritchard had orchestrated an identical arrangement—an encore moment, at the same autopsy table—of Heller's own suffering in seeing Trish lying naked there. Sorenson had desired, needed, perhaps even loved Sandy Lazo-Wasum over that Antarctic winter. Heller had desired, needed, perhaps even loved Trish Wong over the Antarctic winter. Pritchard had desired, needed, perhaps even loved to engineer suffering for all of them.

As for the poisoning? The methodology? Which had maybe started it, unleashing Pritchard's original impulse? *Hey, if I could get hold of a couple of those specimens . . .*

It was science, thinks Heller gloomily. The spirit of inquiry. The spirit of experimentation. Pritchard had experimented first with Dolan's T3, after all, getting to know it, over the years. Then, had moved on to another project. Carefully. Quietly. A zoological and then chemical experiment, his own makeshift, off-kilter version of the experiments of Tallent and Blevins, the competing pharmaceutical researchers.

Pritchard the scientist. Following the scientific impulse. Heller didn't like the darkness of that answer.

And shutting down the station's communications completely? Crazy. Unthinkable. The problem being they had already gotten away with crazy and unthinkable. They had killed and then "found" the body, and no one figured out the cause of death. They had already run the experiment of crazy and unthinkable on Lazo-Wasum, and it was a success.

Seeing if you could get away with it. Part of the very point of the experiment. Pure research. Crazy and unthinkable became the gateway—the gateway drug—to controlling communications entirely. Why not? They were believed. They were partners. Nobody doubts partners. Did T3 play a role? Antarctic stare? The fugue state? The darkness? The winter? All lubricants. All facilitating their dream. Their dream of invulnerability.

And the high price of that dream.

As it got light enough and warm enough to do so, Heller finally made his way out to the water's edge, at the far side of McMurdo, to stand alone in exactly the spot where he saw the puffy red dot of parka—motionless, mysterious—the day he arrived.

He stared out at the vast turmoiled sea spreading north in front of him, just as she had. What were you thinking that day? he had asked Trish, when he realized it had been her red parka, when he realized it had been her. Were you happy? Sad? Contemplative? Awestruck? Absorbed in the ocean's beauty, or in your own thoughts?

All of the above, she had answered with a shy smile.

As he stood there himself, looking out, thinking of her, he felt it just as she said—all of the above.

• • •

The second plane is due in a few hours.

Heller is excited.

The second plane carries three psychologists, coming to interview him, Hobbes, and others about "group delusion." Shared psychosis. To try to understand what happened. How it could have happened. What we can learn.

Picking up where NASA's T3 research left off, thinks Heller cynically.

But that's certainly not what Heller is excited about.

He's excited about the one other passenger on the plane.

The special passenger he's managed to secure a seat for, thanks to Hobbes and Stanford pulling a few strings.

Heller is staying on awhile. A few weeks. Enough time to see the spring take hold. To see some fragile shoots of green push up through the ice. Enough time to have a few more sessions with Professor Green at the eye of the telescope.

Seeing Antarctica come to life beneath the sun. More than just the return of the sun. The return of day itself.

What a perfect time, what a perfect chance, to visit the exotic continent.

With your dad still here.

Yes, Amy's coming.

Still minoring in astronomy.

She's looking forward to the observatory.

• • •

Antarctica.

What an unexpected place to start feeling a sense of home.

Author's Note

In reality, the communications satellite dish serving McMurdo Base is located on Black Island, about twenty-five miles from McMurdo. The signal traverses those twenty-five miles by digital microwave. It would have been impossible for Heller, Pritchard, and Dolan to travel twenty-five miles in the brutal cold and wind conditions of Antarctic winter—it was life-threatening enough for them to make it the single mile from McMurdo to the fictional communications tower I built for them. On the other hand, the distance to Black Island shows that if there *were* a communications issue, the reality could be far more dire than my fiction.

Also, the US observatory is in reality at Amundsen-Scott Station, but I located it at McMurdo for this account—among many, many other liberties.

Acknowledgments

Many thanks to my tennis and paddle tennis pals, who lent their names for several of the characters herein. I assure you, my pals have nothing in common with their namesakes. Their behavior and judgment are never short of exemplary (except for an occasional poor line call), and they are fine fellows to play with me.

Thanks also to my son, Roger, who first had the notion for a novel about Antarctica. When we first discussed it, we imagined Antarctica as a lush, temperate, post-global-warming paradise. But as you can see, Rog, your pop, as always, went darker with it.

About the Author

Jonathan Stone writes his books on the commuter train between his home in Connecticut and his advertising job in midtown Manhattan, where he has honed his writing skills by creating smart and classic campaigns for high-level brands such as Mercedes-Benz, Microsoft, and Mitsubishi. Stone's first mystery-thriller series, the Julian Palmer books, won critical acclaim and was hailed as "stunning" and "risk-taking" in starred reviews by *Publishers Weekly*. He earned glowing praise for his novel *The Cold Truth* from the *New York Times*, who called it "bone-chilling." He is the recipient of a Claymore Award for best unpublished crime novel and a graduate of Yale University, where he was a Scholar of the House in fiction writing. He is also the author of *Two for the Show*, *The Teller*, *Moving Day*, *The Heat of Lies*, *Breakthrough*, and *Parting Shot*.